# Racing the Devil

## E. Michael Terrell

NIGHT
SHADOWS PRESS

Cover Design by Michael R. Hicks

Printed in the United States of America

Library of Congress Control Number: 2009930613

ISBN 978-0-9799167-7-9

Nights Shadows Press, LLC
8987 E. Tanque Verde #309-135
Tuscon, AZ 85749-9399

Dedicated to

Chester Campbell
Mentor, critique partner, friend

*Where God builds a church, the devil builds a chapel. – Martin Luther*

*The devil casts a long shadow. – Anon.*

# 1

**E**VEN IN THE DIM light of the bar, I could see the bruises.

Beginning just below one eye, they spread down the side of her face and neck, tinged the blue rose tattoo above the swell of her left breast, and seeped beneath the plunging neckline of her scarlet halter.

She paused inside the door, hugging herself. Her gaze swept the room, lit briefly on one face, then another. Looking for something, or someone. Or maybe for someone's absence.

I looked away before she could catch me staring, and when I glanced up again, she had squeezed onto a slick red stool between two beefy bikers whose low-slung jeans revealed the top third of their buttocks.

One of the bikers tilted his head toward her. Murmured something I couldn't hear.

She flinched away from him and drew in a ragged breath. Said something that made him scowl and turn back to his drink. Then Dani, the bartender, brought her an amber liquid over ice, and she hunched over the laminated bar, stirring her drink with one finger. The fingertips of her other hand rubbed gingerly at her cheek. She flicked her tongue across a split in her lower lip and blinked hard.

Not my problem, I told myself, even as my hand tightened around my glass. There were a thousand reasons why a woman might come to a bar with bruises on her cheeks and tears in her eyes. Not all of them involved some jerk with a sour temper and heavy fists.

I tore my gaze away and told myself again: Not my problem.

It was a sweltering June night, and I was sweating my *cojones* off at a corner table of the First Edition Bar and Grill and trying to forget that Maria, my wife of thirteen years, was spending her first anniversary with a man who wasn't me. We'd married young, two weeks after my twenty-first birthday, and while my mind understood what had gone wrong, the rest of me still felt like someone had thrown a bag over my head and scraped me raw with a cheese grater.

She'd waited a decent year before remarrying, but it wasn't long enough to keep my heart from aching like a broken tooth whenever I imagined D.W.'s hands on her, his mouth against hers . . .

A quavering voice interrupted my darkening fantasies. "Hey, Cowboy. Buy a girl a beer?"

I looked up to see the woman in the scarlet halter top, and the first thing I thought was, *Cowboy. . . Maria called me that.*

The second thing I thought was, *Why the hell not?*

"Sure." I gestured to the empty seat across from me, and she squeezed past a lanky man in leather and slid into the chair. "What's your brand?"

"Bud Lite." She gave me a watery smile and patted her stomach, which was as flat as a whippet's. "Got to watch the weight."

I edged through the crowd to the L-shaped bar and ordered the Bud and another Jack and Coke from Dani. She pushed a stray curl behind one ear and slid two glasses toward me with a nod toward the table I'd just left. "Looking to get lucky?"

"I don't know. She seems a little . . . fragile."

"Afraid she'll glom on?"

"Plenty to be afraid of before it gets to that."

"The boyfriend's out of the picture, if that matters. Or so she says."

"So she says."

"Seemed to me like she could use a little comfort."

"Maybe. But why me?"

"You gotta be kidding." A smile flitted across her face as she reached across the bar and smoothed the front of my shirt with her palm. "Believe me, honey, you're the pick of the litter."

I gave her a goofy grin, stammered a thanks, and stuffed a couple of dollars into the beer mug she'd set out for tips. Then I wended my way through the sweat-sour crush of bodies and the cigarette haze back to my table, where a burly guy who looked like someone had Super-glued a tumbleweed to his face was putting the moves on my new acquaintance.

He was about five-ten to my six feet, built like a barrel and reeking of cigar smoke. When he saw me, he rocked back on his heels and glared at me through slitted eyes, maybe gauging if he could take me. I was pretty sure he couldn't.

The muscles in my shoulders tensed, and we stared each other down for a long moment. Then he dropped his gaze, adjusted his crotch with one massive hand, and mumbled to my tablemate, "Aw, he ain't man enough for you." He ambled toward the pool table, throwing a gap-toothed, tobacco-tinged grin back over his shoulder. "You want a real man, give me a holler."

I set the lady's beer in front of her and slid into the seat across the table from her. She scooted her chair closer so I could hear her over the din. "Cockroaches. If there's one in the room, he'll find me. You come here often?"

I smiled at the cliché. "I stop by for a beer and a burger most Friday nights."

"No beer tonight." She nodded toward my glass.

"Nope." I thought of Maria, and a bitter taste came into my mouth. "Tonight called for something stronger."

She glanced at my left hand. "You're not married."

"Divorced."

"Kids?"

"One." I tugged my wallet out of my hip pocket, flipped to my son's school picture. I handed it over, watching her face as she studied it.

3

The corners of her mouth twitched up. No pity. No revulsion. "He's cute," she said.

"He has Down Syndrome."

"I have a cousin with Downs," she said. "Sweet kid."

Something in my gut relaxed. She handed back the wallet and said, "I've never been here before. Seems pretty rough."

The First Edition was originally conceived as a retreat for journalists and reporters—cozy and intimate, with a clientele who wore tweed jackets with suede patches on the elbows. It had changed hands several times since then and had finally evolved into a cramped sports bar catering primarily to good ol' boys and bikers.

The decor retained vestiges of its past. Ancient printing presses and yellowing early editions of *The Tennessean* and *The Nashville Banner* shared shelf space with NASCAR photos and neon Bud Lite signs. A Jeff Gordon ball cap hung from the half-empty potato chip rack, a rubber arm jutting from beneath it.

Beside the bar, a bulletin board labeled "Wall of Shame" was covered with candid photographs—a grinning man in a neon pink construction helmet, a shot of someone mooning the photographer, a bearded man at the pool table shooting the cue ball into the V of a young woman's spread legs.

No pictures of yours truly.

The lettering on the front window read, *First Edition Bar and Grill. Bikers Welcome.*

"It's not as rough as it looks," I said, pointing to a sign beside the Wall of Shame. It said, *No vulgar language.* "They don't even allow cussing in here."

"It's noisy, though." She slid her hands beneath her hair to rub the muscles of her neck, then leaned forward and placed her forearms on the table, giving me a good view of her cleavage. "Can I ask you something?"

"Sure."

Her cell phone rang, a tinny blast of "Born to Be Wild." She startled, rummaged through her purse, and fished out a shiny silver phone that looked like a miniature spaceship. She squinted at the name on the screen, and a shudder ran through her body.

"Oh, God," she said.

I felt my eyes narrow. "Is that him?"

She nodded.

"Tell him to get lost."

Her voice was a whisper. "I can't."

Her hands trembled as she fumbled with the phone.

I laid my hand over hers. "Ignore it then."

"I can't." She flipped open the front cover and held the phone to her ear. "Hello? Baby?"

I couldn't make out the words, but I could hear him shouting from where I sat. She blinked back tears and listened, her whole body trembling. "No, sweetheart, I didn't mean . . . I didn't . . ."

I gave her three minutes. Then I took the phone away. "Back off, buddy," I said into the speaker. "The lady wants to be left alone." Then I hung up.

"Oh, God," she said again. "He's going to kill me."

"You're not thinking of going back to him?"

"No, no, you don't understand. He'll find me." She flicked her tongue across her injured lip again and crossed her arms across her breasts. "What am I going to do?"

"The first thing you do is get a restraining order."

With a sharp, bitter laugh, she gestured to her battered face. "I had a restraining order when he did this. For all the good it did."

"I have friends on the force. I'll check on it tomorrow. You'll file charges."

It wasn't a question.

She gave a hitching sob. "I can't . . . I don't know . . . I mean, okay. Only ... Will you stay with me? Tonight? You don't know how he is."

She was looking for a protector, not a lover, which was fine with me. Still, there were probably a million reasons to

5

say no. I considered telling her I had a previous engagement and getting the hell out.

But there was no previous engagement.

"Why not?" I threw back the rest of my drink and pushed away from the table as the alcohol burned its way down my throat. "You want to take one car or two?"

"Let's take yours." She wiped at her eyes and forced another smile, revealing a smudge of cherry lipstick on one tooth. "He'll be looking for mine."

Since the parking lot was packed, I'd left my truck a little farther up the street. We walked past the antique boutique and the Tae Kwan Do school where I took lessons and occasionally taught. From there, it was less than a three-minute stroll to the strip mall where my black and silver Chevy Silverado sat glistening like a water bug beneath the street light.

"Nice wheels." She ran a loving hand over the front fender. The diffused light of the parking lot softened the hard angles of her face and made her almost beautiful. "You okay to drive?"

"I'm okay." I opened the passenger side door for her, and she slid across the seat as I closed the door behind her. When I climbed behind the wheel, she wriggled into the hollow under my arm. Poked the bobble-head Batman on the dashboard and giggled. Her hair still smelled of cigarette smoke, but underneath that was a musky perfume that, combined with the whiskey I'd been drinking, made it hard to think clearly. I said, "I don't even know your name."

"It's Heather." Her fingers squeezed my knee, trailed up my thigh.

I closed my hand over hers. "You don't have to do that."

"Sssh." She lifted her other hand and pressed the index finger to my lips. "I want to."

Maybe she wanted more than a protector, after all. I had a feeling I was headed for a night of raw and meaningless sex that I should probably feel guilty about but didn't.

"I'm Jared." I tried to keep my voice steady as her hand

continued its northerly migration. "Jared McKean."

"I know. I asked the bartender. Jared McKean, Private Eye." This time, her smile was wicked. "Or should I say, Private Dick?"

# 2

W<small>E STOPPED TO PICK UP</small> a bottle of Sangria and a couple of wine glasses. Then she directed me to a seedy motel off Lebanon Road. Twenty-four hour porn, rentals by the night or by the hour.

Nothing classy about it, but that was just as well. Class would have been wasted on us.

By the time she slipped the electronic key into the slot and pushed the door open, I was lightheaded with alcohol and muzzy with lust. I like to think of myself as a fairly centered, thoughtful kind of guy, but by then my center had drifted considerably south.

I thought briefly of Maria and felt a pang of guilt. But hey, I wasn't married anymore. I wasn't even dating anyone. And it wasn't like Maria wasn't giving it up to old D.W., probably at that very moment. So what difference did it make if I had sex with someone I had hardly met?

We squeezed inside the room, and Heather pushed me back against the door and pressed herself against me. Her tongue explored my mouth, flicked across my lips, and fluttered down my neck. Her breath was ragged with excitement, warm, and scented with beer. Her hands were everywhere.

I pulled away long enough to gasp, "You don't have to do this. I'll stay anyway."

"Don't," she whispered. "I need . . ." Her voice trailed off.

I thought of Maria again and nodded.

I needed, too.

Let's just say it took us a while to get to the Sangria.

I remembered the condom, barely.

There is a kind of sex where two people have learned each

other's preferences and rhythms, where one person's curves fit into the other person's spaces like the pieces of a puzzle. It's a slow, comfortable sex with a rightness and intensity, and it takes years of time and love to get there.

But there is another kind of sex, all animal ferocity and passion, sweat and thrust and howl and moan. Heartbeats pounding like primeval drums. Your body rises and she's there to meet it, and you think she might devour you, and you wish she would. Heat. Shuddering. Her legs around you, and you feel each tremor of that drenched and pulsing place between her thighs.

Three guesses which we had.

Afterward, we lay entangled with each other and the sheets. The sweat cooled on our bodies, and the room smelled heavily of musk.

"Mmmm. That was nice." She leaned over and planted a wet kiss firmly on my lips. "Wait here and I'll go get us a drink." She peeled the condom from between my thighs, kissed the place where it had been, and swung her legs over the edge of the bed. "I'll get rid of this on the way to the fridge."

I watched as she padded to the wastebasket, then to the refrigerator. She was thinner than my ex-wife, with sharp, jutting hipbones and a small, flat behind. Her breasts were soft and pear-shaped, with long pink nipples that stood up like the ends of a big man's thumbs. I could count her ribs and the vertebrae that ran like a knotted chain down the center of her back.

She had two tattoos in addition to the rose on her left breast. One was a circle of barbed wire and blue roses around her right ankle, the other a small yellow butterfly on her left shoulder. Her lipstick was smeared, and there were dark smudges in the hollows beneath her eyes where her mascara had run. Her hair was tousled, and since I was the one who had tousled it, I found it both erotic and endearing.

"Service with a smile," she said, and held out a brimming

9

wine glass. She slipped beneath the sheet and sipped her drink, holding it delicately, between two fingers and a thumb. "I know it's not expensive, but I love sweet wine. Don't you?"

"Mm." I tipped my head noncommittally.

She brushed her fingers across my upper arm, where a thin white scar stood out against the skin. At her touch, the pale hairs on my arms prickled.

"What happened here?" she asked.

"Vice squad. Undercover. Crackhead with a switchblade."

"And this one?" Her index finger traced a short jagged scar a few inches to the right of my navel. At her touch, the muscles of my stomach jumped.

"Broken bottle."

Her hand swept upward, palm flat against the hard contours of my abs. Her fingers tugged gently at the blond hairs on my chest, slid across my pectoral muscles, and came to rest beside the small round scar halfway between my armpit and my heart.

The one that had ended my marriage.

"And this?" she said. Just before her finger touched the puckered skin, I closed my hand around hers and said, "That one, I don't talk about."

"Ah." After a moment, she cleared her throat, slipped her hand from beneath mine, and said, "So. What's it like being a detective? It sounds exciting."

"Sometimes." I brushed my lips across the butterfly on her shoulder. "Mostly, it's a lot of waiting."

"Waiting?"

"Waiting for a cheating spouse to come out of a motel room. Waiting for a guy defrauding his insurance company to sneak out of his wheelchair and go dancing. Waiting for interviews. We talk to a lot of people. That's about it."

"You think about it being car chases and murder mysteries."

"P.I.'s don't do murder," I said. "Once in a blue moon, if we're hired by an attorney. But mostly, it's missing persons, insurance fraud, personal injury claims, spousal misconduct . . . that's the kind of stuff we do. We leave the homicides for the cops."

She made a wry face. "Too bad. I think a murder would be interesting."

"I worked homicide for seven years," I said. "And believe me, murder isn't interesting. It's nothing but a waste."

We moved on to other topics then. She told me about Ronnie, the soon-to-be-ex boyfriend.

"He seemed so sweet." She wrapped one arm around her knees and held her Sangria glass with the other hand. "Guess you never know, huh?"

"Guess not," I said, though there had probably been signs.

"Here, hold this." She handed me her glass and headed off to the bathroom.

When she came back, we had another glass of wine, made love again, and sometime after that I drifted into sleep, her body curled against mine like a Siamese cat's. I woke up once, with my head spinning and my stomach roiling, realized it was still dark out, and sank back into a sleep too deep even for dreams.

MORNING. A SLIVER of sunlight sliced through a gap in the curtains and seared through my eyelids, setting off a small nuclear explosion in my head. I scrabbled for the digital clock beside the bed and squinted at the readout. 10:45.

Great. I had to pick up my son, Paulie, at noon. I lay with my palms over my eyelids long enough to realize that my bladder was also on the brink of implosion. What a dilemma. If I got up, my skull might blow apart. If I stayed put, my bladder might burst. God. I clenched my teeth, pressed the palms of my hands to my temples, and stumbled into the bathroom to take a leak and inspect my tongue, which was coated with a white scum that looked and felt like dryer lint.

Heather was gone. She'd taken the wine glasses and the bottle of Sangria. And on the table, she had left a note.

11

*I'm sorry*, it said.

Shit. How could I have been so stupid?

I picked up my jeans. My belt hung from the loops, my cell phone still clipped to it. I checked my wallet. Everything was there. I felt for my keys. Still in the pocket.

So, sorry for what? For not saying good-bye? She hadn't left a number, so I guessed we'd had a one-night stand.

Too bad. I wondered vaguely if she'd ever get away from Ronnie, and if she did, if I would ever know about it.

Then I told myself there was nothing worse than a maudlin, thirty-something single guy with a hangover. I'd gotten laid, and if the worst that could be said was that the lady liked her sex with no strings attached, who was I to try and complicate things?

Still feeling muzzy-headed, I showered, dressed, and went down to the lobby, where a canister of stale coffee and a pile of day-old bread and pastries masqueraded as a continental breakfast. I couldn't manage much but coffee and dry toast, but even that calmed my churning stomach. While I ate, I skimmed a couple of sections of the *Tennessean,* which someone had left on the corner of the table.

There was an article on the legislation to remove the waiting period from handgun permits, a questionnaire for football fans, a story on the Society for Creative Anachronism, and a column on the RC and Moon Pie Festival in Bell Buckle, which was where I'd planned to take Paulie this afternoon.

According to the article, the festival had been a great success. I shook my head and read the article again.

Had been. As in, having already occurred. As in, something was terribly amiss.

I glanced at the header at the top of the page, and a hollow feeling settled in the pit of my stomach.

The header said *Sunday*. But I'd left the First Edition with Heather on Friday night. How the hell could it be Sunday?

Numb and disoriented, I scooped up the paper, and a headline on the front page of the local section caught my eye:

*Woman Slain in Hotel Room. Ex-Police Officer Sought for Questioning.*

Ex-police officer. I'd lost touch with most of the guys I used to work with, but I still felt connected to the force. Once a cop, always a cop, as Maria used to say. I'd skimmed most of the other stories, but I read this one word for word.

The victim was Amanda Jean Hartwell, known to friends and family as Amy. The grainy photograph showed a smiling, bespectacled young woman. Her hair, a tumble of shoulder-length curls pulled back by two barrettes, was either light brown or dark blond. It was hard to tell from the black-and-white photo.

Her body, which had been shot and mutilated (no details), had been found at the Cedar Valley Motel in Hermitage. Survived by a husband (Calvin J. Hartwell), two daughters (Katrina E. and Tara D. Hartwell), and a sister (Valerie C. Shepherd).

Her lover was wanted "for questioning"—a euphemism for "we know you did it, son, we just can't prove it yet"—and a description of the lover and his license number followed. NRL-549.

A trickle of ice water seeped though my bloodstream and settled in my bones.

NRL-549. That was the number on my license plate.

And the name at the bottom of the article . . . *Wanted for questioning: Jared McKean* . . . that was mine too.

# 3

I TUCKED THE NEWSPAPER under my arm and sauntered out to the parking lot, trying not to look like a man who was wanted for murder. Sun and humidity basted the asphalt and turned the outdoors into a sauna. Through ripples of heat, I could see my truck a few spaces to the right of where I'd left it. I'd been distracted at the time, but I was sure I'd parked closer to the streetlight. I peered inside and saw a key jutting from the ignition.

On the floorboard, the handgrip of a Glock .40 caliber protruded from beneath the driver's seat. Not mine, I told myself, as if wishing it might make it so. Mine was in the glove compartment, and I'd locked it with a combination that was not my son's birth date (too obvious), but my horse's.

My stomach tumbled, and my mouth tasted suddenly of bile. For a moment, I struggled to hold down my meager breakfast. Then I pulled my key chain from my pocket and counted. House key, office key, keys to Maria's place and my brother's house.

The key to the truck was gone.

My temples throbbed dully.

I'd missed picking up Paulie yesterday, and it wasn't looking good for today, either. It was already 11:30, and if the police wanted me for questioning in a murder case, I'd be lucky if I managed to extricate myself by midnight.

I tugged at the door handle. Unlocked. The Batman on the dashboard looked reproachful.

I punched in the glovebox combination and popped it open. Stared at the empty compartment as if I could will the gun into its accustomed place. For a long moment, I stood there, considering. I could take the Glock with me, wipe it

14

down, pour acid down the barrel, and drop it in the Cumberland River. I could throw it down a manhole or bury it in some vacant field. It would be easy. My hand stretched toward the pistol . . .

And pulled away. I shut the door and shoved my hands into my pockets. I'd made too many mistakes since Friday night. One more wouldn't make things better.

Besides, I'd rather be jammed up for doing the right thing than for doing the wrong one. At least if things went badly, I'd have the consolation of feeling self-righteous about it later.

I moved into the shade, away from temptation, and called Maria from my cell phone. She picked up on the second ring, sounding breathless, harried.

"It's me."

"Jared." There was a tremor in her voice, and I could see her in my mind, her round dark eyes like the pictures of those big-eyed kids so popular back in the '60s. "Where are you?"

"I'm sorry about yesterday. Missing Paul. I didn't—"

"I know. Just . . . are you all right?"

"You've seen today's paper."

"Yes. And the police were here. They said you hadn't made it home last night or the night before. They said you killed some woman."

I took a long, deep breath, pinched the bridge of my nose between my thumb and forefinger, and told myself not to panic.

This was easier said than done. If the police were actually saying that I'd killed a woman, it meant they had more than a license number. "Who'd they send out? Anybody I know?"

"Frank Campanella. Harry Kominski. Where are you?"

"Parking lot. Did they tell you what they have?"

"They said they had your fingerprints. A lot of other things."

"They couldn't have my fingerprints. I wasn't there."

I could hear the tears in her voice and wanted to rush over there and take her in my arms. But that wasn't my job any-

15

more, and I heard D.W.'s voice somewhere behind her, comforting and reassuring.

"I know you didn't do it," she said, finally. "I'm sure Frank knows it too."

D.W. took the phone. "Look, buddy," he said, "none of us think you did this. But you've got to go and talk to them, get this thing straightened out."

"I will," I said. "Put Paulie on. I've got to tell him I can't come today."

"I'll tell him."

"I'd rather."

I could almost hear him shrug. "Okay. Just a minute . . . Here he is."

"Hi, Daddy. Mama crying." The gravelly little voice made my heart twist. I could see him perched there, maybe on Maria's lap, his stubby fingers curled around the receiver, his slanted eyes crinkling. A little Buddha with Down Syndrome, happy to hear from me, worried about his mama.

"I know, Sport. You give Mom a hug for me, okay?"

"You come get me?"

"Not today, Sport. Something came up. I'm sorry, buddy."

"Moon pie, Daddy. You said Moon Pie."

"Next time, Paulie." The festival would be long over, but he wouldn't care. I had promised him Moon Pies; it didn't matter where they came from. I was proud of him for remembering.

"You come get me," he said again. "Today."

"I'm sorry, Sport. Another day. I love you."

"I love you. Come today."

There was a long pause as the phone switched hands. D.W. again. "He'll be all right. You just get this business taken care of. And call Jay, if you haven't already. He's frantic."

JAY WAS CHRISTENED with three first names. Theodore Jay Ambrosius Renfield. If names are destiny, Jay was destined to be an entrepreneur, an actor, a brigadier general, or gay. His parents, I think, had visions of a wealthy southern gentleman in a white linen suit. Pert blond trophy wife; three perfect, berry-brown children; sprawling estate with a pillared mansion and rolling green hills dotted with walking horses.

When we were in preschool and he preferred paper dolls to matchbox cars, his mother called him "sensitive." When he wore her eye shadow to school in the fifth grade, she called it a phase and took comfort in his manlier pastime of assembling models of plastic horror movie monsters. By the time he reached junior high school, it was obvious to everyone that the trophy wife was out, and that Theodore was, in his own words, a flaming fag. He went by 'Ted' then, and the guys in P.E. called him 'Ted Red'. "Hey, Ted," they'd call, "You on the rag?"

He began to call himself by his second first name (Ambrosius being out of the question). This resulted in a brand new nickname—"Gay Jay." Since, objectionable as that was, it was preferable to being named after a woman's monthly inconvenience, he decided to keep it.

When we were in grade school, we hung out together—Jay and Jared, two tow-headed boys that people often mistook for fraternal twins. But I was no more comfortable with his burgeoning homosexuality than the rest of the guys in our class, and by our junior year, we had pretty much drifted apart. Then one afternoon, I walked into the locker room and found the captain of the football team pushing Jay's head into the toilet.

I didn't think.

I charged.

Two cracked knuckles (mine) and half a dozen stitches (the football captain's) later, I found myself with a seven-day suspension and Jay's undying gratitude.

We lost touch not long after high school. I went to the police academy, got married, got a Criminal Justice degree with a minor in Psych, and had a son. Jay got a scholarship to Vanderbilt and moved in with a leather-clad, B&D biker boy with bleached blond hair and a Marilyn Monroe tattoo. His parents disowned him. He made a small fortune designing computer games and graphics.

I was lucky to get the bills paid.

Needless to say, we moved in different circles.

I hadn't seen Jay in ten years when he called me up out of the blue and told me that the biker boy, to whom Jay had always been utterly faithful, had left him high and dry and HIV positive. A lingering cold had been the impetus for him to get the test, and it had shown him to be on the brink of full-blown AIDS. He hadn't even known his lover was infected. They'd been tested years ago and both been clean.

Months after my divorce, when I had lost my job on the force and was trying to set myself up in the private detective business, it seemed only natural for me to move in with Jay.

All right, maybe not natural, but right. It was a good trade. I got cheap room and board, a place to board my horses—a palomino quarter horse named Tex and a black Tennessee Walker called Crockett—and unlimited use of Jay's swimming pool. He got someone to take care of him.

The boyfriends came and went, but I was his family.

I flipped open my phone again. The battery was low, so I dug through my pockets for a couple of coins, went back inside the motel, and called home.

Jay picked up on the first ring.

"It's me," I said.

He let out an audible breath. "Thank God. Where have you been? I didn't worry when you didn't come home, but then the police were here, and . . . They went through your room. I couldn't help it. They had a warrant."

Worse and worse. If they had enough on me for a judge to issue a search warrant, it was looking very bad indeed.

"What did they take? Do you know?"

"Hair samples. From your comb. They looked through all your clothes. Something about fibers and bloodstains. And they dusted for fingerprints. What a mess." He was quiet for a moment. "They seemed especially interested in your theatrical makeup."

It had been years since I'd done any community theater, but I'd found that a little facial hair could change a man's entire appearance. Back when I worked undercover in vice, it came in handy. It still did.

"It's okay," I said. "I'll call Frank and see what's going on. If they've got DNA, this'll be over with in no time."

"God, I hope so." I could hear the mixture of anxiety and relief in his heavy sigh. "How can they even think you'd be involved in a thing like this?"

"Somebody stole my truck last night. No, night before last." I still wasn't clear on the timing. I'd lost a day at least, but I wasn't sure how. Had the cloying sweetness of the wine concealed something more sinister than fruit? "I'm sure this'll all be cleared up soon."

But something niggled at the back of my mind. I hadn't been in Hermitage on Friday night. I didn't know the murdered woman, and I'd never visited the Cedar Valley Motel.

So why did the police have my fingerprints?

MY NEXT CALL went to Frank Campanella, Metro Homicide. For seven years, he was my partner. Now he was dusting my room for prints. It was his job, but the thought left a hollow feeling in my belly just the same.

He answered on the third ring. "Campanella here."

"It's me."

"Jared. Where the hell are you?"

"Everybody wants to know where I am. Frank, you know I didn't do this."

There was a long pause. When he spoke, there was a tinge of anger in his voice. "You want to hear what we've got so far?"

"You know I do."

"We've got hair and semen. It'll be a few weeks before we get a sure DNA match, but serology results show it's your blood type. AB negative. I don't have to tell you how rare that is."

He didn't. It was a trait my brother, Randall, and I had both inherited from our father. "Okay. So it's rare. There's still plenty of guys in Nashville with AB negative blood."

"We've got your fingerprints. We've got your name all through her Palm Pilot. We've got a message from you on her voice mail telling her she's one dead bitch if she doesn't quit screwing around. We've got a witness puts your truck at the crime scene, and the receptionist there says a man of your approximate height and weight checked into that room. Guy had a beard, but we all know you wear disguises."

"You think I'm dumb enough to leave my hair and semen all over a crime scene? Or forget to wipe my prints? You think I'm dumb enough to leave a threat like that on tape?"

"I wouldn't have thought so. But it's a crime of passion, which as we both know, makes men stupid."

"You really think I did this?"

"I don't know what I think. Why don't you give us all a break? Come on in and tell us how it happened."

"I can't tell you how it happened. I wasn't there."

I heard a long exhalation on the other end of the line. When he spoke again, his voice had softened. "Mac, I can help you, but you gotta give me something."

The nickname was a razor through the heart. I had trusted Frank with my life, as he had trusted me with his, and although I felt that trust eroding like a child's sand castle, if he could still call me 'Mac,' there was hope for it yet. I squeezed a breath past the knot in my throat and said, "Look, I'll get back to you later, when I know what's going on."

I hung up before they could trace the call. Hand on the receiver, I laid my throbbing forehead against the wall and thought about Heather.

*I'll get rid of this on the way to the fridge.* But had she? She'd stopped at the trash basket, but had she actually dropped the condom in it? Or had she put it in the refrigerator when she went to get the wine? I remembered how she'd held the glasses, primly, by the stems, and thought that maybe it was something more than primness that had made her hold them that way.

*Here, hold this.* She'd gotten my prints on both glasses.

Semen, hair, and fingerprints. While there were plenty of people who could have gotten prints and hair samples, she was the only one who'd had access to semen in quite a while.

But why?

How long had she been planning this perfect little murder?

*I think a murder would be interesting.*

Had she chosen me to be her fall guy because I was convenient? Was I just the one she happened to pick up?

But if that was the case, how had she gotten my voice on the victim's voice mail?

And who was the man with the beard? The elusive, abusive Ronnie? Had there ever even been a Ronnie?

I thought about the note she'd left. *I'm sorry.*

Sorry for what, I had wondered.

Now I knew.

# 4

I WIPED A LINE of perspiration from my forehead and left the motel on foot. My shirt was plastered to my back before I even made it out of the parking lot.

I made my next call from the diner across the street and ordered a pot of coffee to occupy me until my ride arrived. His name was Billy, like about a million other good-ol'-boys from the South. I have personally known three Billy Rays, a Billy Don, a Billy Jack, a Billy Bob, two Billy Joe's, and even, once, a Billy Bill. William Bill Burleson. It said so on his birth certificate.

My buddy's name was William Mean, which had, in his army days, been shortened to the more descriptive (and more accurate) Billy Mean. In military fashion, he'd found himself called "Mean, William", which eventually became Mean Billy, or sometimes even Mean Billy Mean.

Back then, he was shaped like a sparkplug, all bone and gristle under muscles packed hard as a buffalo's. Now that bone and muscle was blanketed under fifty pounds of fat. But Billy was no prey animal. He'd been in Special Forces, and he still moved that way, dangerous beneath the flab, like a caged tiger.

He was three years younger than my father would have been, and back in the late sixties, had served two tours in Vietnam. Dad was Air Force and Billy was Army, but I wondered sometimes if their paths had ever crossed. There was no reason why they would have, but I wondered just the same.

Billy swears, and I believe him, that he hardly felt afraid at all in 'Nam. Fear was such a constant presence that he hardly even noticed it. But when he got back home, all that

22

fear crashed down on him like fifty tons of bricks.

He had night terrors. He was petrified of thunder. One afternoon, a woman spat at him as he was buying groceries. Another called him a rapist and a monster and a baby killer. Before long, he could hardly leave his own house.

There was no money. His wife moved out and took their 2-year-old daughter with her, and while Billy said he couldn't blame her, it only made the black depression worse.

One day, a buddy from his old platoon called up and said he had a plan to make them rich. It involved guns and a liquor store.

It was desperate and stupid, and Mean Billy knew it. But he was desperate himself. And besides, it served the commie-hippie-liberal assholes he'd gone to war for right.

The best thing to be said was that nobody died.

After six hard years at DeBerry Correctional Facility in Nashville, he got out with a Bachelor's in Social Science, a handful of grant applications, and a *vision*. Within the year, he'd wrangled a warehouse down on Seventh Avenue and turned it into a shelter for homeless men, mostly ex-vets and ex-cons. He arranged jobs for them and provided transportation in a faded Chevy van on which one of his clients had painted a not-too-shabby replica of Van Gogh's 'Starry Night'. He called it the Dream-mobile.

His clients called it the Mean Machine.

Twenty minutes after I called him, he pulled up in it and honked the horn.

I paid my tab and went outside to catch my ride.

"Think you might announce us to the whole damn neighborhood?" I brushed a petrified French fry off the passenger seat and slid inside. After a few fruitless tugs at the seat belt, I gave up and consoled myself with the hope that he'd drive less like a bottle rocket than usual.

"Aw. Nobody's watchin'." He peeled out of the parking lot, dispelling my misguided optimism. "Now, tell me what you've gotten yourself into."

"I wish I knew. Frank says they've got a boatload of evidence against me in this killing they had out at the Cedar Valley Motel night before last." I told him about the hair, the prints, the tape, and the semen.

"Jesus, buddy. That's almost enough to make me think you did it."

"Don't even joke around about that." My tone was sharper than I'd intended.

"Well, who have you been giving semen samples to?" He tugged at his grizzled beard and laughed at his own joke, his ruddy face reddening to the shade of a country ham.

I shot him an annoyed look. "I know who planted the semen. I don't know how they got the tape. I never met this woman, and I sure as hell never threatened to kill her."

"Which, if you was gonna do, you wouldn't have announced on tape."

"Exactly."

"Nashville's full of actors, buddy. Maybe they just found someone who sounds like you."

"Maybe." It seemed unlikely, but if there was some other explanation, I had no idea what it might be.

We drove to Billy's place and I followed him up a narrow stairwell to the efficiency apartment he'd built above the shelter. He jiggled the key in the lock until it caught, then kicked the door open and made a sweeping gesture toward the living room—sagging brown leather couch, frayed tartan La-Z-boy, scuffed coffee table, and a 29" TV way too heavy on the green. His battered maple desk was jammed into one corner, piled high with bulging manila folders. The room smelled stale, like sour socks beneath a veneer of Pine-Sol.

"Welcome aboard, good buddy. *Mi casa es su casa.*"

"*Gracias,*" I said, which was about the extent of my Spanish.

"I've got a couple of appointments downstairs. Grab yourself a beer and make yourself at home. Stay as long as you need to."

He picked through the precariously balanced folders, eased out two fat files, and nudged the stacks back into place.

"It won't be long, "I said. "Don't want them looking at you as an accessory after the fact."

"I'm already an accessory."

"They can't prove you knew I was wanted when you picked me up. In a day or so, there won't be any question."

His big shoulders hunched. "We'll cross that river when we come to it. I owe you, boy, and I always pay my debts."

The debt he was referring to was one of my first cases: finding his daughter, Cambria, and arranging a reconciliation. The first part was a cakewalk; people who aren't hiding from anything are easy to find. The reconciliation was tougher. Cam hadn't seen her dad since she was two, and the chip on her shoulder was about the size of a redwood.

In the end, she agreed to meet her father, and after a cool year, things had finally begun to warm up between them.

"Hell, Billy, you already paid for that, remember? Two hundred dollars a day, plus expenses."

"Naw, man. You gave me back my little girl. That'll never be paid back."

He said he'd be gone until about 4:30, then took his massive self downstairs. When he was gone, I helped myself to two aspirins and a Dr. Pepper, plugged my phone in on Billy's charger, left a brief message on Frank Campanella's answering machine, and settled in to figure out my options.

I knew I'd have to turn myself in sooner or later, but first, I wanted to find out more about the woman I was supposed to have killed. Amanda Jean Hartwell. Amy. If I knew who she was, maybe I could determine who might have wanted her dead.

And why her murder had been pinned on me.

I still didn't know why I'd been chosen. Had I just been at the wrong place at the wrong time, or did someone hold a grudge against me? There were plenty of candidates: guys whose insurance scams were derailed when I snapped photos of them lifting weights and dancing with their girlfriends, parents who'd lost custody of their children when embarrassing photographs surfaced, husbands who'd been caught with their pants down and lost half their assets in messy divorces.

Not to mention all the scumbags I'd helped put away while I was still on the force.

I grabbed a piece of paper and started jotting names of people who might hate me enough to do this and be smart enough to pull it off.

By the time Billy got back, I had covered most of the sheet. Some of the names weren't really names at all, but descriptions: "scraggly reddish brown hair, scar on left cheek, arrested for burglary;" "big guy, lightning bolt tattoo, arrested on suspicion of rape." Some were nicknames: Ice Pick, Hammerhead, Crossbones, Blade.

I didn't think any of the names would lead anywhere, but it was a place to start.

Billy ordered us a sausage pizza with double cheese, which we washed down with a couple of Heinekens while we watched the evening news.

Sure enough, my name was on it.

My gut lurched when they showed the victim's picture. Dropping my pizza back into the box, I leaned forward for a closer look.

In the photo, Amy Hartwell stood in front of a Tudor-style stone house, her arms clasped around two young girls. Katrina and Tara, said the anchorwoman, ages 12 and 7. Amy's hair and Tara's were the same soft shade of golden-brown, like buttered toast. Katrina's was as smooth and pale as corn silk.

They were all smiling.

The camera segued to an interview with the cleaning woman who had discovered the body. She was a buxom redhead in her fifties with a round, freckled face. Her hands, in her lap, twisted a frayed Kleenex into a corkscrew, and her eyes were swollen, rimmed with red.

"It was early, you know, and she didn't have . . . Ms.

Hartwell didn't have . . . the 'Do not disturb' sign on the doorknob. So I used my key and went in . . . And I went in, and it was . . ." She stifled a sob. "There was a naked woman on the bed. Her legs were spread, like . . . like he . . . Somebody . . . wanted her to be found that way." She held the tissue to her nose and honked into it as the camera cut away to the reporter.

This time, they didn't say I was wanted for questioning.

This time, they said I was a suspect.

I leaned over and flipped the channel to the Nashville station, where local celebrity Ashleigh Arneau was delivering the same news in a breathy, husky voice that made murder seem like seduction. She batted her eyes at the audience, wide blue eyes she insisted on calling "wisteria."

On the screen behind her was a photograph of me with my eyes bulging and my mouth twisted in what was almost certainly a curse. I looked like a man with murder on his mind. In truth, I'd just dropped a hammer on my thumb.

A real Kodak moment.

I could imagine how Ashleigh must have salivated when she realized she had photos of a bona fide fugitive in her own personal archives.

"Aw, shit," Billy said. "Not that bitch."

"I have an idea," I said.

"A bad idea. I can tell. You don't even have to tell me what it is."

"She can help me."

He snorted. "Yeah, when Hell freezes over. Didn't she help you enough already?"

"Billy . . ." I sighed. He was right. It was stupid. Of all the people in the world I shouldn't trust, Ashleigh was at the top of the list. But she was also one of the few people in a position to help me out of the mess Heather had gotten me into.

Besides . . .

I punched the *off* button on the remote and said, "She owes me one."

27

# 5

ASHLEIGH ARNEAU AND I met in high school. She was head cheerleader, vice president of the student body ("president of student body vices," was the joke), drama queen, and star reporter for the *Golden Bear Claw* student newspaper. We didn't date back then, although we did a few shows together. In *The Crucible*, she played Abigail to my John Proctor, which might have been an omen of things to come.

But she was seeing a guy from MTSU, and I was dating a cute little junior who played clarinet in the band. The junior, Belinda Honeyman, was playing Goody Proctor, so there was little opportunity for conquest, even if either of us had been so inclined. By the time I ran into Ashleigh again, she was working as a reporter for a local TV station. She'd nose around the precinct house looking for a story, and I would spout whatever we'd been told to tell the press—usually "no comment."

I swear on my mother's heart, I never slept with Ashleigh. Not while I was married, anyway. Maria has her doubts, but this is the God's honest truth. Until six months after my divorce—by which time Maria was already seeing D.W.—my relationship with Ashleigh Arneau was strictly professional. But after my wife—my ex-wife—got serious about the man who would in time become my replacement, I took the plunge and asked Ashleigh to a live performance of *Johnny Guitar* at a local dinner theatre.

We lasted for four months. Four months of drama, four months of her pleading with me for info on ongoing cases, four months of stimulating conversations and fantastic sex. And in the end, when I was called into the Commissioner's office and relieved of duty for divulging sensitive information, it turned out to be four months of nothing.

I called Ashleigh from a pay phone and told her I'd been fired. She made all the right noises, sympathetic and concerned, and I got home just in time to catch her removing the recording device she had placed in the receiver of my phone.

There was an awkward silence. Then she asked, "Are you going to have me arrested?" Only the slightest tremor in her voice told me she was genuinely frightened of the prospect.

I thought about it. Thought about what would happen to that exquisite body and that gorgeous face in prison. And I decided that, whatever she had done to me, I couldn't put her through it.

I looked squarely into those wisteria-colored eyes and said, "Get out."

She laid a cool hand on my forearm. "I'm sorry, Jared. I didn't mean to get you fired. Only, you have no idea how fierce the competition is out there. If I don't get these stories…"

"Get out," I repeated, and I guess she finally figured I meant it, because she left.

I mailed her the rest of her belongings. There wasn't much. Some lingerie, a few toiletries, and a couple of changes of clothes.

I didn't pee in her shampoo, but I thought about it.

I hadn't seen her since, except on TV, and even then I always tried to change the channel before she came on.

Now, though, I hoped a sense of obligation and the lure of an exclusive would be enough to secure a little loyalty.

Billy hovered over my shoulder as I dialed the number on my cell phone. When she answered, I drew in a breath. Her voice was still enough to drive a sane man mad.

"Ashleigh, it's Jared. Jared McKean."

"Jared!" She sounded surprised and a little eager. "How long has it been?"

*Not long enough*, I thought, but did not say. "A little over a year. I saw you on the news tonight."

29

"Really?" A note of pleasure warmed her voice. "What did you think?"

"Beautiful, as always. I wanted to talk to you about your lead story."

She gave a squeal of nervous laughter. "Yes, I imagine you do. But, Jared . . ."

"Ashleigh, you know me. I didn't kill this woman."

"Oh, I know. I'm sure this is all a big misunderstanding." After a little pause, she added, "I understand they've got your DNA."

"They don't have *my* DNA," I said, though if my suspicions about Heather were true, they very well might. "They have my blood type. But I know that isn't public information yet. You got taps on someone else's line?"

Long pause. "I have a contact on the force."

I took in a long, slow breath. "Look, Ash, enough fencing. I need your help."

Wary now. "Why should I help you?"

Why, indeed. "Let's start with, you used me, you lost me my job, and then you did a story on how I'd been dumped from the force—which was your fault to begin with. Now you've plastered my picture all over the news. Nice touch, by the way, choosing the one that makes me look like a homicidal maniac."

I could picture her on the other end of the line, the little furrow between her brows, the cupid's bow of her lips pursed into an indignant pout. "What is it you want?"

"You've already said you had a contact. You can ask around, find out about the victim."

"You already know more than I do. They say you'd been banging her for months."

*Months?* I shook my head, although she couldn't see it. "I didn't even know her."

"Then why are they saying you do?"

"There was a woman I met..." It sounded lame, even to me, but I ran it down for her anyway.

She was quiet for a moment. Then, "Conspiracy theories really aren't your style."

"You know I didn't do this. If I was going to kill somebody, I would have done you a long time ago."

On the other end of the line, there was a sound like a baby's hiccup. When she spoke again, her voice sounded strained. "Maybe you should just turn yourself in. The police will figure it all out."

This wasn't necessarily true. Metro had a lot of good cops on the job, but like police forces everywhere, the department was overextended. They didn't have time to chase shadows when, thanks to Heather, I'd become a prosecutor's wet dream. It would be tempting just to throw me under the jail and close the books.

Especially considering the conditions under which I'd left.

"Ashleigh, I'm just saying, if I were the kind of guy who would do a thing like this, it would have happened by now. My wife left me, and I didn't kill her. You . . . you were pretty much the devil incarnate, and I didn't kill you."

"Who knows?" She still sounded scared, but she'd gotten back some of her bravado. "Maybe everything just built up."

"Think of the story. 'Local Anchor Woman Clears Innocent Man.' That could be you. That's prize-winning material."

There was another pause. "It would make a good story. But you have to promise me an exclusive."

"It's all yours."

"I need to know exactly what happened last night. What happened with the woman. How your truck ended up at the murder scene. Can you come over and fill me in?"

"I don't know . . ."

"This may take awhile, and I don't want to do it on the phone. I need to see your face, your mannerisms."

I thought about it. There was a chance she'd set me up. On the other hand, she'd climb Mt. Everest with her silk-wrapped, salon-painted fingernails for a story. Maybe she'd be curious enough to give me a day or two.

"Okay," I said at last. "I'll be there in thirty minutes."

When I hung up, Billy flung himself down on the couch with so much force it bounced. "I guess it won't do me no good to tell you this is the damn-foolest thing you've ever done?"

"Billy," I said, "desperate times call for desperate measures. And these, my friend, are desperate times."

BILLY OFFERED TO DRIVE ME OVER. Instead, I walked a couple of blocks to Broadway and caught a cab to Ashleigh's place in Green Hills, an upscale neighborhood south of downtown. I didn't think she'd turn me in until she got her exclusive, but I wanted Mean Billy miles away from the place, just in case she did.

She had a two-story, Elizabethan-style house with a pool in the back yard and a koi pond in the front. The front porch light radiated a washed out glow that turned her dogwoods and azaleas into jagged black tangles. I had the cab driver circle the block twice to make sure there were no cops around. Then I got out, paid my fare, and threw myself to the sharks.

Shark.

Singular.

She met me at the door with a standard high-society hug and kissed the air beside my cheek. The scent of her Bill Blass perfume brought back erotic memories. Rumpled sheets, chestnut hair splayed across my chest, the smell of sweat and flowers on her skin.

"Jared. It's good to see you again. You still look scrumptious." Scrumptious. She actually used words like that. She trailed one finger lightly down the buttons of my shirt and sighed. "Makes me wonder why I ever let you go."

"Your source dried up."

She pouted prettily. "Now, Jared. Don't be cynical."

"Getting canned because your girlfriend sneaked around and tapped your phone will make a person cynical. Not to mention getting framed for murder."

She dropped her hand to her side and took a step back,

averting her eyes. "So, how's Paul?"

She'd never been comfortable with Paulie. I wasn't sure if it was because he was a child or because he had Down Syndrome. Maybe some of both. Ashleigh wasn't exactly the maternal type.

"Fine," I said. "They're keeping an eye on his heart, but for now he's doing okay." Downs kids have a tendency toward heart and respiratory problems. Leukemia too, though we'd been lucky on that count. Knock on wood.

"Well. That's good, then. How old is he now? Six? Seven?"

"He'll be eight next Wednesday."

"My God."

"He was going on seven when you and I were together."

She grimaced. "I was thinking he was younger." She was wearing a tight black miniskirt with a white silk blouse that skimmed all the right places. Her makeup had been flawlessly applied: smoky eye shadow, thick black lashes, pale smooth skin with a hint of blush, siren-red lips. "Well, enough small talk. Why don't you sit down and tell me what happened, exactly? I'll get us a drink. Do you still like Jack and Coke?"

I thought of the last time I'd had Jack and Coke and grimaced. "Nothing for me, thanks."

"Nothing? Bourbon? Beer? Iced tea? Pepsi?"

"Tea, if it's already made."

She sashayed into the kitchen, hips swaying beneath the short skirt. I knew the show was for my benefit. I also knew that I could have been the plumber or the Terminex man, and she would have felt the same need to make me want her. I was easy pickings, but we both knew nothing would come of it.

I looked around while she was gone, noticed she'd changed her security system.

She came back carrying my tea and what looked like a glass of orange juice, but which was almost certainly a screwdriver.

"Made some changes," I said, pointing to the new keypad.

She gave a dismissive wave. "Oh, that. I had a break-in a

few months ago. Someone cut the wires on the system. But I guess something must have scared him away, because nothing was missing. Now . . . Tell me about this woman you met last night. What was her name? Amy something, wasn't it?"

"No, that was the woman who was murdered. I never met her. This girl called herself 'Heather,' but that's probably not her real name."

I told her the story, from Heather's request for a drink to reading my name in the paper.

When I'd finished, she leaned back, crossed her legs at the knee, and said, "That's fascinating."

And all hell broke loose.

A uniformed policeman burst through the door, gun drawn. Another couple of cops poured out of the bedroom.

I knew when I'd been beaten. Even if I'd had my gun, I knew better than to draw on cops. People who draw down on policemen tend to have very short life expectancies.

I put up my hands and let them search me, then went peaceably out to their patrol car, which must have been hidden in a neighbor's garage.

I started to cover my face, but thanks to Ashleigh's photograph, there wasn't much point. Instead I took a deep breath and tried to exude an aura of dignified innocence.

Ashleigh trailed along behind us, looking delicate and shaken for the cameras she had obviously invited.

I looked at her and said, "Once a barracuda, always a barracuda."

Her eyes were wide and innocent, brimming with unshed tears.

The cameras were rolling.

# 6

"**O**KAY, LET'S GO over this again." Frank Campanella paused to take a gulp of the bitter brew that passed for coffee in the interrogation rooms. His partner on the case, Harry Kominski, was nowhere to be seen, probably watching from behind the two-way mirror.

In all the years I'd known Harry, I'd heard him say maybe fifteen words. He was the tallest man on the force, which, combined with his reticence, earned him the inevitable nickname 'Lurch.' He looked like a dumb galoot. He wasn't. Like his namesake, he knew everybody's secrets.

I glanced toward the mirror, told myself to forget about Harry, and focused on Frank's next question. "How long had you been seeing Mrs. Hartwell?"

I sighed and splayed my hands on the table. "For the hundredth time, I hadn't been seeing her. I never even met the woman."

"Then why did she have your name in her Palm Pilot in a dozen places?" He pulled out a small black electronic organizer and read, "'Saw Jared today.' 'Jared and I fought.' 'Jared very angry today.'"

"There are a lot of Jareds in the world."

"It says here in the address part, 'Jared McKean.' Is this your phone number?" He held it up so my lawyer and I could see it.

"You know it is."

"And your address?"

"Yes."

"This *is* Mrs. Hartwell's organizer, isn't it?"

"I don't know. I've never met her."

35

"And yet, she's got your name all over the place."

"So it seems."

"Why would she have your name and address in her organizer if she didn't know you?"

"I don't know."

"You don't know."

Wallace Aaron, an up-and-coming young attorney whose name I had plucked out of the yellow pages, raised his hand in protest. "Detective Campanella, he's already said he doesn't know."

"Swill." Frank drained the last of the coffee and tossed the crumpled cup into the wastebasket. "You remember what swill this is?"

I forced a smile. "I remember."

He stole a glance at my attorney, then turned his attention back to me. "Let me get this straight. What you're saying is, this stranger you picked up in a bar had sex with you so she could steal your DNA and plant it at a murder scene?"

"I know it sounds implausible, but . . ."

"Implausible? Son, it sounds like a bad detective movie."

"Detective . . ." Aaron's tone held a warning.

Frank sighed and scraped his chair away from the table. "You know, Mac, I never believed any of the things they said about you, how you were feeding information to that reporter you were humping. I always stood up for you."

"I know you did, and I appreciate that."

"I wish to God I could believe you now."

I looked down at my hands and forced the words from my tightening throat. "Frank, you know I'm not stupid. If I'd killed the girl, why would I have left all that evidence around? Let me ask you something. Where did you get my fingerprints?"

"You know I'm not at liberty—"

"A pair of wine glasses, maybe? Am I right?"

"Of course you're right. But you could be right because you were there."

36

"You don't have to say anything else," said Aaron. "In fact, I advise you not to."

I ignored him and responded to Frank's hypothesis. "No. Because that's what was missing from the hotel room. Were there traces of drugs in either glass?"

"We're still waiting for the report to come back. Why? Did you drug her?"

"No, but she might have drugged me. In fact, I want a blood test and a urinalysis. As soon as possible, in case it's Rohypnol." Also known as 'roofies', the date rape drug Rohypnol left traces in the bloodstream for up to forty-eight hours and in the urine for up to seventy-two.

"You'll get 'em, but I don't need to tell you a prosecutor will just say you drugged yourself after you killed her."

"Piece of the puzzle, as you always say. What about the bottle? Any prints there?"

"No prints on the bottle."

"Why would I remember to wipe the bottle and not the glasses? And what about the rest of the hotel room? Were my prints found anywhere else?"

"No," he conceded.

"And the lineup. What happened with the lineup?" I'd been sure the clerk at the motel would clear me.

"Inconclusive. The man she saw had a beard and a mustache, but you could have pulled that off with stage makeup. You did it in vice often enough. Besides, with the Palm Pilot, the prints, the serology report, ballistics—we know the bullet that killed her came from your Glock—we didn't need much more." He raked his fingers through his silvering hair. "What I want to know is, why pose her like that? I know you've been through a lot lately, but she was your lover, for God's sake. Why not leave her a little dignity?"

Aaron gave me a warning look. "I really have to recommend you not say anything more."

"I didn't pose her, Frank. I didn't kill her. I didn't fucking *know* her."

He leaned forward and studied my face. Then he heaved himself out of his chair and turned away. "There's something else, too."

He tossed a manila folder onto the table in front of me.

"What's this?"

"You tell me."

I opened the folder, and a slender, pubescent girl with long pale hair and a pensive expression stared up at me from a glossy color photograph. I recognized her from the morning paper as Katrina Hartwell, the murdered woman's daughter. The girl was naked, except for a gold crucifix and a pair of absurdly high heels. One hand clutched at a bit of white cloth that was probably a handkerchief.

"Kiddie porn?" I closed the folder without looking any further. My mouth tasted sour. "You're not serious."

"Found 'em in your truck, right under the driver's seat, along with traces of semen. Also from someone who's AB positive. You want to explain that?"

My head was reeling as if I'd just been struck with a two-by-four. "Frank, you know I didn't . . . I couldn't . . ."

"Don't say anything else," Aaron said to me. "Not another word."

"Doesn't matter what I think," Frank said. "This is going to hurt you. And the tape. That's going to hurt, too."

"I never called her." My voice sounded dull, as if it came from somewhere far away. "I don't know whose voice is on that tape, but it's not mine."

For a moment, his gray gaze held mine. Then his shoulders sagged and the lines of his face went slack with disappointment. He looked away again, but before he did, I saw in his eyes the words he couldn't say: *I loved you like a son.*

"It's not mine, Frank," I repeated.

He ran his hands over his face and said, "The voice recognition boys say it is."

FRANK CAMPANELLA HAD WORKED for the Metro Nashville police force for thirty years. Twenty of those years had been spent solving homicides. For seven of those, he'd been my partner, my mentor, and my friend.

We'd spent many a weekend in his basement sipping ice cold Heinekens and building terrain for his Lionel electric trains: mountains carved from foam and flocked with green, weathered wooden trestles spanning lakes of blue acrylic, forests made of plastic armatures and dried moss, long stone fences made of sealed and painted Cap'n Crunch. Miniature people waited forever for their trains, reading tiny newspapers, clutching tiny suitcases.

We'd been to NASCAR races together and fished from his old dock, and the day a suspect named Caleb Wilford rammed a titanium-tipped arrow into my chest, it was Frank who put him down with a bullet to the head, then held a towel to my seeping wound until the paramedics came.

It had taken a lot to convince Frank I was guilty. I tried to feel angry about it, but all I could summon up was a heavy sadness that made me think of *The Crucible* and poor Giles Corey being pressed with stones.

I sipped at the coffee he had brought me and waited to be taken to Night Court, trying not to think about reasonable doubt and how a judge who knew a hell of a lot less about me than Frank did was about to decide whether or not the evidence against me was compelling.

I'd been through the routine a thousand times, but never from this side of things. Mug shots, fingerprinting, the strip search and cursory shower with the dour guard watching, the orange jumpsuit, being led to Night Court in cuffs. I saw the necessity, but I couldn't say I liked it. I felt embarrassed and ashamed, a little less than human, even though I knew I hadn't done what they'd accused me of.

I used my one phone call to tell my brother, Randall, where I was and what had happened. By the time I got to Night Court, which in Nashville operates twenty-four/seven, he was sitting in the gallery with his wife, Wendy, and their teenaged children. Caitlin, at thirteen, wore a flowered sundress that showed off her blond hair and her summer tan. She looked fresh and young and out of place. Seeing her, I felt old.

Josh, fifteen, sat slumped beside his mother, who looked as pale and anxious as I'd ever seen her. Josh looked like he'd stepped out of *The Rocky Horror Picture Show,* his face vampire-white, his pouting lips outlined and painted black. His long straight hair, which should have been the same light buckskin color as his father's and my own, had also been dyed black. It might have been amusing, except that, even with the distance of the courtroom between us, I could feel Randall's seething embarrassment .

Josh had always been the kind of kid his teachers called a Delight to Have in Class. Bright. Happy. Sensitive. Lately, he'd become a different person, sullen and uncommunicative. Things must be bad, if Randall was letting Josh go out in public dressed like a ghoul.

I forced my thoughts back to the courtroom, where there were six other cases before mine. None involved homicide. Then the charges against me were read in a monotonous voice that barely penetrated the numbness in my brain. "Possession of child pornography," I heard, and "Murder in the First Degree." Some half-cognizant portion of my mind understood that they could go for the death penalty.

I hoped there were enough discrepancies in the crime scene to indicate the murder had been a crime of passion, but I was concerned about the bearded man the receptionist had seen. A disguise could be seen as proof of premeditation. On the other hand, if I were going to a rendezvous with a married woman, it wasn't outside the realm of possibility that I might wear a disguise as a matter of course.

Yeah. Right.

I refused to think about the other charge. It bothered me more to think I was suspected of child porn than of murder.

The Judicial Commissioner set bail at two million dollars.

The pronouncement was like a fist to the gut. I guess I was lucky he'd set bail at all. But I would have to come up with ten percent plus twenty-five dollars, if I could even convince a bail bondsman to take a chance on me, and two hundred thousand dollars was a lot of money.

A lot of money I didn't have.

If I had somehow managed to come up with the cash, and if I could find a bail bondsman willing to guarantee me for two million dollars if I skipped, I could have walked out of the courtroom a relatively free man. Since I didn't have it, the Judicial Commissioner set a date for jail docket, and a balding man whose swollen belly strained at the buttons of his uniform led me out of the courtroom through a side door.

Before the door shut behind me, I heard Randall's voice call after me. "Don't worry, Little Buddy. We'll get you out real soon."

# 7

I SHOULD HAVE KNOWN what was coming next.

The only thing worse than being an ex-cop in jail is being a suspected child molester in jail.

By the time I realized I was being taken to the common dormitory and not the private cell they usually reserved for high-risk types, I was already there.

"I think there's been a mistake," I started, though I didn't want to come right out and tell him why I needed protection from the general population. Not there in front of a bunch of guys who would want to skin me and make gloves from my hide.

"Sure, buddy." The guard, whose nametag read 'Hal Meacham' swung the cell door open. "That's what they all say."

"Look, can we just—?"

He fingered his baton. "You can just get your sorry ass in there, is what we can do. Hey, fellas, guess what's for dinner. Chicken hawk."

At the name, slang for pedophile, every head in the cell turned to face me. For a moment, I knew what a fox must feel like just before the hounds tear it apart.

Meacham gave a hard shove to the center of my back, and I stumbled inside.

The door clanged shut behind me, and I backed up against it and looked around.

"Hey," drawled one of my cellmates, a potbellied good ol' boy with a ruddy complexion made ruddier by a web of broken capillaries.

Shelly, I remembered, my heart sinking. Ryfert Shelly. I could see in his face that he remembered me too.

"I know that boy," said Shelly. "That boy's a cop."

A smaller man who looked to be in his fifties swaggered closer. He smelled of old beer and stale cigarettes, and when he spoke, his breath was foul and fetid with decay. I reckoned he would probably be toothless in a couple of years. "A cop *and* a chicken hawk?" He poked me in the chest with one bony finger. "That so?"

"No."

"He's lyin', Fish. I remember him. He busted me and Roley once."

Fish blinked once, slow and somehow menacing. "I don't like liars, boy."

"I'm not a cop anymore."

"Mm." Fish gave his companions an exaggerated wink. "You know what they say. Once a cop, always a cop."

A Latino with a pencil-thin mustache glowered at me. "And once a *cabron*, always a *cabron*."

Fish grinned broadly. "You know what I think? I think we ought to give our new friend a proper welcome. How about it, pretty boy? You up for a blanket party?"

"Nah." I'd heard of blanket parties, but I had no desire to experience one. "I'm all partied out."

"Tough shit. I'm givin' you a personal invitation." He laughed and walked back to his bunk.

The Latino leaned in and whispered, "Everybody got to sleep sometime. You better sleep with one eye open, *malparido*."

For the rest of the day, they pointedly ignored me. I knew the reprieve was temporary, but took the time to stake out a bunk and familiarize myself with my surroundings.

The cell was dank and crowded with a metal sink and toilet and a concrete tank in the center of the floor for the drunks to throw up in. The stained mattresses stank of urine. Above one of the bunks, someone had scrawled, *For a good time, call Martha Stewart.*

I sat cross-legged on my bunk and tried to sort out who was who and who fell where in the pecking order.

In addition to Shelly and Fish, whose real name was James Roy Breem, my cellmates were a penny ante crackhead by the name of Tyrone Majors, a career thug named LeQuintus, and the Latino, a chop shop mechanic named Jorge Ramirez. LeQuintus, in for assault with a deadly weapon, looked like he could have taken the top three places in a Musclemania competition all by himself.

Shelly and Breem were also in for assault. They'd beaten up a black man with a chain, and it was clear that by the time I joined this happy little family, there had been more than a little friction and a few blows passed between the white boys and the black boys in this cell.

It must have been a relief for them to discover a common enemy who just happened to be me.

That night, lying on the too-thin, lumpy mattress, I fought to keep my eyes from closing. It wasn't hard at first. Anxiety and adrenaline kept me awake, with some help from the bare light bulb in the hallway that shone in my eyes. But as the night wore on, anxiety gave way to exhaustion. My eyelids fluttered, snapped open, closed. I jerked myself awake, swung my legs over the edge of the bunk, and listened to the snores and heavy breathing of my cellmates.

Were they asleep, or faking? Some of each, I thought, but that was just an educated guess.

I must have dozed off at some point, because I awoke with a start as a musty-smelling blanket fell across my face. Rough hands hauled me out of the bunk. My head struck the metal bed frame, and a sharp wet pain pierced my scalp.

"Shit!" I jerked one arm free, and the blanket slipped enough to show a flash of orange jumpsuit before the cloth was yanked roughly across my face. "Motherfu—"

I sucked in a moldy breath, coughed and gasped at what felt like a dried leaf caught in my windpipe.

Then a painful bear hug pinned my arms to my sides. Someone else's arms snaked around my knees and lifted, held me suspended above the floor while I bucked and flailed against a flurry of kicks and punches that rained against my belly, back, and sides.

The blanket muffled my curses, but I knew the guard could hear the ruckus. I also knew he'd take his own sweet time getting there.

I bunched my knees and kicked out with both feet. My range of motion was limited by whoever had me by the legs, but I managed to connect with something.

"Oof! Shit!" It sounded like Tyrone. With my arms clamped to my sides, I couldn't do much in the way of self-defense, so I jerked my head back sharply, hoping to smash someone's nose cartilage into his brain.

"Ow!" The one behind me howled and loosened his grip. My tailbone hit the concrete floor, and a jolt of pain shot through my pelvis. Somewhere down the hall, a door clanged open. At the sound, my cellmates scattered. I lay there for a moment, stunned. Then with my arms free at last, I struggled to untangle myself from the blanket.

By the time the guard got there, I had freed myself, and my cellmates were back on their cots. My lip was swollen, and blood streamed from my mouth and nose. The hair at the top of my head was tacky with it. My body ached, but nothing felt broken. Not much, anyway.

"Okay, buddy." Officer Meacham sounded bored. "Who did this to you?"

I waved a hand to indicate my cellmates. "They threw a blanket over my head and beat the hell out of me."

"Did you see which ones were involved?"

"How could I see that, with a blanket over my head?"

"There's no need to get smart with me, boy. There's nothing I can do, if you didn't see who did it."

"Sure. That's why they do it that way. Because it works."

He shrugged and handed me a handkerchief. "Hey. You can't do the time, don't do the crime," he quoted. "Baretta. Early seventies."

When he had gone, I turned back to my cellmates.

45

"Okay, fellas. Have you got your meanness out, or am I gonna have to beat the shit out of you?"

The one called Fish sat up and grinned. A trickle of blood flowed from one nostril, and his crooked yellow teeth were tinged with red.

"You? Beat the shit out of us? I'd like to see that. I really would."

I shrugged. "I'll take on any or all of you. But let's keep this fair, okay? You've already done this the chicken shit way. At least give me a fighting chance."

I wasn't entirely bluffing. I knew I'd be hurt if I had to fight them all, but I was good enough to hurt at least a couple of them first. It might be just enough to earn a little respect.

"You calling me chicken shit?" Fish's rheumy eyes narrowed.

"Five men ambush one man in his sleep. What would you call it?"

He tapped his forehead with his forefinger. "I'd call it smart. But I tell you what. If you can take LeQuintus . . ." He gestured toward the massively muscled black man. "Then we'll lay off you for a while. Course, ain't nobody never beat LeQuintus."

LeQuintus flashed a set of laser-white teeth and flexed his muscles. "Damn straight."

LeQuintus looked like he ate baby ducks for breakfast and hand grenades for lunch. This was a man who'd skin the Easter Bunny for Sunday dinner. Oh, well. I hadn't expected them to make this easy. At least I wouldn't have to deal with all of them at once this time. Not if they played fair.

I know. Only a fool would have expected them to play fair.

"Okay," I said. "Piece of cake."

"Hell," LeQuintus said. "Maybe I'll fuck you before I kill you."

"What's the matter, LeQuintus? Not into necrophilia?"

He looked blank for a moment, then cracked a smile. "Naw. I like to feel 'em squirm."

46

"Now there's a lovely image," I said, grinning. Then, firmly believing that the best defense is a good offense, I caught him squarely in the solar plexus with the most beautiful spin kick you will ever see.

I didn't give him time to catch his balance or his breath before I followed up with a backfist to the side of his head and a palm strike to the chin.

His head snapped back and he reeled sideways, his eyes already glazed. He threw a weak punch, but I dodged the blow and came up under his guard with a spear hand to the throat.

He gagged and wheezed for breath, his fingers opening and closing like a kitten kneading at its mother's teat.

In the movies, this is where I would have punched his lights out with my fist. In real life, that will get you broken knuckles or a sprained wrist. The bones of the hand are fragile and unstable compared to the hard, flat planes of the skull, and I suspected that LeQuintus had a head as hard as granite and about as dense.

I could have killed him with a palm-heel strike to the bottom of the nose. I knew the technique, but I had never used it.

In twelve years of police work and another as a private eye, I'd never killed anyone. I didn't want to start now.

Instead, I came down with an axe kick to the back of his head and stepped back, hands up in a guarding position, waiting to see if he was stupid enough to get up and try again.

I heard Tyrone move before I saw him. Instinctively, I struck out with my left leg. It sent him stumbling him back against the bunk, where his head struck the metal bed frame with an ominous crack. He howled in pain and surprise, clutching at the back of his head.

"Shit, man! You done broke my skull."

"Good." I stepped over his outstretched leg and spun so my back was to the bars. If they all charged me, no one could move in from behind.

Whistles, cheers, and catcalls poured from the other cells.

"You go, dude!" "Pansies!" "Wassamatter? He too much for you?" "Sooo-eeee! Sooo-eeee!" "This little piggy went to pris-on!"

I looked at Breem. "You said if I took LeQuintus, you'd leave me alone."

He shrugged. "Looks like I lied."

They moved in silently, my death in their eyes. I felt a surge of adrenaline amd a twinge of something that might have been fear.

"Your funeral," I said.

And they were on me.

# 8

"**O**KAY, ASSHOLES, break it up."

I looked up through a bloody blur and saw Frank pitch Shelly aside like a paper doll. Two guards pulled Ramirez and Breem away and held them at bay with their nightsticks. Meacham, looking sullen, blocked the exit.

Maybe it wasn't my day to die, after all.

"You okay?" Frank grabbed my collar and hauled me to my feet.

I put out a hand to steady myself against the bars. "Still breathing."

"Good."

I opened my mouth to thank him, but he held up a hand and said, "Don't. I didn't come here for conversation."

"What did you come here for?"

"Apparently, to save your life. Don't make me regret it." He turned away and pushed past Meacham. "Put him in a private cell, Officer. And no 'mistakes' this time."

Meacham scowled. "Looks like someone's got a guardian angel." He hauled me into the hallway, shoved me into my new cell, and slammed the door behind me. Leaning close to the bars, he said, "Tell your buddy I don't care what he does to me. It was worth it."

I wanted to punch him until there was nothing left of his smirk but shards of bone and shreds of bloody flesh. Instead, I gave him my Cool Hand Luke stare until he looked away. Then I stretched out on my new bunk and pretended to sleep. The voices from the other cells subsided, and eventually I dozed, waking every few hours to listen for the rustle of a blanket or the scuff of footsteps on the cell floor.

Breakfast was cold oatmeal, powdered eggs, and shriveled

49

strips of blackened bacon, after which I spent the morning counting cracks in the ceiling and feeling sorry for myself. My eyes were swollen to slits and crusted with blood. It hurt to move. It even hurt to breathe. If LeQuintus and the boys ever decided to go straight, I figured they could get jobs as meat tenderizers.

It was Friday before the guard on duty came to tell me my bond had been paid, my preliminary hearing had been set for the next week, and a Randall McKean was here to take me home.

As we passed the cell where I'd begun my odyssey, I noticed a stocky, bald man passing out Bibles to the prisoners. An angry red scar trailed from just beneath his left eye to the corner of his mouth. There was something familiar about him. I rifled through my mental files and came up empty.

"Who's that?" I asked the guard.

He glanced over into the cell. "Name's Reverend Avery. That woman you killed went to his church." He gave a dry laugh. "Maybe she should've listened a little closer, huh? Especially the part about 'thou shalt not commit adultery.'"

I paused to peer more closely at the reverend. Clean-shaven. Ruddy complexion. Rolls of fat bulging on either side of the belt he'd buckled too tightly around his waist. His girlish mouth wore a smug smile.

A feeling of revulsion coiled into the pit of my stomach.

"I think I know him," I said.

"Seen his picture on your windshield, probably. You know, those religious flyers about how the Pope's the anti-Christ and Madonna is the whore of Babylon." He nudged me again. "You want to stick around and gab, I'll be happy to throw away the key."

"No. I'm going."

LeQuintus looked up and broke away from the group. I was glad there were still bars between us. "It ain't over with you and me, Cop. That Kung Fu shit ain't gonna help you next time."

"Thanks for the warning." I made a mental note to get another gun. You know the old saying: *Don't take a knife to a gunfight.* I'd probably never see LeQuintus again, but I had a feeling that if I ever did, that advice would come in handy.

I CROSSED THE PARKING LOT in Randall's wake, noticed him limping, and said, "Knee bothering you again?"

"Not again," he said. "Still. It's worse some days than others. Want to tell me how you got yourself into this mess?"

I sighed and rubbed my eyes. "I've told this story so many times I feel like a damn tape recorder."

"Well, hit rewind and tell it again."

I started with meeting Heather at the First Edition Bar and Grill on Friday night. When I'd finished, he blew out a long breath and shook his head. "Women. You haven't picked a good one since Maria. I still can't believe you let her go."

I stared past my reflection in the window, remembering my first meeting with Maria. I could still see the flash of her tanned legs as she fanned her long white skirt, her cascade of dark hair pulled up in careless ponytail, her pursed lips, the tiny furrow between her brows as she bent to inspect one of the hand-tinted prints she'd brought to the craft fair at Centennial Park.

I was in college, one month shy of my twentieth birthday and working part-time for a man whose handcrafted dulcimers were on display in the tent next to Maria's.

Best assignment of my life.

She was four years older than I was, which always bothered her. But she was beautiful then, and she was beautiful now. I suspected she'd be beautiful when she had silver hair and wrinkles.

I looked back at Randall and said, "You can't cage a hummingbird."

"That's a load of bull. She wasn't the one who couldn't be caged." He shot me an annoyed look. "And stop that drumming."

I froze, hands poised above the dashboard. His bobble-head Superman, fraternal twin to the Batman on mine, gave an approving nod. Slowly, pointedly, I placed my palms flat on my thighs and said, "You're mad at me. I get the point. But what I don't get is why. I didn't kill that woman. And as far as Maria goes, I'm not the one who ended it."

"She put up twenty thousand dollars of your bond. She and D.W. You know that?"

"No. I didn't know."

"Maria asked him, and D.W. coughed up the money. No questions asked. They must have liquidated half their assets."

"And the rest?"

"Besides what your lawyer got out of your accounts? Wendy and I took out a second mortgage on the house. Jay cashed in some stocks he had. Some of the guys on the force chipped a little in. Guys you used to work with. Even a couple of your clients. A hundred here, a couple thousand there. We've been raising the money since Sunday night."

"Jesus, Randall."

I know. Tough guys don't cry. But it was almost enough to choke me up.

When he spoke again, his voice was hard. "Had to get you out so you could solve this thing. I don't want to have to visit you in prison."

"You won't." I hoped I sounded more confident than I felt.

We rode in silence for a few minutes. Then I broached another sensitive subject. "What's up with Josh these days? The other night, he looked . . ."

"He looked like shit. I don't know what's going on with him. Wendy says I have to let him have his 'space.'" His knuckles whitened on the steering wheel. "I think he might be into drugs. Or worse. He's into all this occult stuff. Hell, sometimes I'm ashamed to admit he's my son."

I had no idea what to say. In the middle of a family crisis, my brother had taken a second mortgage just to get me out of a jam. And Maria and D.W. Where had that come from?

"I'm sorry," I said at last.

"Yeah, so am I." He gave a bark of nervous laughter. "Hey, I didn't mean to dump this on you. You have enough on your mind."

"Dump away." I stared out at the scenery as we whizzed past. "It's the least I can do."

"Getting yourself out of this jam is the least you can do. Manage that, and we'll call it even."

I caught myself before I started drumming on my thighs. "I'm on the job," I said. And I was. The only problem was, I had no idea where to start.

THAT WASN'T ENTIRELY TRUE. I had a few ideas, but I was hampered by the fact that my name—and, thanks to Ashleigh, my face—had been plastered all over the news. I could disguise the latter, but Tennessee detective licenses were photo I.D.'s. It would be tough to conduct an investigation without showing my credentials.

Before I worried about any of that, though, I wanted a hot shower, a home-cooked meal, and a night in my own bed. With clean sheets. And a real, honest-to-God pillow.

Randall dropped me off at Jay's place in Mt. Juliet and waved goodbye. I watched his blue-black Saturn round the bend. Then, feeling drained, I trudged up the long, winding driveway to Jay's sprawling, two-story farmhouse.

"Jay, I'm home." I pushed open the antique mailroom door with the stained glass insert and walked in. The smell of garlic and cinnamon wafted from the kitchen, triggering a Pavlovian response.

Jay came out of the kitchen wiping his hands on a Fourth of July dishtowel. When he saw me, he stopped short and pressed a hand to his mouth. "Oh my God. What did they do to you?"

I flicked my tongue across the scab on my lip, wondering if I should tell him how much I'd healed since Monday. "Just a little welcoming gift. It's not as bad as it looks."

"I hope not, honey, because it looks awful. Black eye, busted lip, bruises the size of hockey pucks." He wrapped one arm around himself and propped the other elbow on it as he catalogued my injuries. "At least they didn't break your nose."

I thought of LeQuintus, flexing his muscles. "Not for lack of trying."

He stepped closer and gave me a quick and awkward hug. "Well. It's good to have you back. We've all been worried sick about you. Come in. Sit down. I made your favorite chicken. Roasted with garlic, basil, and rosemary. Just a touch of thyme. Fresh corn on the cob. Salad with arugula and baby oak leaves, with Vidalia onion dressing. And apple pie for dessert, with cheese or *a la mode*." He laughed. "Don't I sound like quite the little housewife?"

"I've been eating powdered eggs and country fried mystery meat for days. Not exactly gourmet dining." I kept my tone light. Randall says Jay has a crush on me and likes to pretend we're a couple. I don't know about that. It's not the kind of thing you can come right out and ask. Besides, I'm not sure what I'd do if he admitted it. So I ignore it.

Cowardly? I never said I wasn't.

I followed him into the kitchen. As Jay was drizzling the dressing over our salads, I did a quick survey of his appearance.

A light layer of pancake base covered two small lesions on his cheek. A hint of blush negated his usual pallor. He looked okay, I decided. Keeping up his weight enough to keep from wasting. He was wearing tight jeans and a pale blue shirt with mother-of-pearl buttons. Too uptown for a night at home.

"Hot date tonight?" I asked.

He blushed. "You don't mind, do you? You just getting home and all? I can call and cancel."

"No. I'm going to crash after dinner, anyway. I feel like I haven't slept in a month."

"I didn't know you were going to be arrested when I said I'd go out with him."

"Really, Jay. It's okay. I was going to be lousy company anyway."

"If there's anything I can do to help..."

Over the years, Jay has amassed an impressive collection of murky sources of information. 'Contacts,' he calls them, from the years he spent programming computers for Nashville businesses back before he made his fortune in gaming. This may be true, but I suspect his considerable webmaster skills also come into play. Hacking. Cracking. Whatever you want to call it. Some things I'd just as soon not know.

"Later," I said. "You can try and find out if there was an insurance policy on Amy Hartwell. Tonight, go out and have a ball."

His date arrived as I was finishing the last crumbs of my pie. Jay hurried to the door to let him in, then led him back into the kitchen just as I was pushing my chair away from the table.

"Jared, this is Eric Gunnersen. Eric . . . Jared McKean."

Eric, tall and Nordic-looking as his name implied, gave me a cool once-over and licked his lips. "Mmm. Rough trade. Cute, though. Should I be jealous?"

Jay gave me a playful slap on the shoulder as I carried my dirty dishes to the dishwasher. "Honey, he's as straight as half a dozen arrows."

The Viking gave a deep, theatrical sigh. "Pity," he said. "The best-looking ones are always straight."

Which was not only a shitty thing to say to Jay, but also probably untrue. Sit behind a group of women in a Starbucks sometime. Sooner or later, one of them is going to point to some stranger and say, "That guy's way too good-looking. Ten to one he's gay."

I decided I didn't like Eric Gunnersen.

Jay seemed not to realize he'd been insulted. "Isn't that the truth," he agreed. He picked up the bottle he'd put his evening meds in, flashed me a sad but hopeful smile, and tucked his hand into the crook of Eric's arm. "Don't wait up, darlin'. I intend to dance until the cows come home."

It was bravado speaking. We both knew he'd tire long before the night wore old, probably before midnight. The AZT cocktail kept him alive, but it also left him listless and fatigued.

"Don't forget your red shoes, then," I said, referring to one of his favorite films.

He picked up one foot to show me his snakeskin cowboy boots. "Oh, honey. I have something better than red shoes tonight. I have boots made from the foreskins of the rare and priceless Ming snake. Do you know how many foreskins it takes to make a boot this size? And every one is endowed with incredible virility and vitality."

"Get out of here, you lunatic." I steered him and the Viking toward the door. "Reptiles don't have foreskins."

"They don't?" He turned to Eric and said *sotto voce*, "He knows this from experience, of course. Years of examining the genitalia of a thousand species of *genus reptilicus*. He's considered a giant in his field."

I closed the door behind them just as Eric said, "I'm considered a giant in my field too. Why don't we go to my place, and I'll show you my credentials."

Since Jay wasn't my kid sister and I couldn't fly out of the house and flatten Eric in defense of his honor, I turned on the dishwasher and went out to the barn to feed and water the horses, hoping the blond Viking wouldn't turn out to be a complete shit after all. I didn't have high hopes for that, though. Jay's taste in men had turned out to be a lot like my taste in women lately. He picked the ones most likely to pour acid on his heart.

# 9

I THOUGHT I'D FALL ASLEEP before my head hit the pillow. But there was something eerie about being in my own room, where everything was so familiar, and yet everything had changed. There was a subtle disorder to the room, along with the black residue of fingerprint powder. It looked like Jay had tried to clean it up, but there were still traces of it in the cracks and crannies.

The hairs on my forearms prickled as I realized they hadn't been looking for my fingerprints, which were already on file, but for Amy Hartwell's.

My gun cabinet had been emptied, the rifles and handguns confiscated as evidence. The room looked empty without them.

I ran my fingers over my desk, picked up the framed photograph of my father. I was four when he died. He'd come back from Vietnam with a silver star and a purple heart, spent three years as a patrol officer, went out for cigarettes one evening and was killed while protecting a 70-year-old convenience store cashier from a cranked up junkie waving a .45.

Maria used to ask when I was going to stop trying to live up to him.

Frank Campanella was my friend, and he had seen this picture maybe a dozen times, but the thought of him dusting it for prints made my stomach roil.

Mom's picture smiled up at me from the opposite corner of the desk. She passed away when I was fourteen. Cancer. It happened fast. Diagnosed in February, buried in June, and in between, the radiation treatments, the nausea, and the pain. By the time she died, she'd scream when you touched her. I was both relieved and bereft when she died.

I pictured clumsy fingers pawing at my mother's face, jostling my guitar, riffling through my books: Louis L'Amour and Zane Grey, a couple of John Grishams, a handful of thrillers and graphic novels, and a shelf full of books on criminology, psychology, and horsemanship. I imagined Frank and Harry poring through my photo albums, thick with photographs of Paulie and Maria. I envisioned them searching my closet, rough hands rifling the pockets of my suits and jeans and the linings of my L.L Bean shirts.

And I felt violated.

Don't get me wrong. I understood why these things were being done, and why they had to be done. I would have done the same things, in Frank's place. But that didn't mean I had to like it.

Exhaustion has a way of catching up to you, though, and finally I sank into a sleep so deep it verged on coma.

I didn't hear when Jay came home, but he must have, because when I awoke, the sun was streaming through my curtains and the house smelled of pancakes and fresh-brewed coffee. By the time I'd showered, shaved, and dressed, breakfast was on the table. Jay was humming some romantic tune, something from an old Bing Crosby flick.

"Nice night?" I asked.

"God, yes." His grin was childlike, beatific. I thought he looked a little wan without the makeup, but the lesions seemed a little less noticeable than they had the week before. "He's incredible, Jared. Smart, funny, unbelievably handsome. And, of course, the sex was incredible."

I tried not to envision that. "Well. Good. Good for you. When are you going to see him again?"

He brought a creamer brimming with warm syrup to the table and set it in front of me. "He's going to call me tonight."

"Ah."

He looked pained. "Don't give me, 'ah.' He said he'd call, he'll call. You have no idea what a fabulous time we had last night."

"I know. I hope he calls."

He took a bite of pancake and washed it down with a swig of juice and a pill. He took twenty or thirty pills a day, some every few hours, some on an empty stomach, some with meals. Along with his meds, he took Shaklee food supplements by the handful: C, E, beta-carotene, garlic, calcium, a multi-vitamin, and who knew what all, washed down with a soy protein drink and an ungodly blend of homemade juices. The mixture this morning was carrot, celery, and beet juices, sweetened with orange and pineapple.

It wasn't bad.

We steered away from the subject of Mr. Perfect and moved on to more pragmatic matters. My truck had been impounded, and it might be weeks before I got it back. So if I was going to investigate Amy Hartwell's homicide, I was going to need wheels.

"Oh, please." Jay rolled his eyes. "Give me a real problem. You can just drive mine." He worked from home these days and rarely drove his silver Buick LeSabre. It was tempting, but a man can only take so many favors.

"You've done enough already. Randall told me you helped with the bail. Thanks for that too, by the way."

He shrugged. "What are friends for? I know you'd do the same for me. Besides, with you gone, who would I cook and clean for?"

"I don't ask you do that."

He sighed, touched my forearm gently. I tried not to let it make me uncomfortable, but it was hard not to think of it as seductive. "Honey, I want to do that. It makes me feel needed."

"Jay . . ."

"Ssshhh." He moved his hand from my arm and pressed a finger to his lips. "Don't say it. I know what you are, and what I am. And I know there is no way in this world that you're ever going to feel about me the way I feel about you. But I like to think that when I . . . when the end comes, you'll be here."

59

I toyed with my fork, the pancakes suddenly sodden and unappealing. "You know I will," I mumbled. I wanted to tell him that would be years from now. I wanted to tell him there might even be a cure by then. But we both knew the odds on that.

"All right, then. If you'd do that for me, the least I can do is cook you a few meals. Besides, it's good for me. If it were only me, I might subsist on cold cereal and potato chips."

I forced a laugh. "You? The semi-vegetarian gourmet?"

"Ah, yes." His smile was sad. "But what good is it, if there's no one there to share it with?"

IN THE END, HE DROVE ME to an Avis Rent-a-Car, where I picked up a midnight blue Taurus 2-door sedan. I thanked him for the ride, and he promised to look into the insurance angle. Then I went to the office to check my messages and make a game plan.

My office, Maverick Investigations, was on the third floor of a renovated boarding house a few blocks from Vanderbilt Hospital and University. Two doors led from the outer office, where my desk sat, to the rest of the apartment—shower, kitchenette, and a former bedroom that now housed surveillance equipment, a hodgepodge of indispensible gadgetry, and a walk-in closet for extra clothes and my theatrical kit.

My answering service had been inundated with calls, some from people offering support or condolences, some offering to "do me like you done that woman," one from a fellow P.I. named Lou Wilder asking me to give him a call back, some from clients wanting to know how or if this was going to affect my work on their cases, two withdrawing their business, and a whole slew of reporters clamoring for interviews.

Ashleigh had the gall to leave a message of her own: "Hi, Jared. If you still want my help, I'm available. I hope there are no hard feelings, but, you know, it was my duty as a—"

With no small degree of satisfaction, I deleted her.

I returned Lou's call and left a message on his machine.

Then I pulled out my calendar to see what was on the schedule. I would have liked to devote the day to solving my own case, but unfortunately, the bills still had to be paid.

That morning, I tracked down a deadbeat dad and took a roll of photos of a client's husband and his mistress. Nothing graphic; all I had to prove was opportunity and probability, which meant basically a hotel room and a goodbye kiss.

After I'd filled out the reports, I dropped by Randall's house to borrow a gun. He handed me a Colt .45 with rosewood grips and a blued finish. It was a little heavier than the Glock, and I spent a few minutes getting used to the balance.

"Don't get caught with it," he said. "I love that gun."

"Geez, your concern is touching. Don't worry. I'll get it back to you as soon as I can."

He looked hurt. "Keep it as long as you need it."

"Hey, I didn't mean—"

"Forget it. I'll get us a couple of beers." He stumped away toward the fridge as if his knee weren't screaming in protest, but I knew better. I was sixteen when a construction accident shattered his patella, and I'd had twenty years to learn the patterns of my brother's pain.

I also knew better than to bring it up again.

After the beer, I said goodbye to my brother and looked up the Hartwells' address in the phone book. They lived in Bluefield, a semi-upscale neighborhood off Donelson Pike. Property values there had plummeted when the new airport was built, and after an avalanche of protests about the noise, the Airport Authority paid most of the homeowners for sound-resistant windows and extra layers of insulation. Since it was still early in the afternoon, I decided to drive by and scope out the neighborhood.

I had to learn more about the victim. Even in seemingly random crimes, like Bundy's or Gacy's, the victim is chosen for a reason. Maybe she's a certain physical type. Maybe she risks her own safety to be a Good Samaritan. Maybe it's just proximity. But something about her attracts the killer, and if you know what it is, you know a lot about the person who did the killing.

Out of all the women the killer might have picked, he had chosen Amy. Why?

In the movies, this is where the hero would take out his trusty crowbar, or his trusty skeleton key, and he'd wait until the Hartwell house was empty, and he'd force his way inside.

In real life, this is called Breaking and Entering, and it's an offense for which one may spend a goodly portion of his life fighting off the advances of gorillas like LeQuintus.

Yes, I know. Gorillas are quiet, gentle creatures. But they are also very strong and not too bright, and if you make them angry, they can smash a person's fragile little skull as if it were a pumpkin.

I wasn't desperate enough to break into the Hartwell house.

Not yet.

Instead, I found a parking place about a half a block away and watched, my air conditioner running to combat the heat. Visitors came and went with casserole dishes and cake pans. No one stayed long. At one point, Calvin Hartwell came outside and sat on the porch with his two girls, one arm around each. The smaller girl laid her hand on his shoulder, and he absently kissed the top of her head. The older girl sat stiffly, looking off into the distance, her body a hand's width away from her father's.

I thought of the photos Frank had found in my truck and wondered.

Not long after, a silver Cadillac DeVille pulled up, and a woman with strawberry blond hair blown big like a Charlie's Angel climbed out. Her black sheath dress rode high on her thighs and hugged the taut curves of her hips. She was muscular and lean, and there was something both sensuous and feral in the way she moved.

The girls hung back as the woman gave Hartwell a stiff hug. Then all four of them climbed into the Hartwell's Buick

Park Avenue. Nice car. Nice house, a vine-covered Victorian with arched glass panels on the second floor. The yard was landscaped with perennials, flowering shrubs, and grass so plush and green a dandelion would have been ashamed to grow there. Someone had put a lot of care into that yard.

With the family gone, I turned my attention to the neighbors. They'd probably seen me on TV, but most people have a hard time placing faces in unexpected contexts. It's why you sometimes fail to recognize a co-worker when you meet him in the grocery store.

Besides, most people think once you've been locked up, you stay locked up until you've been convicted or found innocent. They wouldn't expect me to be out on the streets. For once, I was glad it didn't work that way.

I started with the house across the street. The name on the mailbox read, 'Mitchell.' By the time a woman in her mid-to-late forties answered the door, sweat streamed down my face, and not just from the heat. I held up my Private Investigator's license with my thumb partially covering the face and said, "Hello, Ma'am. I'm a private investigator looking into the death of..."

The door slammed. I knocked again.

"Go away," said a muffled voice from behind the door. "We've already talked to the police."

"Ma'am, if you'd—"

"Go away!"

I went. I didn't know if she recognized me, or if there'd been so many cops and reporters around that she was tired of talking. Or maybe it was because I still looked a little like I'd been mauled by a rhinoceros. I took a chance it was one of the latter two and moved on to the next house.

There was no one home at the next two houses. At the third, an elderly man offered me a glass of iced tea and said he didn't know the victim well, but that she always spoke politely to him. The little girls were well behaved, and the husband seemed to work long hours. They went to church on Sundays and on Wednesday nights, but he didn't know where they attended. He wished he could be of more assistance, but he kept to himself and didn't get involved in gossip. I thanked him for the information and the refreshment and moved on.

The fourth door I knocked on flew open, and a middle-aged woman with a disheveled red mane leveled a Beretta 9mm at my forehead. With the clarity that often accompanies impending death, I noticed that the barrel looked immense, a yawning hole from which the bullet would come hurtling toward my forehead. To a man about to have his brains blown out, it looked more like a cannon than a handgun. I forced myself to look beyond the barrel, where a pair of hazel eyes glared back with a wild-eyed, panicked sheen.

I took a slow, deep breath and tried to sound calm and congenial. "Ma'am, I'm—"

"I know who you are," she said. "I saw you on the news. What are you doing here?"

"I'm investigating Mrs. Hartwell's murder."

"Liar! I could blow you away right now, and not a soul would blame me." The weapon bobbled slightly. My bowels clenched.

"Ma'am, that may be true. But until the prosecutor proves me guilty, I have the right to try and clear myself."

Her mouth twisted. "Not here, you don't. Not in this neighborhood. If you're not out of here in ten seconds, you won't have to worry about going back to jail."

I tried to look nonchalant as I backed slowly down the porch steps. I suppose I could have gone for the Colt, but there was no point getting into a gunfight if I could help it. Besides, a shootout in real life is nothing like a shootout in the movies. The bad guys don't always miss, and the good guys aren't bulletproof. Just my luck, the crazy bitch would shoot me, and then where would I be?

The barrel of the gun followed me. "If you step foot in my yard again," the woman said through gritted teeth, "I'll kill you."

I noted the name on the mailbox as I left—L. Falcone—
and sauntered toward my car as if I didn't give a moment's
thought to her and her 9mm. There was an itch between my
shoulder blades where I half expected to feel the impact of a
bullet. I've known guys who say being shot doesn't hurt at
first. It's only later that it feels like someone's set your flesh on
fire. Others say it hurts like hell. I don't know which is right,
or what determines which way it happens.

Adrenaline, maybe.

The arrow in my chest had hurt a lot, though. I had no
desire to add a bullet wound for comparison.

The house I'd parked in front of was a gray stone cottage
with a peaked and gabled roof. What my mother used to call a
gingerbread house.

Glancing back, I saw that Ms. Falcone had vanished back
into her lair. What the hell, I thought. Live fast, die young. I
turned up the walkway to the cottage and knocked on the front
door.

At first, I thought I'd struck out for the way-too-manyth
time.

Instead, the door cracked open and an odd, persimmon-
shaped face with a wide, thin-lipped mouth, small bump of a
nose, and eyes like oversized black currants peered out. An
unruly mass of white hair, most of which had been twisted
into a loose bun, gave her the look of a finely-coifed cotton-top
marmoset. The top of her head barely reached my chest.

"Yes?" Her reedy voice barely carried across the porch.

"Good afternoon, Ma'am," I said. "I'm . . ." I looked into
those wizened eyes and faltered. "I'm investigating the murder of your neighbor, Amy Hartwell."

"Are you a policeman?"

"No, ma'am," I said. Impersonating a policeman is against
the law. "I'm a private investigator."

"Let me see your license."

I showed it to her, not flashing it as if I had something to
hide, but not leaving it out for her to linger over.

"McKean." Her dark eyes glittered with something that might have been fear, but her voice never wavered. "Isn't that the name of man the police think killed her?"

Brave. Spunky. I liked her immediately, with her little monkey face and her bright eyes. "Yes, ma'am," I said. I am a reasonably good liar, but not to little old women who look like somebody's great-grandmother. "They think I did it. But I didn't, and that's why I'm here. To prove that. I don't mean anybody any harm, Mrs . . ."

"Drafon. Birdie Drafon."

"I don't mean you any harm, Mrs. Drafon. I just want to find out what happened to Mrs. Hartwell and why whoever did it wanted me to get the blame."

I didn't have to try to look sincere. I meant every word. Mrs. Drafon looked at me with those black currant eyes as if she could see clear into my soul and said, "Of course, dear. Come right in."

# 10

**"I**'M AFRAID MOST of the neighbors wouldn't be able to tell you anything, even if they wanted to." Mrs. Drafon poured fresh-squeezed lemonade into a pair of frosted glasses. "It's not like the old days when everybody knew everybody and we all got together after church on Sundays. Back in those days, anybody could have told you almost anything about anyone. Nowadays . . ." She pursed her lips. "A person could be dead a week and nobody would know until the stench reached the street. I hope you like a twist of lemon. Henry always liked a twist of lemon in his drink."

She gestured toward the picture of her late husband, Henry Drafon, whom I had already learned more about than most folks know about their daddies.

"A lemon twist is fine," I said.

She set our drinks on coasters on the coffee table and sat primly on the edge of her chair. "I always say, there's nothing like an ice cold lemonade on a hot day."

"Yes, ma'am."

"Of course, Henry always preferred beer. Still, he did like his lemonade."

"Yes, Ma'am." I suppressed a smile. "So, tell me. Did you know Mrs. Hartwell very well?"

"Oh, I don't know." She lifted her bony shoulders. "I'm not sure anyone knew her very well. But I think you could say we were friends. Yes, you could say that."

"When you say 'friends' . . ."

She wrapped her simian fingers around the frosted glass and sipped at her lemonade. When she had swallowed, she said, "Not the kind of friends who go out shopping or to restaurants together. But the kind of friends who share a cup of coffee and a bit of gossip. She was very unhappy, and I think she needed someone to confide in. You know how it is. Or maybe you don't. Maybe men don't need that sort of thing."

"When you say 'unhappy' . . ."

"Her doctor called it depression. Personally, I think it was a simple case of marrying the wrong man."

"You don't think much of Mr. Hartwell?"

"Calvin. If you ask me, that's a case of a man whose head is too big for his britches."

I smiled at the mixed metaphor. "Mrs. Drafon . . ."

"Please, call me Birdie."

"All right. Birdie. Do you think he might have been the one who . . .?" I stopped, mid-question. There was no way to mention what had happened without reminding her that she'd just lost a friend—and that I was the one who was supposed to have killed her.

"No," she said. "I shouldn't think so. But I wouldn't put my marker on it. He's a cold man, at the core."

"And that's what made her so unhappy?"

"That, and other things." She paused, tracing patterns in the frost that was rapidly melting on her glass. "She didn't talk about her childhood much, but I had the feeling it wasn't a very happy one. And then there was the church. Do you know anything about the Church of the Reclamation?"

I frowned, trying to recall. Then I remembered the minister I'd seen back at the jail. "Reverend Avery, right? He's their pastor?"

"That's the one. Those folks make the Southern Baptists look like hedonists. Amy didn't mind most of the rules—she didn't smoke or drink or dance—though what, exactly, is the matter with a little dancing, may I ask? Why, Henry and I could cut quite a rug, and I don't think that made us bad or sinful."

"Dancing is a sexually stimulating activity," I explained. "At least, that's what they told us Nazarenes."

"Son," she said, stifling a chuckle, "breathing is a sexually

68

stimulating activity, if you're with the right person."

I lifted my glass in a toast. "Amen to that, Sister Birdie."

She returned my toast. "Now, what was I saying? About Amy?"

"The Church of the Reclamation. The depression."

"Oh. Yes. Well, I think they were related. You see, Amy was a lovely girl. Not beautiful, in the traditional sense, and a bit full in the hips, but lovely nonetheless. And bright. But she was only seventeen when she married Calvin, and I can tell you it was no nine months before Tara was born."

"Tara?" I frowned. "I thought Katrina was the older girl."

"Katrina is Calvin's by his first wife. Don't ask me about her. They never talk about her. As I understand it, she just packed her things one afternoon and left. And no one's heard from her since."

One wife dead, one vanished. Calvin, it seemed, was batting a thousand.

Ms. Birdie clucked her tongue against her teeth and went on. "Poor Amy. Here she was, seventeen years old, with a brand new baby and a five-year-old who wasn't even hers. No wonder she was overwhelmed." She plucked at her blouse, which puffed out where it tucked into her skirt. "When it got to be too much, Amy used to bring those little girls over here to stay with Henry and me. The girls would dress up in their little costumes and perform for us. Which, naturally, Calvin said was a sin. Let me tell you something, Mr. McKean. A man like that, the kind sees evil everywhere? Well, that's a man with sinning in his heart."

I nodded without answering. The words were flowing, and I didn't want to interrupt.

"It was hardest on Katrina, I think. She was always a lonely little thing—old for her age, if you know what I mean—and Amy . . . well, I think she always felt Katrina was a little bit of a stranger. Not that she was unkind. Just . . . distant."

I nodded, feeling a surge of pity for a little girl who'd been abandoned by one mother and rejected by another. A child who might be vulnerable to a kindly-looking predator with candy and a camera.

"When the girls were both in school, Amy thought she might like to go to work, but Calvin wouldn't hear of it. He wanted her at home, and that was that. If she felt unfulfilled, he said, she could use her talents to create a perfect pot roast." She shook her head in disgust. "Pot roast. I was a good wife, Mr. McKean, but if Henry had tried that with me, he would have been buried with that pot roast firmly lodged in his backside."

"I take it Amy didn't see it that way."

"Amy didn't know how to say no." She sighed and smoothed her skirt across her thighs. "Then about six months ago, they joined this new church. It must have been Calvin's idea, because it's all about how women are supposed to be subservient little doormats and how they're all—*we're* all— Jezebels, tainted with the sin of Eve. Never mind that Adam committed the same sin, and proved he had no backbone to boot."

"Jezebels, huh." I wouldn't touch that one with a ten-foot pole.

"Anyway, Amy went along with it. But she just kept getting sadder and sadder, until finally, her doctor put her on some kind of medicine for it."

"Do you know what kind of medicine?"

"It's that one I keep reading about in the news."

"Prozac?"

"I think so. But she stopped taking it."

"Really. What happened?"

Her eyes glistened, two jet beads in a face as wrinkled as a withered apple. "She went out and got herself a job at a travel agency. Windrider Travel. It wasn't about the *work*. It was about him not thinking she was anything of value. Calvin just about hit the ceiling. I mean, sparks flew out of that house. Amy was in tears when she came over here the next day, and I told her, 'Honey, you are worth more than this.

When the good Lord set us here, he made Eve for a help-meet, not a doormat.' And she said to me, 'Ms. Birdie, you are right.'"

Her eyes brimmed, and a tear rolled down her nose and hung trembling from the tip. "I loved that child, Mr. McKean. She had her problems, but she was a good person." She leaned toward me and half-whispered, "I don't know this for a fact, but I think she might have been planning to divorce him."

"Ms. Birdie, this is a hard question," I said. "But I have to ask it—"

"I know." She heaved a deep sigh. "Was she seeing anyone? Well, I don't know for certain, but I know there was a man at work she was partial to. Ben Something-or-Other. I think she would have told me if anything had come of it, but perhaps not. She might have been ashamed, you know. But anyway, that's how I knew you weren't the one who did it. Because she'd told me who she was interested in, and it wasn't you."

I shook my head. "Ms. Birdie, let me just play devil's advocate a minute. Just because I wasn't her lover doesn't mean I couldn't have killed her. I might have been obsessed with her. Jealous. Enraged by rejection. Any number of things. You really shouldn't have let me come in, once you knew who I was."

She reached across the arm of the love seat and patted my hand with cool, papery fingers. "Son, killers are like crocodiles. You ever see a crocodile's eyes? Flat and cold and empty. People say Ted Bundy was a charmer, but he had crocodile eyes. Your eyes aren't empty, Mr. McKean. You've got caring eyes."

My cheeks warmed at the compliment. "Ms. Birdie, I hope you won't be letting strangers into your house based on what's in—or isn't in—their eyes. Because I don't want the *Tennessean* writing headlines about how some lowlife with the right eyes came in here and killed you."

"Pooh," said Birdie. "Drink your lemonade."

71

Before I left, she told me what she knew about the rest of Amy's family. That her parents were both dead. That she had a sister, Valerie Shepherd—the woman in the black sheath dress—who was the soloist for the church's Sunday morning radio show. ("Not that she's a believer," said Birdie. "But she does have a beautiful voice.") Valerie was involved with a man who had done six years in prison before he straightened out his life and joined the church, where he now did all the mastering for the radio show.

Same old song. Went to jail, found Jesus.

Not that I didn't believe in the transformative power of prayer. I did. Mostly. But I'd seen enough jailhouse conversions to take this one with a grain of salt.

I asked, "How were things between Amy and her sister?"

"Oh, like sisters everywhere, I imagine," she said airily. "Close as nits, and fought like cats and dogs."

"What about?"

"Who knows?" She lifted her shoulders in a dismissive shrug. "They were sisters, and sisters fight sometimes. Brothers, too, if my boys were any example."

I thought of my brother, of all the meaningless arguments we'd had throughout the years. I thought of how his loss would rip through my soul like a black hole.

"I'll come by sometime next week," I said, "and put a peephole in the front door."

"Pooh," she said. "No need."

"What if I'd really been a murderer? I could have forced my way inside and had my way with you before you even had a chance to scream."

She smiled a beatific smile. "I'm too old for you to have your way with, and I don't need a chance to scream." She untucked her billowed blouse to reveal a little silver-plated, snub-nosed .38. "All I have to do is stay in close and pull the trigger."

I grinned back at her. "Yes, ma'am, I guess that's true. But you could put all the hurting in the world on him, and what

72

good will it do you if he kills you for it?"

"Mr. McKean," she said, "I trust the Lord and Misters Smith and Wesson to protect my virtue and my life. And I refuse to live in fear. I've lived eighty-two good years, and I believe I am as good a judge of human nature as ever walked down the pike, and if I should one day misjudge someone, why then I'll be with Henry and the good Lord all the sooner. And when I get there, we'll dance us a jitterbug, Mister Calvin Hartwell and his Church of the Reclamation notwithstanding."

"I'm still coming by to put in the peephole."

She pursed her lips, but her dark eyes twinkled. "I won't stop you."

I DROVE BY THE FIRST EDITION on the way home, on the off chance that the woman who had set me up was there. No such luck. It was Saturday, but it was still early, and the only customers were a couple of guys playing pool in the back. Dani was behind the bar, swabbing the counter with a damp cloth. I ordered a beer and asked her if she'd seen Heather around.

"Heather?" She frowned. "That the lady you took home the other night?"

"Yeah. That's the one. You remember her, then?"

"Sure I do. That girl was a mess. She asked about you. Said you looked like a nice guy. She wanted to know if that was for real or if you were some kind of nut job."

"What did you tell her?"

Her grin was crooked and extremely cute, but there were two gold rings on the third finger of her left hand, which meant she was married, or wanted folks to think so.

"I told her you were crazy as they come." She laughed, presumably at my expression. "Naw. I'm kidding you. I told her you were the quiet type, never made trouble. Told her I would trust you with my little sister."

"Your sister?" I raised my eyebrows.

"Honey . . ." She held up her left hand with the two gold

73

rings. "Not that you're not gorgeous, but I'm off the market."

"Story of my life," I said, and slid a twenty across the laminated wooden bar. "Do me a favor, will you? If she comes in here again, give me a call."

"Look, darlin', she don't want to see you, it's not my place to get involved."

My jaw tightened. "Oh, I guarantee she doesn't want to see me."

"What'd she do, run off with your wallet?"

"I wish she'd settled for my wallet. If you see her, give me a call." I handed her my card before she could process what I'd just told her. "Work number's at the top, home number's at the bottom. There's a fifty in it for you."

"My son wants some shoes that cost a hundred."

It was steep, but not impossible. Besides, I liked her. "Okay. A hundred, if you get me here before she leaves."

Her hazel eyes narrowed. "You're not going to hurt her? 'Cause it looked like she's had her share of that already."

"Never hurt a woman in my life," I assured her. "I don't plan to start."

"I'll think about it."

I wasn't sure she'd do it, even for the hundred bucks. I wasn't even sure Heather would come back. I wouldn't, in her place. Still, a long shot was better than no shot. She hadn't given me a last name, so the First Edition was the only link, however tenuous, I had with her.

I thanked Dani, stopped to pick up some files at the office, and got home in time to watch *Happy Days* and *I Love Lucy* reruns with Jay. After three trips to the kitchen—water, beer, a bag of corn chips—and another to the bathroom, I gave up, exchanged my boots for running shoes, and drove downtown to the riverfront. With the sweat drying on my skin and the smell of the river in my nostrils, I ran like I was racing the devil.

In a way, I was.

# 11

**T**HERE HAD BEEN NO WORD from Mr. Perfect, and Jay was like a pendulum, swinging between devastation that Eric hadn't called and the certainty that he would.

"He's an artist." Jay sat on the sofa, legs curled beneath him, gnawing at his thumbnail. "You know how artists are. No sense of time."

I nodded noncommittally.

"He's probably in the middle of a sculpture."

"Jay . . ."

"I know, I know." He sighed and ran a hand through his short, straw-blond hair. "He isn't going to call." His laugh was sad, bitter. "I sure know how to pick 'em, don't I?"

"I'm sorry, man," I said. "I know how much this meant to you."

"Oh well." He unfolded himself from the couch and gave me a wan smile. "*Que cera, cera.* I think I'll turn in early tonight. I'm not feeling very well."

He'd moved downstairs a few months after his status went from borderline to full-blown AIDS. "I don't want to wait until I have no choice," he'd said. "Until I can't get up and down the stairs." I hated to see him preparing for his own death. It felt too much like giving up, but he seemed to take comfort in it. "Jared," he'd say, "I intend to live another hundred years. But just in case I don't . . ."

When he had gone, I went in and looked up Mr. Perfect's number in the phone book. It was listed. I wrote down the number and address and tucked it into my wallet, just in case. I'd give Eric some time to do the decent thing before I paid him a visit.

I flipped through the Nashville listings, looking for Valerie

Shepherd. No luck. I worked my way through Brentwood and Belleview and finally found her in the Franklin section. I didn't plan to go there yet, but it was good to have. At least I felt like I was gaining information, finding trails to follow. Even blind trails tell you something. They tell you when you're headed the wrong way. Or as Edison once said, "I didn't fail to make a light bulb ninety-nine times; I learned ninety-nine ways not to make a light bulb."

Or words to that effect.

On Sunday afternoon, I drove over to the Cedar Valley Motel and asked for the clerk who'd been on duty the night of the murder.

"You a reporter?" The young man behind the counter had lime green hair and an acne problem.

"Detective." I flashed my I.D., knowing he wouldn't challenge me.

"You want Marcie. Just a minute. She's in the back."

After a few minutes, he came back, followed by a violet-haired girl with a ring through one nostril. She could have been his sister. I bought her a Coke in the motel restaurant and asked her to repeat her story. It had been a slow night, she said. She remembered the man who had rented the room because she thought he was cute.

"Do you think you'd recognize him if you saw him again?"

Frank had said the results of the lineup had been inconclusive, but, presumably, the killer hadn't been in it. If he had been, could she have picked him out? Since she seemed oblivious to the fact that I'd been in that lineup, I didn't have a lot of confidence in her powers of observation.

"I don't know." She swirled her ice around with her straw. "The police asked me to check out some guys, but I wasn't sure. He must've, like, shaved since he killed her."

"Anything else happen that night?"

She shook her head.

"See anyone else?"

"Just the usual. Some guy started, like, pissing on the

76

bushes around midnight, and a couple of crazy-ass women had a few too many and had to, like, help each other across the parking lot. Oh, and some guy got lost trying to find the Waffle House. Had to stop and ask directions, like, three times."

There was nothing else. I paid for the colas, thanked her for her time, and went home to spend the rest of the weekend catching up on my caseload and making sure the pasture was clear of toxic plants. Jimson, buckeye, milkweed, red maple . . . Tennessee is a fertile land. I had other things to do, and this wasn't my favorite part of horsekeeping, but it was better than finding one of the boys comatose or colicking. Or worse. The symptoms of plant poisoning varied from distress to paralysis, permanent neurological damage, and death. In the face of that, a little weeding seemed like a small price to pay.

I woke up early Monday morning with my mind full of dismal thoughts, darkened my hair with a temporary dye, dabbed spirit gum onto my upper lip and pressed on a matching mustache, and changed into clean jeans and a short-sleeved denim shirt. I left the shirt untucked to hide the Colt, which was snuggled into a leather small-of-back holster.

My image had been shown on Channel 3 news, but with a different hair color and a little facial hair, I might as well be a different man. I debated whether or not to wear the cowboy hat and decided it would help the disguise.

Besides, I liked it.

It was a little after twelve by the time I headed south down I-65 toward the small, historic town of Franklin and the address I'd gotten for Amy Hartwell's sister.

I passed the driveway twice before I realized I'd found the place, a sprawling, western-style ranch house tucked among softly rolling hills that undulated like a rumpled quilt. White vinyl fencing made neat stitches across the green. *ValeSong Stables*, said the sign beside the entrance. *Quality Arabians*.

Vale, from Valerie, I guessed.

The third time I passed the driveway, it was on purpose. There was a tack shop, Dark Horse Saddlery, just a little farther down the street, and I went there first, on the theory that a horsewoman who lived this close to a tack shop would probably buy some of her equipment there.

I picked up a new lead rope, a bucket of horse treats, and a jar of Hooflex. Then I left them on the counter while I went into the back room to look at the advertisements.

Business cards and flyers covered one wall. The other three were obscured by boxes of riding boots and helmets. I scanned through ads for equine massage, riding lessons, Quarter Horses, and Jack Russell Terriers, until I came to a stack of business cards that read, "ValeSong Stables. Pure Egyptian Arabians. Training, Breeding, Sales. Victory's Flame at stud."

I unpinned the stack, stuffed one into my pocket, and re-pinned the others. Then I went back out front to show it to the girl behind the counter, a gangly girl with work-callused hands, long black hair, and features like a Greek statue.

"I'm looking for a good endurance horse. This place any good?" I pulled out the card and showed the girl the name.

ValeSong? Sure. I guess so. I jump Thoroughbreds myself." She pointed to a photo under the glass countertop of herself on a light bay mare. "That's me and Moxie."

"Moxie. Good name."

"Yeah. She's still young, but she's got a lot of promise. My trainer says we might be able to make Grand Champion at Shelbyville in a couple of years."

Shelbyville is Horse City. They have the big Tennessee Walking Horse Festival there every year, although that's come under fire because of the soring controversy. As far as I'm concerned, anybody who sores a horse should have to walk across hot coals, then race around a half-mile track with ten-pound shoes strapped to his feet. My Walker is flat shod, and his walk is just as pretty as God made it, which is pretty enough for me.

They don't show only Walking Horses in Shelbyville, though, and I suspected the girl was talking about one of the specialty or all-breed shows held almost every weekend.

"That would be something," I said. "You ever see this Valerie at a show?"

"Sure. Victory's Flame won High Point Champion three years in a row at the Festival of Horses."

"Know her?"

"Victory's Flame?"

"Valerie Shepherd."

"She comes in here a lot. Being so close and all."

I gave her a grin I hoped said Harmless, Friendly, and Not Too Bright. "The reason I'm asking is, if I'm going to consider buying a horse from her, I'd want to know if she's any good."

"You mean, as a breeder, or a trainer?"

"Both. Either."

'Well . . ." She picked at a corner of a photograph that protruded from beneath the glass. "I don't really have a lot of dealings with her, you know. But she does real good at the shows."

"Any complaints?"

"There's always complaints. Some people are never happy. There was something about a horse being abused once, but she fired the guy who did it. And one woman came in and said Ms. Shepherd came on to her husband. But who knows? Could just be gossip. Or paranoia."

I gave a sympathetic nod. "Plenty of that to go around. You think I could talk to any of these people?"

"We don't take their names. But the guy who used to work for her comes in here sometimes. I could give you his name and number."

"The one she fired?"

"Uh huh. He's training for himself now. Does good business, from what I hear." She shook her head. "I don't understand it myself. Would you hire a trainer who was fired for beating a horse?"

"Nope."

"That's what I thought." She wrote the name and number

down for me. Asa Majors.

"Ms. Shepherd and her husband run the place?" I asked, fishing.

"Actually, I think she got the place as part of her divorce settlement."

"Jeez." I grinned. "I'm glad my ex-wife didn't have her lawyer."

"Lotta guys say that." She flashed me a flirtatious smile.

She looked fresh out of college, which made her about a decade too young. Still, it gave me a lift like I hadn't felt in a while. I gave her a wink and a smile and left. I slid behind the wheel of the Taurus, surprised to find myself whistling.

# 12

THE DRIVEWAY LEADING to Valerie Shepherd's house and barn was long, winding, and surfaced with a layer of fine, dusty gravel. The grassy slopes that rose and fell to either side were a lush, uniform blue-green that meant they had probably been seeded with Kentucky bluegrass. In the rippling heat, the white barn with its brick-red roof looked like a mirage.

To my left, several horses, including a couple of spindle-legged foals, grazed in one of the pastures. They looked like fine stock. Sleek, healthy-looking Arabians with good conformation.

I parked beside a candy-apple red Chevy LS with a red and white cooler and a bag of sweet feed in the back. Before I got out of the car, I dabbed at my fake mustache with a Kleenex. It itched, and my upper lip sweated beneath the spirit gum. It wasn't comfortable, but I was pretty sure it would hold.

It was another steaming day, and by the time I stepped into the comparative coolness of the barn, my shirt already had dark patches at the armpits. Sweat trickled down my stomach and into my waistband. I pressed the Kleenex to the beads of perspiration on my forehead and looked around.

Two cement-floored corridors stretched to my left, each with a row of ten stalls along each side. To my right was an arena strewn with rubber granules ground from old tires. They were more expensive than sand or dirt flooring, but eliminated the need to hose down the arena to keep the dust down.

The wash bay and the office were at one corner of the arena, next to a rotating fan and two Pepsi machines. Above it all, on a loft that rested over the entire middle section, were the hay bales that would supplement the feed mix and the sweet Kentucky bluegrass in the pasture. Through the opening at the far end of the corridor to my left, I saw a chestnut mare circling sleepily on a hot walker.

All in all, it was a beautiful setup.

In the arena, the woman I'd seen in the Hartwell driveway was riding patterns. She was a good rider, though a little sharp with the spurs, and I noticed that she kept the sorrel gelding thinking, bending him first right, then left, doing two turns on the forehand, then three on the rear.

I leaned my forearms on the top of the arena fence and watched as she did a near-perfect figure eight. Then she noticed me.

"Hey," she called, then trotted over to the fence in front of me and pulled the gelding to a stop. She was wearing tight jeans, a sleeveless blouse knotted just below her breasts, and a pair of snakeskin cowboy boots with sharply pointed toes. Her strawberry-blond hair had been pulled back into a long braid that lay along her back like a copperhead. A drop of perspiration trickled down the nape of her neck. Watching it, I felt an almost overwhelming desire to trace it with my tongue.

In Calvin's driveway, with the heavy makeup and the big-blown mall hair, she'd looked like just another pretty woman. With her hair pulled back and her skin bare, she had a primal beauty that seemed independent of her wide, mobile mouth and the sharp planes of her face.

"May I help you?" she said. Her voice was sultry and a little hoarse. She sounded like she should be singing from the top of a piano.

I gave her the same story I'd used back at the tack store, that I was looking for a good Arabian horse, a mare or gelding between three and seven, fast and supple, with good wind and a willing temperament. Also, no vices.

She cocked her head and gave me an appraising look. "What would you use the horse for?"

"Trail work. Poles and barrels. Endurance." I'd never ridden Endurance, but Arabians excelled at it. "And I have an eight-year-old son, so whatever I end up with has to be gentle."

"Your son would be riding the horse?"

"Not necessarily. I just don't want anything that might strike at him. No biting, no kicking." I imagined Paulie's head struck by a hard, sharp hoof, his pudgy body falling, the startled look on his moon-shaped face, the fair hair splashed with blood. I imagined myself in slow motion, unable to stop it. Every father's nightmare.

One of many. I have one for every occasion.

"Truth to tell," she said, "I only have one horse for sale right now. Two-year-old. But he's not broke yet, and he's only got one eye. He's still intact, but you could geld him. I could sell him to you cheap."

"Could I see him? When you're finished here, I mean." I gestured toward the gelding she was riding.

"I'll only be a few more minutes." She made a face. "I hate this part of it, but I'm between trainers. Why don't you take a look at the colt? He's in the last stall on that row." She pointed to the corridor that included the wash bay. "Right side. Name's Dakota."

She went back to her training, and I pushed away from the fence and went to look at the colt.

He was about fifteen hands, a rich bay so dark it was almost black, with reddish highlights that rippled across his muscles when he moved. He had one white foot and a small white star between his eyes with three little sworls of hair surrounding it. His conformation was just about perfect.

When I spoke, he startled briefly and swung his good eye toward me. The other was clouded. A jagged scar slashed from the center of his forehead to the middle of his cheek.

His muscles tightened, but he didn't turn his hindquarters to me. His head was cocked, his ears held out to the sides.

Wary.

I slid back the bolt and tugged open the stall door. His ears twitched as the door rumbled on its runners, but since he neither panicked nor charged, I stepped inside and pulled the stall door closed behind me.

After a few minutes, his ears pricked forward and he edged closer.

I gave him my hand to smell, and his nostrils flared, blowing a warm breath onto the back of my wrist. Gently, I blew back.

It took awhile, but he let me run my hands over him, rub his ears, and pick up all four feet. None of his legs seemed sore or swollen, and his hooves were smooth and well shod. When I bent over to look at his front hooves, he nudged my hat off and nibbled at my hair.

It was a gentle gesture, but I knew I needed to put a stop to before it evolved into something dangerous. Horses are big, and they're powerful, and even the sweetest ones can kill you if you aren't careful.

I straightened up too suddenly, and he shied away from me and pressed himself into the corner of his stall, tail clamped tight to his hindquarters.

Behind me, a voice said, "He needs a lot of work."

The horse's skin twitched, and his good eye rolled back so I could see the white.

I said, "What happened to him?"

"I had a trainer, Asa Majors. Went after Dakota with his belt. Nearly took his eye out with the buckle." She slid the door open and stepped in beside me. She smelled of horse sweat and vanilla perfume. "Drinking, I guess. So now, like I said, I'm between trainers."

A violent man in an alcoholic rage. I made a mental note to call on Asa as soon as I could manage it.

I looked at the colt, stretched my hand out, and stroked his flank. Again, his muscles tensed, but he made no move to bite or strike. Nice. But like the lady said, he'd take a lot of work.

"I like him," I said. "But I need to think it over. And I'll want my vet to check him out."

She shrugged. "He's had his vaccinations and his Coggins. I have the paperwork in the office. But if you want your guy to check him out, sure. He colicked a little over a week ago and I spent most of the night monitoring him, but he's fine now." Her lower lip quivered. "That was the night my sister died. Somebody murdered her."

"My God."

She sucked at her lip and nodded. "I can't believe something like that could have been happening to her, and I didn't even know anything was wrong. You'd think I would have felt something."

"You must have been close."

"Since we were little. We used to glue sequins and feathers to old clothes to make costumes. Then we'd dance and sing, do comedy. Drama. Everything. I'm singing at her memorial service on Thursday. I hope I can make it through the song. Channel 3 is planning to televise it. "

"Was she a singer too?"

She gave me a bemused smile. "She could barely carry a tune. And she wasn't much of an actress, either. But we had a good time."

"It must have been a shock when she died."

"You can't believe how I felt when Cal told me. Cal's—he was her husband. But you know, I kind of thought . . . I was afraid something like this might happen."

"Really. What made you think that?"

She rolled her lower lip under her teeth. "I don't know if I should say anything. You might think I was speaking ill of the dead. But you can love someone and not agree with everything they do."

"I think I read about it in the paper. Some guy she was seeing..."

"Exactly. There was a man she was working with, too. I knew she wasn't happy in her marriage, but . . . " She gave a little laugh that sounded more like a sob. "My God, why am I telling you this? You come to buy a horse, and I unload all this on you."

"It's okay," I said, ignoring the pang of guilt that told me I was being a shit. "Sometimes it's easier to talk to a stranger."

"Sometimes it is."

I scratched the colt's withers and eased into a massaging stroke. His eyes rolled back again, his muscles bunched, and then he gave along shuddering sigh and relaxed under my hand. "You want to tell me about these guys your sister was seeing?" It was too early in the conversation to use Amy's name.

"Jared McKean. That prick." She wiped at her eyes with the flat of her hand. "I'm sorry. We haven't even buried her yet. Damned autopsy."

"It's all right. Cry if you want to."

"No. I'm fine. See?" She drew in a quivering breath. "You want to know what I think? I think this Jared found out she was seeing Ben, from work. And I think he went berserk and killed her." She wiped her eyes with the back of her hand and gestured toward the horse. "You want to work him?"

She brought me a halter and a lunge line and whip. Then she parked herself at one end of the arena to watch.

I led the colt into the arena and started him at a slow jog, starting in close and then playing out the line. He danced a little at first, but finally fell into a steady pace. When he seemed calmer, I moved the whip back and forth behind him. Low to the ground, and he slowed; higher, and he went faster. When I cracked it in the air behind him, he spooked briefly and broke into a lope. A lot of people think a lunge whip is used to beat the horse. In truth, you never touch him with it.

While I worked the horse, I tried to think of a way to get back onto the subject of Amy. I didn't want to seem morbid, or worse, raise suspicions. Part of my mind toyed with that problem. The other part noted that Dakota was a supple mover, though a little less flexible on the right. He was shy of the whip, not surprising in light of his past.

"You handle him pretty well," Valerie said, when I led him back to her. "He likes the massage."

"I learned it about four years ago, when my quarter horse started getting a little stiff. Seemed like a good thing to do for him. I do a little TTouch, too."

She raised an eyebrow. "I didn't figure you for all that New Age touchy feely bullshit."

TTouch stood for Tellington Touch, a method of therapeutic touch adapted from the Feldencrais method of working with humans with neurological disorders. It was supposed to make the horses more balanced, more comfortable, and easier to work with. Valerie was right; it did sound like a load of New Age bullshit. I gave her a sheepish grin. "Figured it couldn't hurt to give it a try. I didn't expect much at first, but it seems to work for my guys."

"I guess that's what matters. Anyway, it's probably cheaper than paying somebody else to come out and do it for you." She handed me a rubber curry. "Here. You want to put him away?"

I brushed the colt until he shone, then put him back into the stall and slipped the halter off. She watched while I worked.

"Can I get you a Coke?" I asked when I had closed the stall door.

"It's Pepsi, but sure. Diet."

I fished in my pocket for some change, got a Pepsi and a Diet Pepsi from the machine, and handed the Diet to her.

I followed her to her office area, where she gestured for me to join her on the leather sofa. On a shelf beside the couch was a television with a built-in VCR and a line of videotapes. *Fun Show 1999; Miss Rodeo, age 19; Patches Foaling #4; Dakota Colic, July.* She noticed me looking and gestured to the tapes. "I have a video system set up so I can monitor the horses when they need it. I can hook it up and see from here when they need attention."

"Convenient." I ran a finger along the labels. "You going to be all right?"

She looked puzzled for a moment, then nodded. "I'll be fine. It's hard, but then, life is hard, right?"

I thought about telling her about my parents, but then decided it would be cheap, using them to make her open up to me.

We sipped at our sodas, an uncomfortable silence between us. Then she reached over and ran her fingers lightly over my face. "What happened to you?"

"Mechanical bull," I said, and she laughed.

"I think you'd better stick with horses." She took my left hand, turned the palm upward, and traced my lifeline with her thumb.

"So," I said at last, "is there a Mister Shepherd?"

She gave a bitter laugh. "There used to be. He died a couple years ago. Penniless, in a homeless shelter. Sometimes I think he did it on purpose, so I wouldn't get anything when he died."

I wondered what would make a man lose everything he had to spite a woman he hadn't lived with in years, and what would make a woman think he might. "He wasn't living with you, then?"

"We were divorced. But he stopped paying alimony three years ago. He owed me quite a lot in back payments."

"Looks like you did okay for yourself."

A smile flitted across her lips. "I guess so. But it's the principle of the thing."

"Must have been a hell of a marriage."

"Oh, it was." She swirled her Pepsi and watched as a glistening bead of cola rolled along the inside of the rim. "I'd rather not talk about Tony. It's been a long time, but some wounds heal slow."

She crumpled her Diet Pepsi can in one hand and pitched it into the trash.

"Two points," she said, her voice flat.

The time for revelation was over. I started to get up, and she grabbed the front of my shirt and stopped me with a kiss. A hard kiss, almost angry. Her tongue flicked across my lips, then darted between them.

For a long moment, I kissed her back. Then my senses returned, and I pulled away.

"What's the matter?" Her right hand toyed with the buttons on my shirt, but her eyes were suddenly cold. "Don't tell me you don't want to."

"I don't want to take advantage."

"Bullshit." She twisted the front of my shirt into her fist and thumped my chest. "Don't you go and get all noble on me. Don't you dare."

"It's not nobility. It's—"

"Damn straight it's not. You think I don't know what I want?" She scooted in close against me and pressed her left palm against my crotch. "Poor, grieving Valerie, right? Got to pwotect poor widdle Valerie, right? If you're so damn righteous, why can I feel your hard-on?"

The fingers of her left hand tightened, kneaded. I stifled a gasp. Pleasure, yes, and a touch of pain. I didn't want her to stop. I pushed her hand away gently but firmly, slid out of her grasp, and got to my feet. "I won't say I'm not tempted."

Her laugh was mocking. "Tempted. Yeah, I'll bet you are. Well, have it your way. But I could have rocked your world, my friend."

"Probably."

I jotted down my cell phone number on one of her cards, told her I'd send my vet by sometime next week, thanked her for her time, and told her I was sorry for her loss.

"Sure," she said. "You never even told me your name."

"Ian," I said. "Ian Callahan."

"Right. Well, goodbye, Ian Callahan. Maybe I'll give you another chance sometime."

God, I hoped not.

A man can only be so strong.

# 13

I POPPED A COUPLE of dry aspirins from the bottle I kept in the glove compartment, then eased out of Valerie's driveway and headed north. A few minutes later, I pulled into the Food Lion parking lot, took the spirit gum remover out of my theatrical makeup kit, and got rid of that damned mustache. There was a red rash above my upper lip that was tender to the touch, so I picked up some aloe vera cream from the grocery store and smoothed it into the irritated skin.

It helped some.

While I waited for my lip to stop stinging, I changed my voicemail message to a number-you-have-reached, no name. If Valerie called, the message wouldn't blow my cover. Then I drove back to the office, wondering what exactly had happened back at the stables. There had been real passion in Valerie's kiss, but there had been anger in it too.

Anger at me? At Amy?

Or maybe at death itself?

Back at the office, I rinsed out the hair color. Then I stopped by the hardware store and picked up the parts for the peephole I'd promised Birdie. When I went by her place to put it in, she gave me another glass of lemonade and told me stories about Henry. I asked her what she knew about Valerie Shepherd.

"Not much, to tell the truth," she admitted. "I've never actually met her. But I saw her over at the Hartwells' several times. Christmases, the occasional random visit." She topped off my lemonade, set the pitcher down, and rubbed at her gnarled knuckles. "Something's been weighing on me since the last time you were here."

"What's that, Ms. Birdie?"

"It's about Calvin. I know I told you he was a cold man. But he's always treated me polite-like, and he's mowed my lawn most every week in summer since Henry died. I don't care for the man, but I don't want you to think he doesn't have his good points. I may have been too harsh on him before."

"Everybody has some good points. Must've been some reason Amy married him."

Honey," Birdie said, "love chooses who it chooses. I think she was looking for a daddy, if you want to know the truth. I don't think those girls had much of a father figure, and I think Amy was just wanting somebody like Cal to come along and tell her what to do."

"I reckon she found that."

Ms. Birdie's marmoset face grew still and sad. "I reckon she did. And it must have been a harsh blow for both of them when she realized she'd grown up and didn't want to be told what to do anymore."

I wondered if that was what had gotten her killed.

"Ms. Birdie," I said. "Do you know if Cal was at home the night she died?"

She tapped at her front teeth with a fingernail and frowned. "Actually, he worked late that night. I know, because Amy sent the girls over here after supper. She'd gotten a phone call, and she had to go out and meet someone. So she sent them over here with a note asking if I'd keep them until she or Cal got home. I wish . . ."

I knew what she wished. That she'd somehow known, that she could have warned Amy to stay home with her daughters that night instead of rushing out to meet Death.

"Did she say who she was going to meet?"

"If she'd said, I would've told you."

"And she never came home."

No," Ms. Birdie said, softly. "She never did."

THE NEXT MORNING, when I went out to the barn, I found Tex on his back, cast against the wall of his stall, his eyes half closed and his sides heaving from exertion. He lifted his head and whickered when I said his name.

"Easy, boy." I knelt beside him, stroked his neck. "What have you gotten yourself into?" I'd banked his bedding along the walls to keep this very thing from happening, but somehow he'd managed it anyway. His position and the scattered bedding meant he'd been thrashing, trying to push himself to his feet. One foreleg looked swollen. Injured tendon, maybe. Or something worse.

Damn.

I was six when Mom bought the palomino quarter horse for my brother and me. We climbed over him like lemurs, scrambled under his belly, rode him bareback, practiced trick riding, ran poles and barrels, and roped each other from his back. He never put a foot wrong, never bucked, never kicked, never so much as laid his ears back. He was as close to bombproof as a horse could get, but that didn't mean he couldn't crush my skull by accident.

A steady stream of soothing nonsense kept him calm as I reached across him, grasped his far legs, and gently rolled him toward me onto his side. There were safer ways to do it, and I should probably have used one of them, but I didn't want to leave him there any longer than I had to. Besides, we'd trusted each other for a long time.

He gave me time to get out of his way before struggling to his feet. Then, breathing hard, he hobbled forward on three legs and rested his head on my shoulder.

I stroked his neck, led him to the wash bay, and hosed his leg with cold water. Then, while I was waiting for the vet, I called Information and got a number for Asa Majors.

His answering machine picked up, and I left my number and a message saying I was interested in a horse he'd worked with and wanted his opinion on it.

I knew the morning was a wash.

At 1:00, after the vet had come and gone and the injured leg had been iced and bandaged, Jay brought out a couple of sandwiches and a pitcher of tea. We sat in the tack room and ate while Tex stood munching hay in his stall.

"How is he?" Jay asked.

"He's damaged two tendons and the suspensory ligament in his right foreleg."

"Will he be okay?"

"Maybe. But it'll take time." Time and work. Icing and bandaging twice a day. A couple of months of stall rest with handwalking. Months more of limited turnout and gradually increasing exercise. And still no guarantees. "He may never be completely sound."

Jay nodded, nibbled at the edge of his sandwich. After awhile, he said, "I've put out a few feelers on that insurance thing. Something should shake loose soon."

"Good. Because I have a new assignment for you."

He looked interested, so I went on.

"Hartwell's first wife did a vanishing act. It'd be interesting to know if she's alive and well somewhere or if she's in an unmarked grave."

"You do have a mind for the morbid."

"I know," I said. "It's a gift."

In his stall, Tex snorted, rattled his feed bucket.

"He'll be all right," Jay said, reading my mind. "Just give him time."

Time. I hoped I had time. If I went to prison, who would hose down Tex's leg and change his bandages? Who would handwalk him twice a day? Who would keep Crockett trim and fit? Jay would be willing, but he was in and out of the hospital himself. Some days he was fine; others, he was weak as a kitten.

If I went to prison, who would take care of Jay?

And Paul. I wanted to teach him to hit a baseball, shoot a basketball, catch a fish. Instead, D.W. would do those things, and I would fade from my son's memory like a summer fog.

I couldn't go to prison.

Thinking dark thoughts, I dressed as Ian Callahan and

93

drove to ValeSong Stables. I hadn't found an opportunity to ask Valerie about Hartwell's first wife, but I was sure she'd know the tale; it was the kind of story families whispered over the Thanksgiving dishes. I told myself that was my reason for going back. It had nothing to do with the little bay colt.

And nothing at all to do with the taste of Valerie Shepherd's tongue.

Her red Chevy was pulling out as I neared the driveway. I passed by as if that had been my intent all along, rounded a bend that took me out of view, and hooked a U-turn in front of the tack shop.

I didn't think Valerie had seen my car the last time I'd been there, but I kept my distance anyway, just in case. I almost lost her as she cut across two lanes to the Demonbreun exit. Holding my breath, I jerked the wheel to the right, darted into a space between two semis, bounced onto the ramp, and took a sharp left onto a small access road that curved onto Music Square.

By the time I started breathing again, the red Chevy had cruised to a stop in front of a glass-fronted building with sleek silver letters on the glass. *AudioStyle Recording Studio*, they said.

I cruised by and glanced into the rearview mirror as the door to *AudioStyle Recording* opened and a man with limp, shoulder-length blond hair jaunted out, hands jammed into the pockets of artfully frayed jeans. He looked to be some-where in his thirties, rangy but muscular, and about six feet tall.

My height. My build. About my age.

I looked back at the road. Slowed for a right-hand turn. When I glanced back again, he was climbing into the Chevy's passenger side, and she was leaning across the seat toward him. Their lips met, and the blare of a horn told me it was time to turn.

When I looped around again, they were gone.

# 14

T HE DAY OF AMY HARTWELL'S funeral, I darkened my hair again, applied my Ian Callahan mustache, and put on a dark gray Canali suit with a white cotton shirt and a blood-red tie Maria had given me one father's day. The shoulder holster with my brother's Colt tucked into it made a slight bulge beneath the jacket. Someone who knew what to look for might realize I was packing, but no one at Windrider Travel was likely to notice.

I pulled into the parking lot of the travel agency, noting the single Toyota in the parking lot with some satisfaction. As I'd expected, most of the office workers had gone to the funeral, leaving someone behind to man the phones and handle walk-ins.

I pushed the door open, and the young woman behind the desk looked up from her computer monitor, gave me a distracted smile, and held up one index finger: *Just a minute.*

"And thank you for booking with Windrider Travel," she said into the cordless phone receiver clamped between her cheek and shoulder. Her frosted pink nails extended so far beyond her fingertips that she had to use her pen to punch the hang-up button. With a cheery smile, she swiveled her chair toward me, tucked her hair behind her ear, and said, "May I help you?

Her nametag said *Felicity*, a name so old-fashioned it had gone around the corner and come back into style.

"I'm Ian Callahan. I'm working on a book about Amy Hartwell and wondered if you might have a few minutes to talk."

"A book," she said. "One of those true crime books?"

She looked more intrigued than disgusted, so I nodded

and said, "Nothing lurid, though. I really want to do her justice."

I assuaged my guilt with the knowledge that this much, at least, was true.

"Seems really soon," she said. "It's been what, a week?"

"Just about. I read about it in the paper and thought since it happened right here in town, I might have a unique perspective on it."

"Will my name be in the book?"

"Unless you tell me you want it changed. Then I just indicate that with an asterisk the first time the name comes up. That way, everybody knows which names aren't real."

She frowned, although it couldn't have been easy with her eyebrows penciled into startled arches. "I've never been in a book before. I don't think I'd want my name changed."

She looked so hopeful, I felt bad about the lie that had gotten me in.

Felicity was, in some ways, a P.I.'s dream. Young enough to be excited by the thought of being interviewed and smart enough to observe what was going on around her.

She wasn't too hard on the eyes, either, although she went a little heavy on the makeup for my taste. Her pouty lips were slathered with a waxy layer of coral lipstick, and her eyes were painted with pine green eye shadow and a thick outline of kohl, Cleopatra style. If you took her in your arms, you might end up with an image of her face imprinted on your shirt.

Still, she had a nice figure and long, shapely legs that looked even longer beneath her short skirt. They were a pleasant distraction.

"Do you mind if I tape your interview?" I asked Felicity, holding up my Sony pocket recorder. "For accuracy only. Of course, you'll have a chance to review the book before it goes to press to make sure you've been correctly quoted."

"Oh." She looked at the recorder. "I guess I don't mind."

"What can you tell me about Amy?"

Felicity fidgeted with her pen, then slowly twirled it between her fingers. "I don't know," she said at last. "What do you want to know?"

I gave her an encouraging smile. "Well...what kind of person was she? Did people like her? How did you feel about her? Was she a good worker? Did she ever talk about her marriage? Or her kids? And what about this boyfriend—this Jared McKean?"

"Huh." She gave a nervous laugh. "You really have to think of a lot to be writer, don't you? Let me see." She turned the pen over and began to doodle, covering the margins with sweeping curves and spirals. "She was a real good worker. Always on time. Me, I'd be late to my own funeral." She caught herself, put a hand to her mouth. "I shouldn't have said that."

"It's okay. Just a figure of speech. What else?"

"What else? She was, like, real private. Wore long, flowing skirts, like gypsy skirts, prairie skirts, down to her knees. Bulky sweaters. I think she was self-conscious about her weight."

"She didn't look that heavy in the pictures."

"No . . . Not really." Unconsciously, she sucked in her stomach, slipped a thumb into the waistband of her skirt and tugged. "But she wasn't petite. And she just...well, you could tell by her posture. She wasn't comfortable in her body."

"But you liked her?"

"Everybody did, I guess. I mean, it wasn't like we were friends or anything, but we got along. She seemed like kind of a prude. But then, I guess you never know about that. Her lovers and all."

"Her lovers?"

"You know." She curled her lower lip under her top teeth.

"Not really."

She gnawed at her lip, then flicked her tongue across it and answered. "This Jared McKean, for one. She never talked about him here. Nobody knew she was seeing someone else."

"Someone besides her husband?"

"Well, him, sure. But I meant Ben Carrington."

"Ben..." I wrote the name on my yellow legal pad. "That's C-A-R-R-I-N-G-T-O-N?"

"That's right."

"Who's he?"

"Oh." She giggled. "Ben's her boyfriend. They had lunch together every day. Stayed late 'talking'." She made quotation marks with her fingers.

"Did he know she was seeing somebody else?"

"I don't think so. It just broke his heart when he found out. I mean, he knew she was married and all, but he thought she was this sweet, innocent thing whose husband treated her like dirt. He thought he was the only one she was involved with. At least, until this other guy killed her. He was so torn up about it. He thought the guy might have found out about him and killed her because of it."

"Did he tell you he was having sexual relations with her?"

She bit her lower lip. "N-o-o-o. Not in so many words. He's a real gentleman. He'd never brag or anything like that."

"Did she ever talk about her husband?"

"She told us once he didn't want her working. I don't think it was a very happy marriage."

"What makes you think that?"

"If she'd been happy, why would she go out with Ben?"

"Good point." I tipped my head in acknowledgement. "The night she was killed. Did she say anything about meeting anyone?"

"Not to me."

"Is Mr. Carrington married?"

"No." She lowered her eyes. "His wife died about five years ago. Cancer."

I thought if Carrington wasn't the murderer, he was the unluckiest bastard on the planet.

I pumped Felicity for a little more information, just enough to ascertain that she knew nothing more about the murdered woman. Then I asked if I could take a look at Amy's workspace.

"Well." She bit her lip. "I don't know."

I gave her my best, most charming smile, the one Maria said had made her marry me. "I promise to leave everything exactly how I found it."

She stared into my eyes for a long moment, possibly trying to gauge my sincerity. At last, she said, "All right. But don't mess up anything."

She went back to her own desk, leaving me alone at Amy's.

I slid into the dead woman's chair and scanned her work space, trying to get a sense of who she was and why someone might have wanted to kill her. I sat at her desk and soaked her in, from the jumbled cork bulletin board and color-coded file folders to the family photograph on one corner of her desk. I picked up the photograph and studied it, my tongue worrying at the scab on my lower lip.

I recognized Amy from the pictures I'd seen in the news and Calvin and the girls from yesterday afternoon. Calvin looked stern and solemn in his dark suit. One hand rested on his wife's shoulder. It might have been a protective gesture, but in light of their troubled marriage, seemed possessive and proprietary instead. Amy, wearing a flowered skirt and a peach sweater covered with seed pearls, had an arm around each of her daughters, who looked scrubbed and fresh-faced in their matching jumpers.

I looked into Amy's eyes. *Who are you?* I thought at the photograph. *Come on, baby, talk to me.*

Of course, she didn't talk to me. She stared out of the picture, a strange blend of pride and sadness on her face.

*Who are you?*

A woman who felt overwhelmed by her children. Who had tried—and possibly failed—to love another woman's daughter. Who had given up everything to be what her husband wanted and finally decided she wanted some of it back.

Had it gotten her killed?

Why had she gone to the Cedar Valley Motel?

The calendar on her desk revealed no clues. Daily appointments were marked in a careful, even hand. Doodles framed the printed squares, not the usual hearts and spirals, but real drawings: a lone palm tree on a tiny hump of island, a cartoon Volkswagen with flat tires and a sad face, a cute-as-hell fly in a multi-sleeved turtleneck trying to pull free from a piece of flypaper, a chorus line of dancing raisins wearing clown noses and Groucho Marx mustaches. Escape and isolation. The raisins looked happy enough, but wasn't the disguise really just another way to escape?

The drawers of her desk were neatly organized: brochures, contracts, pens, and paper clips. In one drawer, I found a Nora Roberts paperback , a copy of *Chicken Soup for the Soul*, and a hardcover volume called *The Incest Survivor's Handbook*. I thought of the photos Frank had found in my truck and wondered if Amy had known Katrina was being exploited.

I went back to Felicity's desk.

"Did Amy work on Friday?" I asked.

"Yes, of course." Her startled eyebrows tried to lift a little higher. "Why wouldn't she?"

"No reason. Just covering the bases. Did she say anything about going to see anyone that night? A date? An appointment?"

"No. She said she was going home. But when I left, she and Ben were outside in the parking lot, talking."

"Could you tell what they were talking about?"

The look she gave me was withering. "I don't eavesdrop."

"No, of course not. But you might have overheard something in passing. Sometimes you can't help but hear something."

"Oh." She seemed somewhat mollified. "I guess that's true. But no, I didn't hear anything."

"Did they seem upset? Angry?"

"They looked like a couple of high school sweethearts saying goodbye after school. You know. One more thing, then one more thing. Like they couldn't stand to leave."

"Did you go straight home after work?"

"No. I had dinner at Ruby Tuesday's, then went home and watched *Silverado* on cable."

I grinned. "I saw that movie six times. Tell me you're not married."

She smiled, eyes downcast. Demure. Flattered and embarrassed. "I'm not married."

"Woman of my dreams," I teased. Then, "I don't guess you'd let me take a look at Ben's desk, would you?"

She frowned. "Well . . ."

"I won't bother anything."

"I'll tell you what." She nibbled at a long, almond-shaped nail. "I'll let you take a peek on the way out. But you can't touch anything."

I held up three fingers. "Scout's honor."

Ben's desk had a few scattered Post-its and brochures.

*Call Margaret.*

*Corey. Ballet. Sat. aft.*

There was a picture of a woman holding a baby, a smaller photo of a smiling little girl in a pink tutu tucked into the frame.

"Corey?" I asked, pointing to the picture."

"Mmhm. That's his daughter. She's six now."

"And Margaret?"

"Baby-sitter."

"Ah."

"Is that all you need?"

I thought about asking for her number, but what would I say if I called her? *Hello, I'm not really an author and I lied to you about pretty much everything, and I'm the only suspect in the murder of your colleague. Want to go out sometime?*

Right.

"That's everything," I told her.

After an awkward silence, she flashed me a smile and said, "Well. Why don't you just take my card? In case you need to ask me anything else."

She handed me a business card that said, *Felicity Ambrose. Windrider Travel Agency. We've planned more trips than Timothy Leary.*

I don't usually like drug jokes, but it was so unexpected, I laughed when I read it. "Well. Thanks, Felicity. Thanks for everything." I gave her an appreciative smile and tucked the card into the inside pocket of my suit jacket.

Then, regretfully, I got into my rental car and left.

THAT NIGHT, JAY AND I watched as Ashleigh's station broadcast a memorial service at Amy Hartwell's church. Ashleigh looked pained and sincere as she introduced the show in front of the Road to Glory Church of the Reclamation. The cameras returned to her throughout the program to show us how touched she was. This was done primarily by showing her dabbing at her eyes with an embroidered handkerchief, with an occasional close-up of her quivering lips. Ashleigh Arneau, compassion incarnate.

Yeah, right.

"I really hate that bitch," Jay said. I'd told him where and how I'd been arrested. "Let's burn her in effigy."

"She'll get hers someday," I said, but I didn't believe it. People like Ashleigh never get theirs.

The thing is, if I'd really thought she'd turned me in out of some sense of duty, or honor, or citizenship, I might have actually admired her. But I knew better. Ashleigh was a glory-hunter. If she'd ever had a noble instinct, she'd long since choked it into catatonia.

The service started with a welcome and a prayer. The choir sang 'Amazing Grace.' Then members of the congregation stood up and said some complimentary things about Amy. They mentioned their love and sympathy for Calvin, along with their hopes that he and the girls could get over this and go on with their lives. Calvin stood up, red-eyed, and said he hoped the Lord would show his dear wife mercy. Then the honorable Reverend Samuel Avery stepped up to the podium.

I sat up straighter. He was the same minister I'd seen at the jail. Same porcine build. Same balding, egg-shaped head. Same angry scar. He opened his mouth, and the voice that came out was soft and slithery like the serpent in the Garden of Eden. The very sound of it made me want to punch someone.

I'd heard that voice somewhere before.

Amy Hartwell, he said, had fallen into temptation, but he held out hope that she'd had time to repent before her grisly death. The Lord was merciful, he said, and so, despite her fall from grace, she might yet see the glorious face of the Almighty. If she had repented with her last breaths.

If.

Beside me, Jay murmured, "My God. In front of the children."

When Avery had finished, Valerie Shepherd sang a dramatic rendition of 'How Great Thou Art.' Her voice rose high and clear, ending on a note that must have made the stained glass windows tremble. She didn't sing like someone who should have been lying on top of a piano. She sang like she'd been born to it. Although her cheeks were streaked with tears, the smile on her face was orgasmic.

She was good, even by Nashville standards, where your waitress, your pharmacist, and the guy who services your car might all be Garth Brooks wannabes.

The camera panned to the blond man Valerie had picked up at the recording studio. He nodded and bobbed to the music, turning knobs and dials on a console that had probably cost as much as my truck. After the song was over, he gave Valerie a thumbs-up and a broad, gold-studded grin.

Jay shook his head in admiration, "Now there is the next Streisand."

"Which? The singer, or the blond guy?"

"The singer. Blondie would look like hell in drag. Not that he isn't gorgeous."

I looked more closely at Blondie. His knuckles sported

jailhouse tattoos, LOVE on one hand and HATE on the other. Probably the black sheep boyfriend Birdie had mentioned. I wondered why, if he was Valerie's boyfriend, she had planted a long hot kiss on Ian Callahan.

I wondered about the man who had used my name to rent a hotel room and then killed a woman in it.

"Gorgeous aside," I said. "Does that guy look anything like me?"

His gaze swung from me to the blond guy and back again. "You're of a type," he said.

"Enough so a hotel clerk might think he was me?"

He shrugged. "Fake beard, cowboy hat, pony tail tucked under to make the hair look shorter . . . your hair's a little darker and your teeth are better, but if they weren't paying attention, I guess maybe."

I made a mental note to learn more about Blondie.

After the final prayer and as the congregation poured out onto the sidewalk, Ashleigh thrust her microphone into Tara Hartwell's ashen face. Kneeling beside the child, Ashleigh said in her sweetest voice, "Sweetheart, is there something you'd like to say about your mama?"

There was a long silence. Ashleigh, knowing the value of a dramatic moment, waited. I saw Calvin Hartwell's hand tighten on his daughter's shoulder.

Tara said sadly, "My mama's in Hell."

"What?" Ashleigh blinked. Her mouth twitched, as if it couldn't decide whether to protest or smile.

In other circumstances, I would have enjoyed seeing Ashleigh gaping and speechless on live TV. But I couldn't get that kid's face out of my head, or that small, lost voice.

Then the moment was gone. Calvin Hartwell picked his daughter up and whisked her away to his car. Katrina, the twelve-year-old, scurried after them, one hand clutching at the tail of her daddy's jacket.

# 15

IT ISN'T ALL THAT HARD to follow a man who doesn't know he's being followed. On Friday morning, after I'd taken care of the horses and left a message from Ian Callahan on Reverend Avery's answering machine, I sat in my rental car, my Sony digital camera and a briefcase full of surveillance equipment on the seat beside me, and watched Cal Hartwell and the girls leave their house bright and early the next morning. I let them get a half a block away before pulling out after them.

The tricky part was while we were in still in Hartwell's neighborhood, because traffic was so thin it was almost non-existent until we turned onto Lebanon Road. Technically, it's the Sergeant Lance Fielder Memorial Highway, but no one calls it that, because it takes almost as long to say as it does to drive. I know, I know. If someone had named a road after my dad, I'd want people to know it. But it's been Lebanon road for as long as anyone can remember. Old habits die hard. Look at the metric system.

I stayed three or four cars behind the champagne Park Avenue, except on the side streets, where there were no cars for cover and I had to drop back to almost out of view.

Cal dropped his daughters off at an elementary school not far from their house. *Welcome to Fun Factory,* said the sign out front. *Summer Activity Program.* I'd figured a guy like Hartwell would put his kids in a private school, but here they were, the younger girl in pink slacks and a *Spongebob Squarepants* T-shirt, the elder in a light blue jumper. They got out of the car, and Cal called them back for a final hug. Then they entered the building hand in hand, clutching the straps of their backpacks like two lost souls.

They didn't look back.

For a week after Dad died, Randall stayed home from school. He says he still remembers his first day back in his third-grade classroom. It looked exactly the same, but he felt strange and different from the other children. Something terrible had happened to him and his family, and it set him apart. He couldn't have said how or why, but it was true. "I'm half an orphan," he remembers thinking, "and my daddy is a hero."

Something terrible had happened to the Hartwell girls, but they couldn't console themselves with the thought that their mother was a hero. Instead, they would have to cope with prying questions and judgments. *Why was your mother at that motel? Why was she with another man when she should have been at home with you?*

Watching them go into that big building all alone made my stomach feel hollow.

With the girls safely at Fun Factory, Cal took I-40 West toward downtown and turned left off the Broadway exit. Another surprise. Calvin had been quoted both in print and on the evening news as saying he worked as an architect out of an ultra-modern, glassed-in suite not far from the Convention Center. But to get to the Convention Center, and thus to his office, he would have had to turn right onto Broadway.

So where was he headed?

I trailed him past the fork where Broadway split and turned to West End. Past Ruth's Chris Steakhouse. Past Stone Mountain, Nashville's best known psychedelic-retro-hippie head shop. Past the little strip mall that housed Borders Books and P.F. Chang's.

He turned onto a side street just as the light turned red. If I'd been closer, I would have gunned it, but there were three cars between my rental and his Park Avenue. I fretted through the red light, drumming on the steering wheel and swearing under my breath until the stream of ongoing traffic broke enough for me to bolt through.

Of course, I lost him.

I drove straight for about three blocks, and when I didn't spot the Park Avenue, swung left onto a residential street. I cruised slowly up and down the cross-streets, driving a grid like the one I'd walk if it were a crime scene. Then something happened that I'd almost given up on since I'd met up with Heather in the First Edition Bar and Grill.

I got lucky.

I spotted the Park Avenue just as Cal was starting up the walkway of a three-story traditional-style brick house with ivory lace curtains and a dried-flower wreath on the door.

Suddenly, things got interesting.

The woman who met him at the door wore tight jeans and a see-through blouse with no bra underneath. My telephoto lens showed me a gold cross nestled between her breasts. The hello kiss she and Cal exchanged said more than just hello.

I thought, *You son of a bitch.*

Had he strayed from the straight and narrow after Amy went to work, or had he been dipping his wick in someone else's oil the whole time his wife was at home scrubbing toilets and popping Prozac?

I snapped a couple of photos of the liplock at the door. Then, when they had gone inside, I took pictures of the front of the house with the Park Avenue in front of it, so that the license plate and house number were clearly visible.

It didn't prove anything, except that Calvin Hartwell was a hypocrite, but it might be enough to raise at least a few doubts about my guilt in his wife's murder.

I got out of the car and skulked around the house until I ascertained that, a) I couldn't see or hear whatever Calvin and the woman were up to, b) I'd gotten the woman's name—G. Mathis—off of the mailbox, and c) if I stayed around much longer, I'd either be caught trespassing or be late for my preliminary hearing. Then I laid my camera gently in the passenger seat and drove away.

Of course, I wasn't late. I could have waited several hours

and still had time to spare, because nine tenths of most people's court dates is spent waiting. Since my case fell late in the schedule, Randall, Jay, and I sat in the gallery and listened to a dozen cases before my name was called.

The D.A., with a little help from Frank and Harry, presented all the evidence, both physical and circumstantial, that the state had amassed against me, and the judge ruled that, yes, there was plenty to justify sending the case to the Grand Jury, at which time Frank and Harry would present their evidence again, and the Grand Jury would almost certainly decide that, yes, there was enough to justify a trial and set a date for one.

In the meantime, I was a free man, and if I wanted to stay that way, I had to solve Amanda Hartwell's murder. It sounded simple until you realized that a murder unsolved after forty-eight hours is unlikely to ever be solved. It was a crucial window, and I'd already missed it.

Frank followed Randall, Jay, and me out of the courtroom. "Got a minute, kid?"

Randall's face flushed a virulent red. "No, he doesn't have a minute. What did you think you were doing up there?"

Frank sighed and ran a hand through his silver hair. "My job, Randall. Just my job."

"Yeah? If my job was railroading my friends, I think I'd go home and shoot myself." Randall had drawn up to his full six-two. He looked puffed out, like a rooster about to fly into a cockfight.

I laid my hand on his shoulder and squeezed. "He's just doing what he has to. In his place, I'd do the same thing."

"Like hell, you would. I want to hear him say he thinks you're innocent."

Frank looked like he'd swallowed a fish hook. "I'd like to think that, Randall. But the voice print . . . That hurts."

Randall set his jaw. "Innocent until proven guilty, remember?"

"Son," Frank said. "We can prove him guilty. We can

prove it beyond any reasonable doubt." He turned to me. "Officially, this case is closed. Nobody wants to look like they're trying to protect you just because you used to be one of us. Plus, there's a lot of ill feeling over how you left. The story the Arneau bitch did on you made the whole department look bad."

I grimaced at the memory. "I understand."

"Mac." He searched my face. Met my gaze and held it. "No head games. Just a simple yes or no. Did you do it?"

"No, Frank. No, I didn't."

"Okay, then."

"What? Suddenly you believe me?"

"Don't make me regret it." It was the second time he'd said that to me. His hand clapped my shoulder. "You get what I'm saying? Unofficially, I'll do what I can."

I nodded. Wondered what it meant to our friendship that he'd thought me capable of murder. If it could be mended by a word of encouragement and a hand on the shoulder. "Whatever you can do," I said. "I appreciate it."

Randall looked away. "I hate this."

"I know," Frank said. "We all do."

I told him about Cal Hartwell's morning liaison and the pictures I had taken of it. He told me the lab had found gray carpet fibers on Amy Hartwell's body.

"The carpets at the motel are sandy-colored," he said. "The ones in the Hartwell house are mauve and cream. The carpet in the Hartwell cars is taupe for the family car, and red for Amy's. The carpets in Jay's house are blue, and your truck has a gray interior, but not the right gray."

"So we have mystery fibers."

"That's about the size of it."

How many gray carpets were there in Nashville? Only about a million. But if we found a good suspect, and we could link him to a gray carpet, we could match the fibers.

"What about the phone call?" I asked. "The one she got that night just before she went out?"

He shook his head. "Came from a pay phone downtown. A couple of blocks from your office."

I forced a laugh. "It just never gets any better, does it?"

Harry stood beside the courtroom door, looking embarrassed, and I wondered if he thought I'd murdered a woman and taken pornographic pictures of her child. He noticed me looking and glanced away.

Frank scuffed at a smudge on the floor with the toe of his shoe. "You might want to know, we got your lab work back. Traces of Rohypnol. So you were right about being drugged."

I nodded.

Randall looked from Frank's face to mine. "That's good, right? It means he's telling the truth about being set up."

"Not necessarily. The D.A. is already working on the theory that he took the drug himself. It's not that unusual. You can get a hell of a high from roofies and alcohol—if it doesn't kill you. And it would make sense, if he was trying to make it look like he was being framed."

"What about the glasses?" I knew this was important. I just wasn't certain why.

"Residue in both. And traces of the same drug found in the victim's body. None of which is any help to you."

"What about my motel room? If my glass with the drug residue was found at the murder scene, what did I put the roofies in when I took them back at my motel?"

He shrugged. "Dropped it down the garbage chute, carried it out with you when you left. Or maybe you took 'em before you left."

"How'd I drive back to the motel, if I'd already downed the drug?"

"I dunno. Guys drive high all the time, but it was a hell of a chance to take. The good news is, the Rohypnol doesn't hurt your case. The bad news is, it doesn't help either."

Which was what I'd known all along, but it still hurt like hell to hear him say it.

AN HOUR AFTER THE HEARING, I was at Ms. Birdie's kitchen table eating grapefruit salad and nibbling on Italian wedding cookies. "You said Hartwell was late the night Amy was killed," I said. "What time did he get home?"

"It was after two." She pressed her lips together to show her disapproval. "The girls were sleeping in the spare room, and instead of waiting until morning to wake us all up, he came a-pounding at the door about two-thirty. Said Amy wasn't back, and wanted to know where she'd gone. I said I didn't know where she was and furthermore, if I did know, I wouldn't tell him. He barged in and took the girls, and after a cup of tea, I went back up to bed and went to sleep."

"How did he seem? Rumpled? Disheveled? Any blood?"

"Flustered. Angry. His tie was loose. But I don't think I'd call him rumpled. I didn't see any blood, but he was wearing a dark suit, so I mightn't have seen it anyway. I do remember that his cuffs were white, and I didn't see any bloodstains on them."

So Hartwell didn't have an alibi for the night of Amy's murder. Or maybe—I thought of G. Mathis—he did. The million-dollar question was, even if she did give him an alibi, how reliable would it be?

I finished my lemonade and gave Ms. Birdie a kiss on one withered cheek. The skin was dry and soft and smelled of violets.

"I'll be seeing you, Ms. Birdie," I said.

She reached for my plate and stacked it on top of her own, crossing our forks on top like swords. "I'll have the lemonade ready."

# 16

**"W**E'RE NOT ALLOWED to talk to strangers." Tara Hartwell jutted out her jaw and poked a chubby finger in my direction.

"Hush," Katrina said. "He's just a reporter."

I rested my arms on the Hartwell's backyard fence and shrugged. "How about I stay way over here, and you stay way over there. That way, you'll know I don't have anything nefarious in mind."

A little line formed between Tara's eyebrows. "What's nefarious?"

Katrina said, "It means 'bad.'"

I nodded. "Bad. Wicked. Nefarious means evil."

There was a swing set in the yard, and Tara scooted onto one of the narrow plastic seats and scuffed at the dirt with the toe of her shoe. She was a sturdy little girl in pink shorts and a Snoopy T-shirt, buttered-toast hair bleaching to honey, tanned skin with *Peanuts* Band-Aids at the elbows and knees.

Katrina wrapped a slender arm around the swing set's support pole and rested a pale cheek against the metal. "What do you want?"

"It's been a rough couple of weeks for you," I said.

Tara nodded. "My mama's gone to Hell."

"Shut up," Katrina said. "She hasn't."

"Has."

Katrina looked at me and rolled her eyes. "She's got this idea in her head."

Tara pouted. "Reverend Avery said so."

"Reverend Avery doesn't know everything." Katrina gestured in my direction. "What do *you* think?"

I pretended to consider it. "I don't think she's in Hell."

112

"I don't either. *Are* you a reporter?"

"Detective."

She tilted her head to one side and raised one eyebrow. "Oh."

"I know it's hard. But do you think you could go over it again? What happened that night?"

"Huh." Tara gave a little grunt. "Mommy went out with Aunt Valerie. Then she went out with her boyfriend. Then she got killed-ed. Then she went to Hell."

"Killed," Katrina corrected. "You're so naïve. She didn't go out with Aunt Valerie. She just said that so we wouldn't know she was going to meet her boyfriend."

From the house, Calvin Hartwell called the girls.

Tara pushed herself out of the swing and ran toward the house, but Katrina sidled closer to the fence. "Do you believe in Hell?" she asked.

"Only for bad people," I said. "Really bad."

She sucked at her lower lip. "Like adulterers?"

"Like murderers," I said. "Rapists. Child molesters."

"That's what I think too," she said, and was gone.

On Saturday, I finally reached Asa Majors, who gave me directions to his farmhouse in Smyrna. I put on my Ian Callahan disguise and drove out to a modest farm a few miles southeast of town. The barn was weathered, with traces of peeling red paint, but it looked sturdy. In back were a round pen and a small arena. I saw half a dozen horses, one of them a foal, grazing in the side pasture.

A black man with graying hair and a wiry mustache sauntered out of the barn, wiping his hands on a grimy bandana. "Mornin'," he said. "You must be Callahan." He stuffed the bandana into his back pocket and stretched out a hand.

I shook it, stepping in close enough to smell alcohol on his breath, if there was any. There wasn't.

He said, "You say you're looking at a horse I trained?"

"Two-year-old bay Arabian. Owner calls him Dakota."

His eyes narrowed. Hardened. "He's a good horse. Or was,

before he lost his eye. Best I ever worked, maybe. But I haven't seen him in awhile."

"Owner says you almost blinded him with your belt buckle."

He stared out across my shoulder, and a muscle in his jaw twitched. "She said that, did she?"

"I saw the scars."

He lifted a shoulder. "She told me it was an accident with barbed wire. I couldn't say otherwise." He glanced away. Guilty conscience? "Look, she was my employer. We had differences. That's all."

"I'm not going to pass on anything you say," I told him. "But I don't want to take on a horse that's been abused."

His tongue made a meandering bulge in his cheek as he considered. "She has a temper on her, that girl. You mind if I clean stalls while we talk?"

"No. Go ahead."

I followed him inside. There was a pitchfork propped beside the door of the first stall and a wheelbarrow in the center aisle, empty except for a few wisps of hay and a crust of gritty brown residue. He nudged the wheelbarrow closer and picked up the pitchfork. Scooped up a forkful of soiled bedding and pitched it into the wheelbarrow tray.

I stuffed my hands into my pockets and drew in a deep breath. The building smelled of sawdust, hay, old wood, and horse. Call me crazy, but I liked it.

"Tell me about her temper," I said.

"It didn't happen very often," he said. "Those fits. Mostly when something else was bothering her. Not quite a year ago, she had a really bad one. That's when the colt got hurt, and that's when I finally quit."

"You quit?"

He paused with the pitchfork in mid-swing. "She tell you otherwise?"

"She said she asked you to leave."

His laugh was just short of bitter. "Shoulda known."

"You ever meet her husband?"

"Ex. I knew him. Fact is, he's the one hired me. Had a problem with the substances."

"What kind of substances?"

"Most all of 'em. His family thought she encouraged it. Thought that was what killed him."

"Did she?"

"Neither one of 'em was what you'd call temperate. But seemed like she could handle it better. All I know is, they divorced, and he lost his job, and after awhile he ended up in some kind of shelter. Killed hisself, I heard."

"She got a good chunk of his money when they split."

"She had a lot of ammunition. Photos, witnesses, letters from some other woman."

So. He'd cheated on her. That explained the bitterness.

"Ever meet the sister?"

"Once or twice." He jabbed the pitchfork into the straw. "You know, you ain't talking like a man who's after a horse."

Busted. I'd been too eager. Now I had two choices—bluster through, or come clean. I gave him a sheepish grin. "Guilty as charged. Actually, I'm a private investigator looking into Amy Hartwell's death."

"Guy who's supposed to've killed her was a P.I. You working for him?"

"Yes."

In his eyes, I saw, not hostility, but wariness. "What if he did it?" he asked.

"He didn't."

"They say they've got a airtight case."

"I've found a couple of holes in it."

He scooped up another pitchfork full of horse droppings. "Man who kills a woman like that. He don't deserve to be got off."

"You're right." I bent to move the wheelbarrow closer to the stall. "Couldn't agree more. One more thing."

"Shoot."

"I saw a lot of empty stalls at ValeSong."

"She's lost a lot of business over the years."

"The mood swings?"

"That, and she has some problems with women. Mostly on account of men."

Remembering her aggressive sexuality, I nodded. "Women find her threatening."

He stopped and leaned his elbows on the pitchfork. "She has a way with the gentlemen, Mr. Callahan, but whether anything comes of it, I couldn't say."

"But she's lost business because of it."

"I'd say so. But if you're thinking maybe she killed her sister to get some kind of inheritance, you're way off base."

"What makes you say that?"

"'Cause she don't get nothin' if her sister dies. Calvin gets it all. Calvin and them little girls."

Two witnesses. Two conflicting stories. I liked Asa, but he might have shown a darker side if I'd met him after a few shots of vodka. He'd denied blinding Dakota, but that meant nothing. If he had done it, he would certainly have lied about it. He'd changed the subject when I'd asked him about Amy. A guilty conscience, or justified caution? There were still some folks who might be glad to blame a black man with a history of violence for the murder of a white woman.

He might even be guilty, but as far as I could tell, he had no reason to frame me for the murder, so I guessed that left me still at square one.

I pulled over and punched Frank's number on the speed dial. Home was one, Maria and Paulie two, Randall three, and Frank four.

"I got good news and bad news," Frank said. "You want the good news first?"

"Bad news first. Save dessert for last."

"Okay. Bad news is, the semen in the victim and on the photographs is yours."

I'd known it, but that didn't stop a knot from forming in

116

my gut when he said so. "The good news had better be damn good."

"The semen in the victim had traces of spermicide."

"People use birth control, Frank. That's not unusual."

"Yeah, but the semen on the photographs . . . They found traces of spermicide in that, too."

It wasn't exoneration, but it was a crack in Heather's flawless plan. There was no reason for a man to use a spermicide while masturbating over pornography. Which meant that the semen on the photographs and the semen on the victim had come from the same source—the condom Heather had taken from the hotel room.

I took a deep breath and asked, "Is it enough?"

On the other end, I heard his chair creak as he shifted his weight. "Not for the D.A., probably. But it's a start."

ON MY VOICE MAIL was a terse message from Reverend Avery saying he wanted no part of Ian Callahan's true crime book, so I drove home and spent an hour dying my hair red and applying a matching beard and mustache. In winter, it wouldn't be too bad, but I dreaded wearing it out in the July heat.

Every trade has its downside.

When I'd finished, I pulled on a pair of faded jeans and a short-sleeved madras shirt worn outside the belt to hide the Colt. A pair of scuffed work boots completed the ensemble.

"You look like a lumberjack," Jay said, when I strolled into the kitchen. His hair was rumpled, and he was wearing pajama bottoms and a blue velour bathrobe, belted at the waist. The robe gaped open at the top to reveal a flash of pale white chest with a livid purple lesion under one nipple.

Noticing my glance, he flushed and clutched the gap closed with one hand. "Very rugged."

"That wasn't exactly what I was going for."

"Oh? What were you going for?"

I shrugged and went to the refrigerator for a beer. "Just

something different."

"Well, honey, I think you succeeded. If you went to the Pearly Gates in that get-up, I don't think God himself would recognize you."

"You did."

He laughed. "Well, I knew it was either you, or you'd spent the night with a delicious-looking lumberjack, the odds of which were something less than minuscule. So what's the occasion?"

"I just moved to town with my wife and two kids. We're looking for a church to go to, and I saw the Reverend Avery on TV the other night, so I thought I'd drop in at the parsonage and see if he was what we're looking for."

"What do you do for a living?"

"Computer programmer."

"No." He shook his head. "You don't know enough about computers."

"I've heard you talk about them often enough."

"Yes, but if you say you're in the computer business, he'll tell you that his system's down, or that he can't access some file or other, or that he keeps getting error messages, and he'll want you to fix the problem while you're there. It's kind of like being a doctor. Suddenly everybody has a sore throat." He took a bite of cereal and closed his eyes, as if in ecstasy.

"What is that? Captain Crunch?"

"Mmhm." He opened his eyes. "I know it's not good for me, but sometimes I just get a craving for the stuff."

"Sounds good." I thought about pouring myself a bowlful, decided Cap'n Crunch would probably be incompatible with beer. "So, no computers. What's your suggestion?"

"Why not tell him you're a cop? Between jobs, so you don't have to deal with that 'impersonating a policeman' problem. Your wife is in computers, and you followed her here when she got a job offer she couldn't refuse." He grinned, little gobs of yellow cereal stuck between his teeth. "And tell him that your kids are still small. Toddlers, maybe."

I nodded. "It's good."

"You haven't started work yet. You're still in the application process. Which is why you can show up at the parsonage in the middle of the day, dressed like a lumberjack."

"You think I should change?"

"No. It's kind of sexy, actually." He dabbed at his mouth with a napkin and pushed himself away from the table. "So, of course, you're going to waste it on a heterosexual man of the cloth."

# 17

REVEREND SAMUEL AVERY lived in a red brick, new-money McMansion a few hundred yards from an old-money golf course. I'd called Avery on the way over, introduced myself as Herman Abernathy, and given him the cover story Jay had come up with. Avery seemed pleased with my interest in his church and told me to come on by.

A balding man with thick, wire-framed glasses, he met me at the door wearing tan slacks and a short-sleeved white dress shirt with large wet circles under the armpits. The top button of his collar was buttoned, and a fold of fat bulged over the cloth like a roll of Jimmy Dean sausage with a split in the package. His neck and face were red, as if the circulation had been cut off at the neck. It made him look like a petulant Pillsbury doughboy with a sunburn.

With a fake beard and mustache, could he be said to match my description?

Maybe to a blind man.

"Reverend Avery," I said.

He grasped my hand in a sweaty paw and gave it a half-hearted pump. "Mr. Abernathy?" he said. The smooth, soft voice still made my gut recoil. I could almost place it.

I ducked my head in an awkward nod and answered, "That's right. I called earlier."

He stepped aside to let me enter. "Come in, Mr. Abernathy. My wife left us a pitcher of iced tea. Can I pour you a glass?"

"Thank you," I said. "Much obliged."

The tea was strong and very sweet. I sat at his kitchen table, sipped my drink, and glanced around the room. Sparkling marble counters, Italian-style mosaic tiles, white lace tablecloth crisp and pressed and freshly laundered. The curtains were some kind of embroidered silk fabric that had probably cost enough to feed a small village.

He glanced at his watch. It looked like a Rolex, and not a knock-off, either. "I don't mean to rush you, but I have an appointment in about an hour. What can I do for you?"

"I saw you on TV the other night," I said. "That was real sad, that lady getting killed."

His head bobbed, jiggling the skin beneath his chin. "Indeed it was. Very sad. It's always sad when a young life is snuffed out, but even more so when that life has fallen from grace."

"You said something like that at the service," I said, as if I'd just remembered. "You think she'd turned her back on God."

"I'm afraid she did. The manner of her death attests to that." He cleared his throat and took a sip of tea. "Mind you, I'm not saying she deserved to die in such an . . . unsavory manner. No, that is not for me to decide. But she certainly reaped what she'd sown. Tell me, Mr. Abernathy, what made you decide to follow your wife across the country?"

I shrugged. "It was a good job. It meant a lot to her. Me, I can work anywhere."

"I don't mean to be critical, but if you mean to join my congregation, you should know I disapprove of a man relinquishing his place as head of the home. Especially when there are children to consider. Your wife has usurped your place at the head of the family, and if you're to live your life as the Good Lord meant it to be lived, you must reclaim it. As Christ is the head of his church, so must a man be the head of his household. Tell me, who cares for your children?"

"We take them to day care," I said, giving the answer I thought would bother him most.

"Day care." His velvet voice resonated with the rhythms of a Southern fire-and-brimstone preacher. It was a strange dichotomy. It reminded me of—

121

Before I could remember, he went on. "Son, I'm glad you came to me today, because your family is in peril. Your children are growing up without their mother, without a strong moral foundation."

"I don't think that's—"

"There are children killing children every day in this country. Why? Because they aren't being taught values at home. Their mamas are out working, and there's no one there to guide them to the Lord."

"Reverend, she loves her job."

"More than she loves the Lord?" His green eyes glinted behind his glasses. "More than she loves you? We live in a sinful world, Mr. Abernathy. Don't let her draw you into it. Take your lesson from Adam and bring your wife under control."

"What do you suggest? A hickory switch?"

His splayed hands slapped the table. "You say it with derision, sir, but I say, you must do what you must do to regain your place as head of your household. I do not condone battery, Mr. Abernathy, but neither am I opposed to corporal punishment. If your wife behaves like a spoiled child, you must treat her like one."

"Is that what happened to that lady who died?" I asked. "Her husband use a little corporal punishment?"

His mouth tightened. "Calvin Hartwell had nothing to do with his wife's death. If anything, she died because he failed to do what was required."

"Meaning?"

"A woman who is properly submissive to the Lord and to her husband will not stray. Amy Hartwell strayed. Calvin lacked the strength, or perhaps the courage, to put an end to it."

Maybe, I thought. And maybe he just found a way to stop it permanently. Capital, not corporal punishment.

I said, "What if it's the husband who strays?"

The reverend gave me an oily smile. "A man who strays

does so for one of two reasons: his wife has failed to meet his needs, or a wanton harlot has ensnared him. Remember, it was Eve who tempted Adam in the garden, and it is woman who continues to tempt man today."

I turned this over in my mind, and Herman Abernathy, my lumberjack persona, gave his head a slow nod. "So if I cheat on my wife, it's her fault?"

Avery leaned back in his chair with a smug smile and laced his hands across his stomach. "Oh, not entirely, of course. You do bear some responsibility. But the fault lies largely with her, and with her failure to support your marriage as she should."

I could see why Calvin Hartwell found the Church of the Reclamation appealing. Christian man seeks validation for un-Christian behavior. Film at eleven.

"Do you have to discipline your wife?"

His smile made crescents of his eyes and round mounds of his cheeks. It was a familiar-looking smile.

"My wife, sir," he was saying, "is a model of Christian womanhood. A good wife is more valuable than gold. I have never needed to discipline Margaret."

Lucky Margaret.

"I'm not sure I want to be married to a Stepford Wife," I said.

"Son." His voice was kindly, dripping with false concern, and suddenly I knew where I'd heard it, or one much like it. It reminded me of a voice I'd last heard in a courtroom thirteen years ago. The only problem was, it belonged to a dead man.

He was getting into the sermon now, his blue eyes shining and his ruddy face flushing ruddier. "You've fallen victim to a modern misconception—that a woman must be like a man to be fulfilled. But nothing could be farther from the truth. Believe me, Margaret is neither enslaved nor oppressed. She submits to me as the church submits to Christ, and I cherish her as Christ cherishes the church. There is no better recipe for marriage."

I couldn't say much, considering the fate of my own marriage, but somehow I didn't think the reverend's philosophy would have made our relationship better. If anything, it would have ended sooner and a hell of a lot more acrimoniously.

"I'll have to think it over," I said. That, and why he reminded me so much of a man who was supposed to have been killed ten months ago. "Do you think I could have a copy of the church directory? I'd like to talk to some of the members of your congregation."

"Of course you can, son. As soon as you're a member of the church. Meanwhile, come join us for services. Sunday School at ten, sermon at eleven, Sunday and Wednesday nights at seven."

I could tell from his forced jocularity that he wasn't going to give up the directory. I couldn't really blame him. Even if I were nothing more sinister than an insurance salesman, his congregation would hardly appreciate his giving out their names and addresses to strangers.

I said, "I hear you have a Sunday morning radio show."

"That's right. It airs on WPRZ at ten and two."

"You record it in the church?"

He nodded. "We record both shows on Saturday, and then the man who does it takes it back to his recording studio and edits it."

"Really. Which studio does he use?"

"Why do you want to know?"

"I play a little music myself. I was thinking maybe I might make a demo tape, see if anybody might want to buy some of my stuff."

"I don't remember the name," he said. "It's in one of our pamphlets." He rinsed out my glass and set it in the sink, gave me a stack of brochures, and ushered me politely out the front door, saying he had an afternoon appointment to anoint a man with cancer.

"I'm sorry about the lady who died," I said, just as the door was closing.

The Reverend paused. "That woman cheated on her husband and left two young girls at home to fend for themselves. I don't condone murder, but if Amy repented before she died, then the man who killed her did the work of God."

THE DEAD MAN WITH THE velvet voice was a pedophile named Walter Christy. I'd first seen him in front of the child care center he and his wife owned back when I was a patrol cop, driving from one end of my sector to the other, taking calls when they came in and looking for trouble the rest of the time. I don't know what it was that made me notice him. He was a plain-looking, stocky man already beginning to bald. One hand clutched a Raggedy Ann. The other held the hand of a little girl in a yellow dress.

As they disappeared around the corner of the childcare center, something in his body language set off an alarm. The stroke of a hand on the little girl's hair. A moment of unguarded eagerness on his face. I honestly don't recall.

What I do recall is parking the car and radioing for assistance, following him around to a shed at the back of building, and finding him with the girl's dress up above her waist and his hands stuffed down her white cotton panties.

I remember that my voice was calm as I sent the child back to the house and told Walter he was under arrest.

And the next thing I remember is Barry Sheldon, who had taken the backup call, hauling me off Walter Christy's sobbing, shuddering body. My hands were bruised, and I was covered with blood, and most of it was Walter's.

He almost walked.

His lawyer screamed police brutality, and the D.A. screamed resisting arrest. The D.A. screamed louder. Or maybe it was just that no one wanted Walter back out on the street.

There was plenty of evidence. Walter had been molesting little girls for fourteen years, and he had hundreds of photographs of his victims. The stream of young witnesses took days. His wife and younger daughter were among them, and after the trial, Walter found himself with divorce papers in his hand and a sixteen-year prison sentence. His wife gave up her childcare license, and a few years later, I heard she had packed up both girls and moved away.

Remarried. Put the past behind her.

And that was the last I'd heard of Walter Christy, until ten months ago, when, after an elaborate escape attempt, he'd gone screaming off in a prison trustee's SUV and crashed into a gasoline truck.

The explosion was spectacular.

I was sorry for the driver of the truck, not sorry at all that the world was rid of Walter.

I knew my distaste for the honorable Reverend Avery was probably related to his resemblance to Walter. Maybe I was biased, but I pulled over and made a quick call to Frank anyway.

"Walter Christy," I said.

"What about him?"

"How sure are you he's dead?"

"Nobody could have survived that crash."

"Could he have switched places with someone else before the wreck?"

"No time."

"'Cause this guy, Avery, he reminds me an awful lot of Walter."

"Jared." Frank's voice had that patient tone a person might use with a retarded child. "I'm telling you, Christy's dead."

Frustrated, I thanked him and said goodbye.

All right, so Samuel Avery wasn't Walter Christy.

Still, I could imagine his broad, plump hands around Amy's neck, his fleshy lips twisted with anger and flecked with spittle as his thumbs duck deep into her windpipe. "Repent, harlot," he might have said. "The wages of sin is death."

And I could easily imagine him luring Katrina Hartwell

126

into his office and enticing her to pose for the photos Frank had found in my truck.

Driving back down I-40 to my office, tugging at the beard and mustache to relieve the itching, I wondered if the reverend had an alibi for the night of Amy's murder.

# 18

On SUNDAY, AFTER I'D TURNED OUT Crockett and taken Tex for his morning walk, I called Ben Carrington. Since I'd already used the Ian Callahan persona with Felicity at the travel agency, I gave Ben the same story, that I was researching a book on Amy's murder and that his name had been mentioned by several witnesses.

There was silence on the other end of the line. Then he sighed. "You've heard the rumors about me and Amy."

"From several sources."

"It wasn't what you think."

"Why don't you meet me this afternoon and tell me what it was?"

"Did you see the memorial service on Channel 3?"

"I saw it."

"It was a lousy excuse for a memorial. It didn't do justice to Amy."

I squeezed my eyes shut and said, "That's what I want, Mr. Carrington. Justice for Amy."

*And for me.*

There was another silence. Then he said, "All right. Why don't you come to my place? Six o'clock. After dinner."

While I waited for six o'clock, I perused the pamphlets Reverend Avery had given me.

According to the literature, the Church of the Reclamation had been founded seven years ago in Louisiana. The founder, Samuel Zebedee Avery, was a Tennessee transplant convicted by God to combat the decadence and debauchery of Bourbon Street. During his ministry, God had led him to a new understanding of original sin and how Eve's legacy still ensnared even godly men. In time, he'd been led to establish other churches. He left his original ministry in the hands of his most trusted deacon and returned to his home state to pass on the word.

There was no web site listed, but I pulled out my laptop anyway, plugged it into the network, and typed "'Samuel Avery' AND 'Church of the Reclamation'" into the search engine.

A hundred-and-fifty-two hits. They'd come late to the information age, because the oldest one was dated seven months ago. I read every one. Then I logged into a couple of data providers I subscribed to and began the tedious process of collecting background and financial information on Avery and his church.

One thing was certain. There were big bucks in the redemption business. Cheating on your wife? It's okay, it's not your fault. But just to be safe, send a check to Reclamation Ministries and your conscience can be clear.

Reverend Avery's message appealed to a narrow audience, but collectively, they had deep pockets.

I ran a quick check on Avery's wife, found a homely woman with a generous inheritance. Avery had covered all the angles.

Scowling, I exited the program. If the bio on the web was right, Walter had been in prison while Avery was building his church. *If* it was right and not some manufactured biography. Either way, it ticked me off. People like Avery weren't real Christians, but they gave Christians a bad name.

After dinner, I showered and transformed myself into Ian. Dark hair, mustache, tailored suit, Colt tucked into the shoulder holster beneath the jacket.

At six o'clock sharp, I pulled into Carrington's driveway. There was a sandbox out front, and a dark-haired girl of about six was sitting on one of the seats, making designs in the sand with her bare toes. When she saw me, she pushed herself up and padded over to me, brushing her long bangs away from her forehead with grubby hands. The gesture left streaks of grime on her face.

"Are you the man who's writing the book?" she asked.

"That's me." I held out a hand, which she shook solemnly. Her palms were hot and damp. When she withdrew her hand, I surreptitiously wiped my own on the underside of my jacket. "You must be Corey."

"That's right. Daddy's inside. He said I could come in and get a Popsicle when you got here, but I can't stay and listen, because you're talking about grown-up things." She grimaced.

"I have a little boy about your age," I said. "I don't let him listen to grown-up talk, either."

"Is he six?" she asked, cocking her head to one side. "Why didn't you bring him?"

"He's eight, but he's small. And I didn't bring him because he's staying with his mom."

"I don't have a mommy," she said, matter-of-factly. "Next time, bring your little boy."

She escorted me into the house, where her father was watching from the window, assuring, I assume, that I had no evil intentions toward his daughter. Good for him.

"Mr. Callahan?" he said. "Can I get you something to drink? I have Coke, Orange Slice, and apple juice." He scooped his daughter up and planted a kiss on her cheek. They looked alike, same fair skin, same dark eyes, same unruly brown-black hair. "And who is this little rag-a-muffin? What have you done with my daughter, you little pig-pen?"

Corey giggled and squirmed in his arms. "Oh, Daddy. It's me!"

He tilted back her chin and scrutinized her features. "I suppose it's possible there's a girl in there somewhere. I'll tell you what. Why don't you go get yourself a bath and put on clean clothes, and we'll make popcorn before bed."

Her forehead puckered. "What about my Popsicle?"

"You can have a half of one before your bath. But no coming in while Mr. Callahan and I are talking. And no listening around the corners." He gave her another kiss. "Okay, sweetheart. Go on."

I waited to laugh until she"d padded up the stairs.

"I'm sorry," Carrington said. "I guess I spoil her."

"I spoil mine too," I said. "A son."

A little of the tension lifted, and he gestured toward the living room. "Have a seat. What can I get you to drink?"

"Whatever you're having."

He came back a few moments later with two Cokes over ice and sat down on the sofa. I had chosen an overstuffed chair that sat kitty-corner to the couch.

"You wanted to talk to me about Amy," he said, and suddenly the tension was back, so thick you could almost taste it between your teeth.

I nodded. "You know about the rumors that you and Amy were . . . involved."

He studied his drink. "Amy and I were friends."

"You didn't have a sexual relationship with her?"

His fingers tightened on the arm of the sofa. "We did. For about a month. Then the stress got to be too much."

"What stress was that?"

He laughed, more nerves than humor. "You've obviously never had an affair."

"Humor me."

"The girls, for one thing. If Cal found out about us and she lost custody."

"The girls." I tapped at Ian's mustache. "I understand Katrina wasn't hers. That there was tension between them."

"Amy had a hard time bonding. Not just with Katrina. With anybody."

"That have anything to do with why she ended the affair?"

He didn't meet my gaze. "Maybe. She had intimacy issues."

"And it didn't bother you? That she stopped sleeping with you?"

"I had mixed feelings. She was married, after all."

"But you kept seeing her anyway."

"She was thinking of leaving him. I could wait."

"Mr. Carrington," I said, "was Amy in love with you?"

He swirled the ice in his glass for a long time. "I believe she was," he said, finally. "She said she was. I was certainly in love with her."

"And this other man? This Jared McKean?"

"She wasn't sleeping with him."

"You're sure of that."

"If she were going to cheat on Calvin, it would have been with me. Does that sound arrogant?"

"Not really."

"She had her issues, Mr. Callahan, but she had a good heart. Maybe this guy told her he was in trouble and she was trying to help. Maybe she'd been trying to help him out for a long time and he killed her when she wouldn't give him more. But she wasn't having an affair with him."

"Her sister said she was."

He looked like he'd just been gut-punched. I felt like a heel for saying it, but it needed to be said.

"She was mistaken," he said at last, his voice weak.

"You don't sound so sure."

"She may have said she was *seeing* him. Like *going to see him*. Not sleeping with him. No."

"But her marriage was troubled. Do you know how long she and Calvin had been having problems?"

"From the beginning. She was pregnant when they married, and he . . ."

"He what?"

"He held it against her. Like she was the only one in the bedroom. She was seventeen. He was twenty-four. So whose fault do you think it was?"

"But he married her."

"For what it was worth. He cheated on her from the very beginning."

"She cheated too. With you."

He looked away. Blinked. "I know. But it was years later, and she ended it. I'm not saying it was okay for her but not for

132

him. And I'm not saying Calvin's a bad man. But he was bad for Amy."

"You said Amy had issues. What were they?"

He squeezed his eyelids together and took a deep breath. When he looked at me again, his eyes were wet. "Intimacy issues, like I said. Trust issues. Guilt issues. You name it. She couldn't believe I loved her, because she didn't believe she was worth loving."

"Any idea where she got that notion?"

He rattled the ice in his glass. "Where does anybody get that notion? From her family, I assume. Or maybe she got it from Cal. He wasn't exactly Mr. Warmth. In fact, when I heard Amy had been . . ." He stopped, choked on the words. "That she was . . . Gone . . . I thought he'd done it."

"And yet, you didn't think he was a bad man."

"Amy said he wasn't. She said he tried to be a good man. He just couldn't keep . . ." He gave an embarrassed laugh. "He couldn't keep his pecker in his pants."

"Ben, I have to ask you this. Where were you on the night Amy was killed?"

He took a deep breath and calmed himself. "I took Corey out for pizza, then we rented *The Lion King* and came back home. She went to bed at nine, and I stayed up and read until eleven. Why?" Every muscle in his face tensed. "You don't think I killed her?"

"McKean said he didn't do it."

"Well." He shook his head, bewildered. "Of course. What *would* he say? But they said on Channel 3 the cops have DNA, and DNA doesn't lie."

I decided not to educate him on the time it took to get back DNA results. "Don't you think Amy would have told you if she was trying to 'help' this man? The police say she'd been seeing him for months."

Ben studied his cola intently. "I would have thought so," he said quietly. "But I guess I was wrong."

I returned to something he'd said earlier. "Mr. Carrington, you said Amy had guilt issues."

"That's right." His nod was wary.

"What did she have to feel guilty about?"

He picked at a loose thread in the upholstery of the sofa. "She wouldn't go into detail."

"But she told you something."

He looked away, the little net of lines around his eyes tensing. "There were sexual issues. She wouldn't talk about it, but I wondered if maybe she hadn't been raped."

"Calvin?"

He didn't look surprised, so I figured he'd thought about it. "I don't think so. She didn't talk about him that way."

"And she never said who?"

"Like I said, she never even said that's what happened. It's just a feeling I had."

"She was in love with you, but she never talked about it."

He looked away. "Seems like lots of things she never talked about."

# 19

AT SEVEN-FORTY-FIVE Monday morning, I parked half a block from the three-story brick house where G. Mathis lived. There was a royal blue Ford Escort ZX2 in the driveway. I hoped it was hers.

At eight twenty-two, she came out of the house wearing a cranberry skirt cut modestly below the knee and a white blouse with lace at the neck. In one hand, she carried what looked like a black leather Bible, and in the other was a turquoise vinyl case that might have held her lunch. Her purse was slung over one shoulder. Very demure. Nothing like the wildcat who had greeted Hartwell at the door.

I followed her down West End, onto Twenty-First Avenue North, and to a little shop shaped like a log cabin. "Angel Food Cafe," the sign out front read. "Christian Books and Gifts. Coffee. Sandwiches. Desserts."

I drove past the shop, bought a Coke at a McDonald's on West End, then tooled back down Elliston Place and back to Twenty-First, where I parked across the street and three buildings down from the Angel Food Cafe.

I waited until ten, when most of the breakfast-and-coffee people had gone, then girded up my loins and went inside. (I have no idea what that means. Prepared myself, I think it means, maybe for a kick in the balls). There were two customers inside, a chunky woman who looked to be in her mid-fifties, and a pretty young woman about eight months pregnant. While I waited for them to finish up their Danishes and coffee, I browsed through the racks of Contemporary Christian music, inspirational literature, stick pins, jewelry, and knickknacks bearing images of every kind of angel imaginable.

135

G. Mathis glanced up from the magazine she was reading behind the counter. "May I help you?"

I looked at her nametag. Glenda, it said.

"No, thanks. Just looking."

At ten fifteen, the older woman left with an Amy Grant CD and a cranberry muffin. At ten twenty-six, the young woman paid for a tape of Christian lullabies and a baby quilt with Precious Moments angels stamped all over it. When it was just me and G. Mathis, I picked up a small gold angel pin and sauntered to the counter, as if to pay.

Her smile was cheerful, practiced. "Will that be all, sir?"

I smiled back. "Not quite. Glenda Mathis, isn't it?"

Her forehead furrowed. "How do you know my last name?"

"Glenda Mathis." I rattled off her address.

She picked up the phone, knuckles white, nails filed short and coated with clear polish. "I'm calling the police."

"Sure." I nodded pleasantly. "No problem. I bet they'd be real interested to know about your affair with Calvin Hartwell."

"Oh." Her voice was weak, her skin suddenly chalky beneath her makeup. "Oh, dear."

She laid the phone back in its cradle and slumped onto a tall, three-legged stool behind the counter. Her mouth opened, closed, opened again.

"Who are you?" she managed. "How do you . . ."

"I have an interest in finding Amy Hartwell's murderer," I said.

"The police have Amy's murderer. They took him into custody a week ago yesterday."

"He didn't do it," I said. "I know this for a fact. What's more, the police are also finding evidence to that effect."

"I don't understand. I thought . . . Cal said they had DNA. Fingerprints. He said they had an ironclad case."

I shrugged. "Unsinkable. Like the Titanic."

She nibbled at a fingernail. Squinted across the counter at

me. Then she paled as recognition crept across her face. "Oh. Sweet Jesus," she moaned. She slid off the stool and backed away until her backside bumped into the wall.

"Don't be an ass," I said. "If I meant to hurt you, I'd have come to your house."

She shook her hands, as if you could shake off fear as easily as water.

"What do you want?"

"How long have you been sleeping with Cal Hartwell?"

"I don't see what . . .," she started. Then she must have realized what a predicament she was in. She heaved a deep sigh and frowned, counting silently on her fingers. "About four months. Give or take."

"And you met, how?"

"At church." She lowered her eyes. They were brown with a reddish cast, like Coca-Cola in the sunlight. It was easy to see what Hartwell saw in her.

"You knew Amy too?"

"Not well."

"How'd the affair start?" I hoped by firing questions at her, I could keep her off guard and answering me.

"I . . . We were at a church supper. Amy was over at the buffet table talking to some other ladies, and Cal and I got to talking. He said his wife was getting so independent that pretty soon she wouldn't need him anymore. He laughed when he said it, but I could see how hurt he was. And we just . . . started talking. That was all it was at first. We'd meet for lunch, or dinner sometimes, and we'd talk."

"And then?"

"Then one day, I told him I had always wanted to build a big house in the country. I could see it in my head, but I didn't know how to make it work. And he said he was an architect, and he could make the plans for me. So he came over to my house one evening after work, and one thing led to another, and . . ." She made a rolling motion with her hand. "He was very unhappy."

"Because his wife was working."

"No. Because she was no kind of wife at all. He'd come home, and dinner wouldn't be made. She'd heat up leftovers, or make boxed macaroni and cheese, or even order out for pizza. Sometimes she'd bring home fast food. Calvin put a stop to that. He said he wanted good meals on the table for those children, and if she didn't, he was going to divorce her, and he'd see that he got custody. He could, you know. And I'd have been happy to take care of them."

I tried to keep my tone neutral. "You discussed this? His divorcing her and marrying you? You two taking the girls?"

"It was never just a cheap affair." Her chin lifted. "He loves me. And I love him. I would be a much better wife than she was. And a better mother."

"You'd quit your job here, I suppose."

"If Calvin asked me to."

"He asked Amy to."

"It wasn't the *job*," she said. "It was the way she started putting everything before him and the girls. And she was cheating on him."

"So was he," I pointed out. "Cheating."

The look she gave me would have shattered nails. "She started it," she said. Then her gaze slid away again, and she sighed. "Oh, I know it wasn't right. We should have waited. But there he was, so unhappy. And there she was, rubbing his nose in her new liberated-ness. It was a sick family, anyway."

"How so?"

"First Amy gets herself pregnant and snatches Cal from her sister. And then the sister turns around and tempts him right back to *her* bed. Sick. No wonder he wanted out. And there we were, falling in love and knowing we were perfect for each other. It was like God had given us to each other."

"Oh," I said, nodding. "God told you it was okay."

"No," she snapped. "God didn't say it was okay. He would have preferred we wait. But Amy was unfaithful, and Cal would have gotten a divorce soon, and we'd be together then, anyway. And I'm sure God would forgive us for...anticipating things."

"Soooo." I frowned, trying to absorb this. "You and Cal were having an affair, which was all right, because Cal was unhappy and because Amy was also having an affair, which wasn't all right, whether she was unhappy or not."

"I don't expect you to understand." She had almost recovered her equilibrium by then, perhaps having decided that I wasn't there to kill her. "I'm not saying what I did with Cal is all right. I'm just saying that, as sins go, it wasn't all that much of one, considering the circumstances. I really feel that God meant for us to be together."

"How convenient of Amy to get herself murdered," I said, between gritted teeth.

She turned her face away. "That isn't what I meant."

"Tell me, do you know where Cal was the night Amy died? Because some of his neighbors say he didn't come home until after two."

"That old busybody down the street," she said. "Cal told me about her. The answer is, of course I know where he was. He was with me."

What a surprise. The question was, was she telling the truth? And if she was, were she and Calvin busy making the beast with two backs? Or busy murdering Cal's wife and setting me up for it?

Again, I came to that sticky question. Why me? Their motive for Amy was clear, but neither of them had a reason to destroy my life. I'd never heard of either of them before Amy's murder. Maybe they just figured a disgraced cop would be easy to frame.

And where did Heather come into the equation? Another of Cal's lovers, maybe? Would Glenda be so anxious to give Cal an alibi if she knew there was a Heather?

"I take it you're not married," I said, though at that point nothing would have surprised me.

"Divorced," she said. "It was a long time ago. He was an

alcoholic. Not a Christian man at all."

"Not like Cal."

She gave me a hard look. "No. Not like Cal."

"Children?"

"No. But Cal and I were going to, as soon as we were married."

"Do you know if he had insurance on Amy's life?"

"I've no idea. And I think I've answered enough of your questions. Are you going to buy that?" She gestured toward the angel pin.

"Sure." I tossed it onto the counter and reached for my wallet. "Never know when you might need a little divine intervention."

"It isn't a rabbit's foot," she said, striking the cash register keys with more force than necessary. "It's just to remind you to live a Christian life. Like the WWJD bracelets. 'What would Jesus do?'"

"Oh." I slipped my receipt into my pocket and slid the pin back toward her. "In that case, maybe you should keep it. Here's another couple dollars. Buy one for your boyfriend too."

I left before she could throw me out.

As I passed her Ford Escort, I glanced inside to see the color of the carpet.

It was gray.

*

# 20

AMY AND CALVIN. VALERIE and Calvin. Younger sister tempts older sister's boyfriend, older sister seduces younger sister's husband.

Valerie had said Dakota colicked on the night of Amy's murder. But what if he hadn't? Valerie was a beautiful woman, but she was also tall and lean, with strong features and an interest in acting. With facial hair and bound breasts—and a distracted witness—she might pass for a man. She was smaller that I was, but with a bulky jacket and lifts in her boots . . .

I laughed aloud at the thought. Not in a million years. Even considering the possibility meant I was more desperate than I wanted to admit. Of course, she could have waited in the car while her boyfriend rented the hotel room. I didn't like having these thoughts, but I couldn't afford not to have them.

I called her from a pay phone at the strip mall down the street, in case she had caller I.D., and in a gravelly voice, said I had a rescued Arabian mare with show and breeding potential who had to be re-homed immediately because my other horses were bullying her. I said I'd gotten ValeSong's number from the folks at Dark Horse Saddlery, and that I'd give the horse away if someone would come and get her. Then, feeling like a heel, I gave her an address that would take her thirty minutes to get to.

The eagerness in her voice told me she'd taken the bait, and forty minutes later, the red Chevy passed, a white two-horse trailer wobbling behind it.

There were no other cars in ValeSong's driveway. Presumably, if there were boarders, they were at work, which was just as well for me.

I stopped to give Dakota a pat before ducking into the

office. Maybe I'd see nothing on the colic tapes but the colt pacing in his stall, but if she'd gone in to check on him . . .

I pushed the first tape into the machine. The time and date flashed in the lower right-hand corner of the screen. 4:00 PM June 23$^{rd}$. Too early. I fast-forwarded through half a dozen videos before I found the ones that accounted for the time between ten PM and seven in the morning.

The picture was grainy, but I could see well enough. Dakota stood in his stall, pawing at the ground. He curled his upper lip, butted at his flanks with his nose. A few minutes later, he kicked at his belly. Rolled. Stood up, paced and pawed some more, rolled again. Clearly, he was suffering.

Valerie had gone into his stall once every half hour to rub his belly and tempt him with a few wisps of hay. No time to drive thirty miles, murder her sister, and stage the scene.

Relieved, I rewound the tapes and put them back where I'd found them.

I called Frank from the car and told him about Glenda Mathis and the gray carpet. Thought about telling him about Valerie and Calvin and decided to keep that to myself for the moment. Then, to make up for missing the RC and Moon Pie festival with Paulie, I went by Maria's to pick him up and keep him until his birthday party on Wednesday. Maria had invited Jay and me, along with Randall and his crew. Oh boy. The first family picnic with D.W. I could hardly wait.


MY SON, PAUL ANTHONY MCKEAN missed being a July Fourth baby by a mere six minutes. I was twenty-eight, and Maria thirty-two.

She'd refused the amniocentesis, which her doctor recommended to all pregnant woman over thirty, because of the potential for miscarriage. It wasn't a huge risk, but any risk was more than she was willing to take.

"I want this baby so much," she told me. "I never knew I could want anything so much."

"Gee, thanks," I said dryly, and she poked me in the bicep and said, "You know what I mean."

Enlightened guy that I am, I accompanied my wife into the delivery room. Piece of cake, I thought. As a cop, I'd seen autopsies and cadavers. I'd seen gunshot wounds and knife wounds and victims of bludgeoning. I'd seen more blood and pain than I knew what to do with, and I felt worldly and jaded and extremely prepared.

I wasn't.

There's nothing more painful than watching someone you love more than life suffer, knowing there is nothing you can do for her except say, "You're doing great, honey. Breathe."

Then it was over, and I saw a glimpse of my son, limp and blue, slick with Maria's blood and coated with a waxy substance that resembled nothing else so much as cream cheese.

The doctor and his entourage of nurses surged around the baby with an urgency I knew meant trouble.

"Is he dead?" I asked, the fear in my gut like a cannonball. "Is he . . .?"

Maria clutched at my hand as if she meant to crush it. Tears streaked her face, and I could see her lips were pressed together, holding in the panic.

I heard phrases like, "Apgar three," and ". . . parents out of here," and ". . . poor little thing."

Dr. Beach pushed out of the clump of nurses, who were doing something to our baby I couldn't see and didn't understand. The look on his face was one I'd seen too many times, on Frank's face, on Harry's. I was sure other people had seen it on my own and dreaded what it meant. It was the face we wore when we were bearing news that shouldn't have to be borne.

"No," said Dr. Beach. "He isn't dead. But it might be better if he were."

"DADDY, I GOT BIRFDAY COMIN'," Paul said.

"I know. Wednesday. How old will you be?"

"Seven." His forehead puckered in concentration as he worked to hold up the correct number of fingers. "I seven."

"No, sport," I corrected. "You're seven now. Wednesday, you'll be eight."

"Be eight?" He sounded puzzled.

"That's right. On Wednesday, you'll be eight years old."

"Eight," he repeated. Then, "What happen to seven?"

I shook my head and laughed. "Sometimes I wonder the same thing." What happened to seven and seventeen and twenty-seven? How did I become one of the men I used to call "sir"?

We stopped at Blockbuster and rented a video.

I parked in the shade and left the motor running and the air conditioner on so that Queenie, the twelve-year-old Akita I'd had since she was six weeks old, wouldn't overheat. I got her, like Paulie, every other weekend, plus two weeks in the summer and certain holidays. I'd taken her with me when Maria and I separated, but Paulie cried for her until I had to take her back.

"Want *Annie*," Paul said.

He'd seen *Annie* about a hundred times. So many times, in fact, that he knew almost all the songs and most of the lines. Worse, so did I. "You have *Annie* at home, sport. How about *Homeward Bound*? Or *Hercules*?"

"*Annie*," he said. "Or *Snow White*. Hi ho, hi ho."

I sighed. "Okay. You win. Pick the one you want."

We went home with both.

When he saw the *Snow White* box, Jay tried without success to hide an amused smirk. "Hi ho, hi ho," he said to Paul, and received a pudgy high five in return.

While I took care of the horses, Paul helped Jay make veggie cheeseburgers and oven-baked potato wedges. Paul will eat almost anything, unless it's sticky. His teachers call him "tactilely defensive," which is a fancy way of saying he doesn't like to get his hands dirty. He hates clay and fingerpaint. When he paints, he uses a brush and makes short, precise strokes, careful not to get any on himself.

After dinner, we watched the movies for the hundred-and-first time. He took his bath (mostly by himself), I helped him into his Batman pajamas, and after pushing aside a small army of Beanie Babies, tucked him into bed.

Queenie put her paws up on the bed and whimpered, so I boosted her up too. Before her arthritis, she could jump over a car, one of the few impressive tricks I ever taught her.

With Paulie in bed, I went downstairs and called Frank.

"Randall?" he asked, when I said hello.

"No, it's Jared. Why would Randall be calling you?"

"He called earlier to see how the case was going. I thought he was you."

"We don't sound that much alike."

"Whatever you say."

I filled him in on what I'd learned, which wasn't much, and pumped him for information.

"We found pollen in her clothes," he said. "And a couple blades of grass. The lab guys think it's possible she was killed or drugged someplace else and brought to the motel."

"That helps my case, right?"

"Maybe."

"Why would I stage a crime scene specifically to incriminate myself?"

"That's a good question. I can't imagine why. If you're lucky, maybe the Grand Jury will think the same thing. Only, it's not a given that's what happened. They said it was possible. It's just as possible that she went for a walk before she met her killer—I'm assuming it wasn't you—and picked up the pollen and the blades of grass then."

"So we're still nowhere."

"Every piece of the puzzle helps make the picture."

Frank's favorite platitude. It was a good way to work, adding a piece of the puzzle here, another piece there. Only this time, I had little patience with it. I wanted a bolt from Heaven to illuminate the real killer—or killers. I wanted to be

145

cleared of Amy's murder, and I wanted it now.

As my mother used to say, *People in Hell want ice water, too, but they ain't gettin' it.*

"What about the time of death?" I said.

"A little after one."

Which gave Cal Hartwell plenty of time to kill his wife and get back home by two-thirty to haul the girls out of Ms. Birdie's spare room. If he were guilty, I wondered, would it have been smarter to leave them where they were and say he'd gotten home at midnight?

"And the body? There was semen. I know that. But was she penetrated?"

Frank coughed. "There was vaginal bruising and abrasions. The forensics boys think it may have occurred postmortem."

"Necrophilia?"

"Maybe. Or the perp might have used an object of some kind. Bottle, maybe. The body was posed. Spread-eagled. So the first thing you'd see coming in the room was her crotch."

I winced at the image. That kind of posing sent a message: *This woman is a whore.*

"There was something else, too," Frank said. "Someone laid a pillow across her face."

So the killer had a moment of remorse. Or at least some sense of guilt. Usually, a killer covers his victim's face because he knows her, or at least thinks of her as human, and doesn't want her corpse to look at him. Covering the face alleviates the sense of guilt, because, with her eyes covered, she can't accuse him anymore.

I'd read somewhere that people were murdered because they got too close to evil. But evil doesn't always have horns and a tail. It's not always easy to recognize.

"Anything on Heather? Anybody hear of her?"

"Not so far."

"Figures."

"It's okay, kid. We'll get 'em."

146

I heard him shift his weight, and his breathing changed.

"What is it?" I said.

"Just . . ." He stopped, cleared his throat.

"Go on."

"You're concentrating awful hard on Amy. Ever thought this might be more about you?"

"What? Somebody killed a girl at random so I could be framed for her murder?"

"I'm just saying. Somebody knows a lot about you. Your schedule. The combination to your glove compartment . . . What were you wearing when you met this Heather?"

"I don't know. Jeans. T-shirt. Boots."

"Cowboy boots?"

I looked down at my feet. Dusty black boots that could have been riding boots or work boots or motorcycle boots. "Not so you could tell."

"Cowboy hat?"

"No."

He gave me a minute to think about it before he asked, "Then how'd she know to call you 'Cowboy'?"

# 21

**W**HEN I'D HUNG UP, I looked up to see Jay leaning against the doorframe, watching.

"How's it going?" he asked. "The investigation?"

My shoulders sagged. "I don't know. We're getting closer. I've got motive for the husband and the lover. But I think we're looking for at least two people. Heather and some guy who seems to be about my height and build. Calvin Hartwell's about the right size, but there's no reason he'd want to ruin my life. I've never met the guy. Besides, Amy would know if she was having an affair with her own husband."

"Maybe he hired someone to sleep with her. And maybe he picked you because of the scandal over Ashleigh. Couldn't he have thought you'd be believable as a suspect? Because of how you lost your job?"

"Maybe." It was no less plausible than Frank's theory that I was the intended victim and Amy was an afterthought. It made my head hurt to think about it, and I changed the subject. "Did he ever call? The blond bombshell?"

He sighed. "No. Let's face it. It was just a one-night stand. And who can blame him? How many guys want a relationship with someone who's already got the disease? It would be like volunteering for perpetual nurse duty."

"You're not that sick."

"Not yet."

"Eric is an asshole," I said. "That's all it means. It has nothing to do with you."

"Darling," he sighed, "it has everything to do with me."

"Look, Jay," I said. "Maria left me, Ashleigh screwed me over six ways come Sunday, and Heather set me up to take the fall for a murder. Some kind of loser, huh?"

He fixed his gaze on me. "Maria loves you. And the only thing you did wrong with Ashleigh and Heather was choose the wrong woman."

"Which is exactly my point." I asked the next question, even though I wasn't sure I wanted to hear it. "You didn't say what I did wrong with Maria."

I'll give Jay this: he doesn't rush the important stuff. He thought it over for a moment, then said, "You almost died."

"The guy with the arrow."

"The guy with the arrow, the guy with the knife, the guy with the broken bottle. She said it was always something. You'd come home late and she'd be worried sick that this would be the time you didn't come home at all. She said you had some pathological need to be a hero and you wouldn't stop until it killed you. She couldn't take it."

"She thinks I have a death wish."

"Not exactly."

"It's not like I'm not careful. I gave up undercover work because she thought it was too dangerous."

"And started hunting murderers. Not exactly the safest field of work."

"I don't need to be a hero," I said. When Maria first talked about leaving, I started spending less time in the field and more behind the desk, away from the messy stuff. It worked for awhile. Then Caleb Wilford cut his wife's throat and fled to his weekend hunting lodge. He took his ten-year-old daughter, Melody, with him.

I closed my eyes and remembered how it had been, Bonnie Wilford's body crumpled on the tiled hall, the puddle of blood around her already growing tacky.

*Frank steps around the puddle and, hands sheathed in latex gloves, picks up a letter from the hall table. He holds it out between us so we can both read Caleb's crabbed scrawl. A dozen rambling pages.*

*'...Bitch left me no choice, she meant to take my little girl*

*away from me. My beautiful princess is mine we will be together for all eternity, a father should be with his daughter...”*

*Frank looks up and says, “My God. He’s going to kill her.”*

“I wasn’t trying to be a hero when I went after Caleb Wilford,” I said. “I was trying to save a child.”

“I know that,” Jay said. “Maria knows that. She’s proud of you for that.”

“Then—”

“You asked me why she left you,” he said. “I’m telling you why. She couldn’t stand to watch you die.”

She’d told me the same thing. She needed someone safe, she said. D.W. was safe. It bothered me that he could give her that.

“Everybody dies,” I said.

He gave a humorless laugh. “Tell me something I don’t know.”

“WHAT DO YOU WANT to do today?” I asked Paulie after a breakfast of Rice Crispies, milk, and orange juice.

“Doddywood.” He grinned, the tip of his tongue protruding from between his teeth.

“Sorry, sport. No Dollywood this weekend. It’s too far. ”

His eyes filled. “Want Doddywood. Boofrog Creek. Bwazing Fooey. Wibber Battle.”

“Maybe in a few weeks,” I said. “We’ll go ride Bullfrog Creek and Blazing Fury then. River Battle, too.”

His lip quivered. “I be good,” he said.

Knife in the heart. “I know you are, buddy. But I can’t take you to Dollywood. It’s too far. How about we go for a ride on Crockett, then go swimming? Then we can go over to Opry Mills and play video games.”

“Pizza Hut?”

“Why not?”

I locked Queenie in the house because, with her arthritis,

she couldn't make that kind of trek anymore. Some dogs will trot after you a little ways and go back home when they get tired, but Queenie was stoic—or stubborn. She'd make it to the end of the trail, even if she had to crawl there.

Jay says she takes after me.

Since Tex was out of commission, I strapped Paulie's Li'l Buddy saddle behind mine on the Tennessee Walker. The black gelding was as gentle as a cotton ball and had a gait so smooth you could drink a glass of bourbon at a running walk and not spill a drop. We took a slow jaunt through the woods behind the house, then turned Crockett out into the pasture and went for a dip in Jay's pool while Queenie lounged in the shade of the porch.

Jay joined us for dinner at Pizza Hut, then sprang for the video games, after which we drove down to Riverfront Park to watch the fireworks. Paul's face was awed and bright as he watched the dazzling bursts, hands clamped over his ears to shut out the sound of the explosions.

"Pretty, Daddy," he squealed, as one burst into the shape of a heart. "Yook, Jay! A hawt!"

When he was born, all I could think of were the things he'd never do. He'd never ride a skateboard, never make the honor roll, never play in Little League. I'd never teach him how to drive, or share my favorite books with him, or see him married and with children of his own. He'd never go to college or follow me onto the force.

But he is not the placid doughboy Dr. Beach predicted he would be. There is no Little League, but there are Special Olympics. There will be no college, but he can read a dozen words, and he is learning more. There will be no job on the police force, but there are sheltered workshops. As my mother used to say, for everything taken, there is something given.

After years of Early Intervention, Special Education, Speech Therapy, Occupational Therapy, and all the other exercises and interventions we've gone through with him, he can dress himself (mostly), feed himself (except for the cut-

151

ting), ride a gentle horse, swim. I sometimes wish things were different, but I can't imagine now how I could love him any more.

He fell asleep on the way home, and I carried him in, his body a warm weight over my heart.

THE CALL CAME SHORTLY AFTER BREAKFAST. I recognized the voice—sultry, with a hint of annoyance—the minute she said my—my alter-ego's—name.

"Ian? It's Valerie. I was just calling to see if you're still interested in the colt. I haven't heard from you or your vet."

"Sorry about that. I've been pretty tied up. But yeah, I'm interested."

"Why don't you come on out and see him again? Bond a little? And . . . I thought I might fix you lunch."

There was a breathless silence on the other end while I weighed the advantages and disadvantages. On the positive side, I might learn more about the Hartwell's marriage and the rumors that Valerie and Calvin had been lovers. On the negative side, what if she gave me that second chance she'd mentioned?

"Don't make any rash decisions," she said, an edge to her voice. "I understand if you need to consult your calendar." She didn't sound as if she understood.

"I'd love to."

"Oh." After a moment of surprise, her tone turned warm and buttery. "All right. I'll see you about eleven-thirty."

Thirty minutes later, I came downstairs as Ian Callahan.

Jay and Paul lay on the living room carpet, crayons strewn across the floor, a Disney coloring book open between them. Jay was using the edge of his crayon to give elaborate shading to Snow White's dress, while Paul clothed three of the seven dwarfs in clashing neon. Jay was humming to himself. Paulie looked intent, the tip of his tongue protruding from the corner of his mouth.

I watched them for a few minutes before I said, "Can you watch Paul for awhile? Valerie just called."

Jay looked up. "Sure. We'll keep each other entertained."

Paulie giggled when I kissed him goodbye. He tugged at my fake mustache and mumbled, "Funny, Daddy."

"Be careful," Jay said. "And don't do anything I wouldn't do."

SHE CAME OUT TO GREET me wearing tight jeans, no shoes, and a red bikini top that tied at the neck and back. Her breasts were full and firm, the nipples hard little points beneath the cloth.

My breath caught in my throat.

"It's so hot," she said, gesturing toward her chest. "I didn't think you'd mind."

"I don't mind."

She led me into the mud room, where a wave of cool air hit me. "Shoes off," she said, pointing to my boots.

I bent to pull them off, and when I straightened up, she sidled in close, hooked two fingers into my waistband, and tugged me toward her. Her hips gave a little push that bumped my backside against the washing machine and positioned my hard-on between her legs.

Her mouth was hot and fresh with mint.

After a moment, my brain started functioning again, and I laid my palms against the side of her face and tilted her head back. "Hey," I said. "What's all this?"

Her breath was warm in my ear. "I always get what I want."

"You don't want me."

"How do you know what I want?"

"I wouldn't be good for you."

She gave a high-pitched, bitter laugh and pulled away. "Neither was my ex-husband. Neither was the guy who just broke up with me. Why should you be any different?"

"I'm sorry."

She wrapped her arms around herself, sniffled, blinked. "I know who you are," she said.

Ashleigh and her damn cameras. I blinked back and said, "What?"

"I thought it was you, and then I saw how you were with Dakota, and I thought, no, it couldn't be, he couldn't have killed anybody."

"I didn't."

She held back a sob, hiccupped instead. "Then why did the police say you did?"

"It's a long story." I gave her the short version.

She nodded and rolled her lower lip under her teeth. "Were you sleeping with her? With Amy?"

"No."

"She said you were."

"Somebody's been planning this for a long time."

"You think some guy started an affair with her and said he was you? That sounds farfetched."

"Maybe, but I can't think of a better explanation."

She thought about it for awhile, then drew in a trembling breath. "I believe you," she said. "I think."

I waited, and after a long silence, I said, "As long as we're clearing the air, you ought to know, I talked to Asa."

"Why? What did he say?"

"He said you were the one who blinded Dakota."

Her nostrils flared. "Asa's a liar. I'd never hurt Dakota."

"He says you have a temper."

She laughed, but there was anger in it. "So what if I do? I went through a bad time a few months ago. It was just after my mother died, and I wasn't very nice to him after the thing with Dakota. But I wouldn't beat a horse."

Poor kid. First her mother, then her sister. "Been a hell of a year," I said.

She nodded. "It's not like Mama hadn't been real sick. She had a couple of strokes in the last few years, and she didn't even recognize us anymore. But still, it was a shock." She rubbed her upper arms, as if to warm herself. "I'd just stepped out to the vending machine, and when I came back, she was gone. Choked on a bite of chicken."

"Jesus. I'm sorry."

She fiddled with her braid and changed the subject. "You believe me about Dakota? *I* believed *you*."

"Yeah. I believe you." Unless something proved otherwise. "What do we do now?"

"I don't know." She pulled her braid around and rubbed it absently between her fingers. "I don't like being lied to."

"It's not personal. It's an investigation."

Her smile was tight. "License to lie?"

"Something like that."

She nibbled at the tip of the braid. It was a gesture Maria might have made. "You think you can catch this son-of-a-bitch?" she said at last.

"I'm pretty sure I can."

"All right, then." She slid back into my arms and rested her head against my chest. It felt good to have her there.

This time, when she kissed me, I didn't object.

# 22

"WELL?" SHE LAY CURLED along my side, one arm across my chest, fingers toying with the hairs around my nipple. "Did I rock your world?"

I bent down and kissed her shoulder. It tasted of salt. "What do you think?"

"That you should tell me you've never been so fantastically fucked."

I kissed her again. "Consider it said."

Something dark flickered in her eyes. "What's the matter, lover? Can't shell out a compliment?"

I raised an eyebrow. "All right. My world has been completely, thoroughly, utterly rocked."

She unwound herself from me and tugged free of the sheets. "Forget it."

"Hey." I sat up and stroked her hair with the back of my hand. "It was great. *You* were great."

"Best you ever had?"

Maria was the best I'd ever had, but it wasn't fair to compare. I loved Maria.

"Yes," I said.

Mollified, she leaned back against me, and I slipped my arms around her. Her body was still tense; she hadn't quite relented yet. "Swear you never slept with Amy."

"I never slept with Amy."

"What can I do to help you catch the bastard who killed her?"

I buried my face in her hair and took a deep breath. She smelled of sex and strawberry shampoo. "Tell me about Calvin."

She stiffened.

"It's all right," I said. "Just talk to me."

She made a little strangled sound. "You won't understand."

"Try me."

"I don't want you to hate me."

"I won't. Water under the bridge."

She rubbed her cheek against my jaw and squeezed her eyes shut. The words came hesitantly at first, but as she unburdened herself, they came faster, as if a dam had broken somewhere inside her. She'd kept it to herself a long time.

She'd met Calvin during her freshman year at college. She was a theatre major, and he was fresh out of his first marriage, raising a daughter and pursuing a Masters in architecture. They met at the Laundromat, a hot babe washing lingerie and a good-looking guy in dress clothes fumbling with his daughter's rompers. He seemed shy, but there was an instant chemistry.

Then one day, she said, she realized she was in love with him. They talked about marriage. She took him home to meet her family, and five months later, he broke it to her that her seventeen-year-old sister was pregnant with his child. He assured Valerie that he loved her, but he had to do the right thing. He had to marry Amy.

"Must have been tough," I said.

"We didn't talk for years. I didn't even go to her wedding. It was so stupid. But they'd not only broken my heart, they'd hurt my pride."

She went by her sister's house one afternoon, not to talk to Amy, but to hash through unfinished business with Calvin. The discussion had been heated, but somehow they ended up making love in the Hartwells' bed.

"I know it was wrong," she said, wrapping her arms around my hands so I couldn't let her go. "But it turned out to be a good thing. Because I knew he still wanted me. And after that, I could forgive them." She gave me a weak smile. "I guess you could say we were even."

"Did Amy ever know?"

"No."

"You're sure?"

"She never said anything about it. And, believe me, she would have."

"Was that the only time?"

"Why would I want to do it again? I knew I could have him if I wanted him. But after he'd picked Amy, why would I want him?"

"Did he have other lovers?"

She slithered out of my arms and swung her legs over the bed. "I imagine he did. Calvin may or may not love the Lord, but he never could resist a willing piece of ass."

AT FIVE O'CLOCK, with the Ian mustache gone and my hair back to its natural buckskin, I drove Paul, Jay, and Queenie to the house I used to share with Maria. It still gave me a hollow feeling in the pit of my stomach, seeing D.W.'s car in the drive, knowing he was keeping my lawn mowed and my gutters cleaned. Of course, they were his lawn and his gutters now. He drove my son to school. He sat with my family in church.

The house sat on the edge of Old Hickory Lake, a single-story white stucco with Spanish archways and a fountain out front. Out back, there was a barbecue pit, a swing set, a picnic table, and a boat dock with no boat. As we unloaded Paulie, the dog, one overnight bag, my guitar, and the wrapped gifts, I heard voices from the back.

"Who talkin'?" Paulie asked, bouncing on the balls of his feet. "Dat my birfday?"

"I think that's your Uncle Randall and his brood," I said, slamming the trunk. Paul and Jay were already headed toward the backyard. Josh met them halfway.

"Josh!" Paulie threw himself into his cousin's arms. "You look scary. Rrrrr."

"Rrrrr," Josh growled back. I thought I glimpsed a hint of a smile, but it was gone before I was sure I'd seen it.

Paulie gave hugs all around, while I put my gifts on the table with the others.

"Jared. I'm glad you're all right." Maria came into my arms as if she belonged there, then pulled away awkwardly and ran a thumb over what was left of my black eye. "You are all right, aren't you?"

"Mostly," I said. "I still don't know who set me up."

"You will." Her smile settled somewhere in the bottom of my stomach. "You're a good investigator. Frank's a good investigator. Between the two of you, I know you'll solve this thing."

"I wanted to thank you and D.W. for helping out with the bail."

"Oh, that." She waved a dismissive hand. "I could hardly let the father of my son languish in some jail cell, could I?"

She was wearing denim shorts and a pink T-shirt with a picture of mountain gorillas on the front. Most of Maria's shirts have wildlife on them. So do about half of mine, mostly because she gave them to me.

Her thick, dark hair was pulled back in a high ponytail, not so much for looks as to keep it off her neck. It was too hot to do much else. Her shoes were leather sandals I'd given her three years ago, imports from Spain. They showed her small, tanned feet with the toenails painted pink to match the shirt.

I fought the urge to plunge my tongue into her mouth. The look on her face said she was having the same thought.

Or maybe it was wishful thinking.

"You look great," I told her, meaning it.

"So do you," she said, "except for the bruising."

There was something else in her eyes, a tentativeness, a holding back. You couldn't be married to a woman for fourteen years and not know when something was bothering her.

"Okay," I said. "Spit it out. What aren't you telling me?"

Her smile was sad. "You always could read my mind, couldn't you? All right. There is something I want to discuss with you. But later. Right now, I have to go finish the potato salad." She turned and called to Jay and Randall's wife, Wendy, who was showing Paulie how to blow his party favor. "Wendy, Jay, could you come and help me in the kitchen?"

With Jay and the two women gone, I decided to bite the bullet and say hello to my replacement.

He was using a spatula to put raw hamburger patties on the grill. Besides hamburgers, he had hot dogs, chicken breasts, and corn on the cob, still in the shucks. I stifled a wave of jealousy. It was a new gas grill, not the one Maria and I had cooked out on. But it was my job he was doing.

"Hey, D.W." He was a little shorter than my six feet, maybe five-ten, with a rugged, square-jawed face, a receding hairline, and the beginnings of a paunch. He wore knee-length khaki shorts with a navy and green golf shirt and white tennis shoes, no socks. Jay said he looked like a man you could depend on.

I couldn't help but resent it.

"Thanks for the bail-out, man," I said.

He shrugged, not meeting my eyes. "It meant a lot to Maria, getting you out."

"Because of Paul."

He jabbed at a burger with his spatula. "I expect so. She says you absolutely couldn't have done this thing. She knows you, I guess."

I felt a flush creep up my neck. "You think I did it?"

He stopped what he was doing and met my gaze. "I don't think you did it," he said. "But I don't know you didn't. All I know is that my wife thinks you didn't do it." *My wife*. I tried not not to wince as he went on. "It means a lot to her that you didn't do it. So if you did, I'm telling you right now, you'd better never even dream of hurting her the way that other poor woman was hurt. If you so much as breathe on her wrong, I'll tear out your spleen with my bare hands."

*You and what army*, was my first thought. Then I thought again and knew that, if our places were reversed, I'd be giving him the same speech. "D.W.," I said, "I would eat hot coals before I'd hurt Maria. Or Paulie. Or you, for that matter."

"Well." He sighed and flipped the burgers. "Well, that's kind of what I thought. But I felt it needed to be said."

My jaw felt tight. "Consider it said."

He nodded.

"Thanks for the bail-out, anyway."

He looked at me blankly for a moment, then said, "You're welcome."

I wandered over to the picnic table, where Randall sat glowering at his soda.

"Your face will freeze that way," I told him, quoting Mom. "What's eating you?"

"Look at that." He pointed toward Josh, who was pushing Paulie on the swing. Josh looked like a sullen, undead creature, Paulie like a smiling Buddha in a striped T-shirt. In the next swing, Caitlin pumped her long, sun-browned legs. With her blond hair and her yellow shirt and shorts, she looked like a human sunbeam.

"Caitlin's growing up," I said, knowing Caitlin wasn't Randall's problem. "You're going to have to fight the boys off with machine guns."

"Not Caitlin. Josh. Look at him. He looks like..." His shoulders lifted. Drooped. "Like some kind of freak."

"It's just a phase," I reassured him. "Like when we grew our hair long and drank beer up in the loft. We didn't even like it."

"There's a lot worse things out there than beer," he said. "You've read about these vampire cults. How they drink blood and worship the devil and then start killing people."

"I don't think Josh is worshipping the devil."

"You ought to see his room. Everything in black. Posters of that Marilyn Manson. What kind of sick shit names himself after a woman and a mass murderer?"

"The kind who wants to shock people. Remember Kiss? Remember Ozzy Osborne? I used to hope that son-of-a-bitch would catch rabies or something, biting the heads off bats."

161

"That's what I mean. We might have drank a couple beers in our time, but we knew you had to be a creep to bite the heads off live animals. I'm not sure Josh knows."

I watched Josh standing behind my son like some kind of bloodless ghoul and wondered.

"He's good with Paulie," I said.

Randall's sigh was heavy. "I don't know who he is, Jared. I don't know what I did wrong."

"You don't have to have done anything wrong."

He looked away from his son. "Then how did he turn out this way?"

I couldn't answer him. Instead, we sat in silence for a moment. Looking at my brother, I realized how much alike we looked. He was two inches taller and four years older, but we had the same gray eyes, the same shock of buckskin-colored hair, the same dimples at the corners of the mouth.

From the time we were kids, he'd planned to follow Dad into the Air Force. He enlisted at eighteen and was four months into his stint when our mother passed away. I was fourteen and probably a pain in the ass, but he left the service to take care of me without a backward glance. Then a construction accident shattered his knee, and the dream was over. At my graduation from college and later the police academy, he'd clapped louder than anyone else. He'd stood by me through my divorce, the mess with Ashleigh, and my decision to go into business for myself as a P.I.

He never once blamed me for the end of his Air Force career.

I blamed myself enough for both of us.

I was grateful when D.W. announced that the food was done. Wendy and Maria came out, bearing deviled eggs, potato salad, and coleslaw. Jay followed with the watermelon wedges.

"Save room for cake and ice cream," Maria said, though how she expected anybody to leave room for anything after such bounty was a mystery. Somehow, we all managed.

Maria got out her camera and Paulie blew out his candles with a series of staccato, spit-filled blows. Perhaps anticipating this, Maria had placed all eight candles in one corner, thereby preserving the rest of the cake.

"Yuck," Caitlin said, grimacing. "He spit all over it. I don't want a piece from that side."

"Hush," her mother scolded, as Paulie's smile dissolved. "Paulie, you did just fine."

"I don't want any cake, period," Josh said. "Cake is an unnecessary extravagance of the bourgeoisie."

"The bourgeoisie is the working class," Randall said. "And there's nothing wrong with being a member of it."

Josh glared at his father. "You're just like Marie Antoinette. Let them eat cake, she said. And all the time, the people are starving."

"Josh, don't." Wendy laid a hand on her son's arm. He jerked away. She pretended not to be upset. "Your father is the foreman of a construction company. I'm a kindergarten teacher. That hardly makes us members of an oppressive upper class."

"My life sucks," said Josh, and laid his head down on his arms. His black hair splayed over the shoulders of his black turtleneck.

Maria said, "You'd feel better if you weren't dressed for Siberia. If you'd go put on a T-shirt, you might not feel so cranky."

His head jerked up, eyes blazing. "I am *not* cranky!" He swung his legs over the picnic bench and stalked down to the boat dock.

"Kids," Wendy said. "I hope he gets out of this phase soon."

"If he talks to you like that again," Randall said, "he may not live to."

I wondered if Josh was under the influence of one of the many mind-altering drugs kids find so readily available these days. People talk about the sixties, but what they had back

163

then was like candy compared to what's out there today.

"Me make wish," Paulie said, proudly.

"I made a wish," Maria corrected. "What did you wish for, honey?"

Paulie's grin was almost as wide as his head. "Cake!"

After the presents, I played a few songs on my guitar, and everybody sang, sans Josh, whose life was apparently majorly sucking.

Maria slipped among the guests, camera whirring, saving moments for posterity.

"I think it's gone well, don't you?" she asked, as I was putting my guitar back into its case. It's a 1956 Martin, not too pretty to look at, but with a sound like a million bucks. "I'm glad you and Randall came. I know it was a little awkward."

I laughed. A little awkward was an understatement. But Maria wants everyone to live in peace and harmony, her married to D.W., and me a part of things like one of the family. A brother, perhaps, or a very close cousin. It didn't seem quite fair to D.W. or to me, but both of us were willing to give it a shot if it would make her happy. I was surprised to find that I resented it, especially since it was probably the best thing we could do for Paul.

"Was it too terrible?" she asked. "You seemed to be having a nice time."

"It was all right," I said. "It will be easier next time."

She smiled her relief. "I think so too."

I snapped the clasps shut on my guitar case. "So, what's this really important thing you wanted to talk to me about?"

She leaned against the table, arms crossed in front of her like a shield. She shifted from one foot to the other, uncrossed her arms, pulled her ponytail to the front and twisted a section of hair between her fingers. I knew it would find its way into her mouth before long.

"You're moving to Australia," I guessed. "You've been asked to go on the next space shuttle mission to take pictures of space aliens. You've signed up for a sex change operation."

"I'm pregnant," she said.

And I said, "Oh."

"It changes things, doesn't it?" she asked, her voice small. "I've been thinking and thinking of how to tell you."

"'I'm pregnant' was okay."

"Too blunt? I know. I've rehearsed this a thousand times, and then when the time actually comes, I mess it up."

"It's all right. What do you mean, it changes things?"

"I don't know." Her eyes welled. "It's like . . . I've really lost you."

My head felt suddenly light. "You didn't lose me. You—"

"I know. Threw you away." She grabbed a napkin and wiped at her nose. "But you were still there. You know, for Paul, and for me too, in a way. I know it's selfish, but . . . I always felt like you were still mine. I was so jealous of that Ashleigh woman."

"You never had to be jealous of her."

"I know I have no right to feel this way."

"I'm still here," I said. "For Paul, and for you. You know that. Nothing's changed."

"But this baby." She drew a deep, quivering breath. "It means it's really over. Our marriage. Us."

"Maria," I said, as gently as I could, "it was over with us when you married D.W."

"I know. But it didn't feel over."

I tried to gather a few coherent thoughts. "Are you saying you don't want the baby? That it was an accident? Or that you want us to be back together?"

"No. Not . . . No." Tears spilled down her cheeks and into the corners of her mouth. "I can't live like that, never knowing when they might bring you home in a body bag."

"They don't bring you home," I said. "They take you to the morgue."

"You know what I mean." She stretched out a hand, touched her fingertips to the place where the arrow wound had been.

165

"Maria, I have no idea what you mean."

"The last time you got hurt, I thought you were going to die. And then I thought *I* was going to die. But now, you come home late, and I don't have to worry, because I don't know about it. I can pretend you're safe at home."

"I would have quit," I said. "I could have joined a construction crew, learned to make cabinets, tried to sell insurance. I didn't have to be a cop."

"It's not about being a cop. It's about who you are. How every time we pass a convenience store, you scope the place for robbers. How we walk down the street and you're looking for muggings or drug deals, or God knows what. And what happens when you see one? I love you, Jared, but I'm not strong enough to live with that."

"I can handle myself."

"So could your father, and look what happened to him." She touched my chest again. "You're a hero waiting for a place to happen. That doesn't change just because you turn in a badge."

"So now you've got Safe. Everything should be hunky dory, but it isn't. What's bothering you?"

"I'm afraid of what it will mean for us. You and Paul and me. Do you take just Paul on weekends? Are you going to be Uncle Jared to our baby? Or just that man who picks up Paulie? Will Paul be jealous of the baby? Will the baby feel left out because Paul gets to go with you?"

"What are you asking me? To take D.W.'s child on weekends too?"

"I don't know. Not right away, of course. But maybe when it's older, if you want to. If you like him. Or her."

One big happy family. Right. "What does D.W. think of this idea?"

"He says it's all right with him if it doesn't bother you. He says he gets to have your child five days a week and every other weekend, so you might as well get to spend some time with his, if you want to."

"D.W. said that?"

"Well, he agreed to it. Don't make a decision now. I know it's a lot to think about. But I want Paulie and the baby to be like real brothers—or brother and sister. So why should Paul get to have three parents and the new baby only two? It's like penalizing him—or her—because of our mistake."

"And what mistake was that?" I asked, my voice more brittle than I meant for it to be. "The marriage, or the divorce?"

"You're making this so hard."

I sighed and put my arm around her, glancing around to see where D.W. was.

He and Jay had gone inside with Wendy, Paul, and Caitlin. Randall and Josh stood chest to chest on the boat dock, faces flushed and fists clenched.

I said, "Does D.W. know you're telling me this today?"

"That's why he's gone inside."

I chose my words carefully. "I'm not trying to make anything hard for you. You know I'll always be here if you need me. You know I'll love your baby, just like D.W. loves Paul. But it won't be easy, and it will take time. I'm still getting used to the idea of sharing my son with another man."

Not to mention my wife.

"I'm so scared, Jared." More tears leaked from her eyes. "I'm just so damn scared."

"Scared? Maria . . ."

"What if it isn't normal?" Her voice was a strained whisper. "I can't talk to D.W. about this. He's so happy about the baby and all. But what if there's something wrong with this one too?"

"Maria." I tilted her chin up and looked into her beautiful, tear-stained face. She smelled of oranges and French Vanilla. "Your baby will be beautiful. Your baby will be perfect. Your baby will be fine."

I would have flayed myself alive for the look she gave me. Standing there in the deepening dusk with my ex-wife in my arms, I felt a crushing grief for everything I'd had and lost.

Maria had D.W. I wondered if I'd ever find another woman who would fill my spaces like a missing piece.

Down on the dock, my brother shouted, "And cut your hair! You look like a fucking faggot!"

And Josh's voice, not yelling, calm—too calm, in fact—cutting through the dusk like a thrown knife, "Dad. I am a fucking faggot."

# 23

JAY TOLD ME ONCE that the most painful moment of his life—more painful than having his head shoved into a toilet, more painful than being told he had been given an incurable, terminal disease by a lover he'd thought had always been faithful, more painful than watching that lover walk out of his life without a backward glance—was the moment his father looked him in the eye and said, "You are not my son."

I didn't know what I would do in Randall's place. Paulie's sexuality would present a different set of complications, but I somehow doubted this would be one of them.

It never rains but it pours, Mom used to say. With my brother's family crumbling and a prison sentence hanging over my head, now I had Maria's pregnancy to think of too. What would it feel like to see her with D.W.'s child? To share my weekends with my son with D.W.'s flesh and blood? It wasn't normal, and I didn't know if we could make it work.

But assuming I didn't spend the rest of my life in a prison cell, I was willing to try. I would be as good a man as D.W.

Jay was asleep by the time I finished with the horses. I would have liked to talk to him about Josh, but decided it could wait.

Besides, I felt like I'd been wrung out myself.

There was another call from Lou Wilder on the answering machine, but it was late, and I didn't feel like talking. I made a mental note to call him in the morning.

I was too tired to dream.

THE NEXT MORNING, after I'd doctored Tex and turned out Crockett, I played another round of phone tag with Lou, left a "when-can-I-see-you-again" message on Valerie's machine, and drove downtown to trade the Taurus for a silver Chevy van. I'd learned enough of Hartwell's damning secrets, and it was time to give the honorable Reverend Samuel Avery his share of attention.

At ten o'clock, a woman in a flowered blouse and white Capri pants came out of Avery's house carrying a basket. She was tall and bony, with a prominent nose. A wide-brimmed hat shielded her face from the sun and threw her homely features into shadow.

Margaret, I supposed.

She set the basket down beside a strip of earth that had been planted with marigolds and rose bushes, pulled on a pair of flowered gloves, and puttered in the garden until the heat drove her inside. There were no further signs of life until shortly after dusk, when Avery and his wife came out to sit on the front porch together, sipping what looked to be iced tea.

At one point, Margaret reached out and laid a hand across her husband's forearm. He said something that made her shrink back inside herself like a snail sprinkled with salt.

Trouble in Paradise.

I watched until they went back inside and I saw the flicker of the TV against the blinds. Then I drove back home to get ready for another night of Heather-hunting.

I WAS GETTING OUT of the shower when the phone rang. I threw a towel around my waist and rushed to answer it, just in case it happened to be Frank.

"Jared McKean," I said.

"Jared. It's Wendy." My sister-in-law's voice was breathless, shaken. I imagined a car wreck, an accident at the construction site.

"What's wrong? Is Randall all right?"

She laughed, shrill, nervous. "Cut to the chase. That's you. Randall's fine. It's Josh."

My imagination shifted gears. Suicide. Drug overdose. "What's wrong with Josh?"

"He's gone. He and Randall got into an awful fight last night. This morning when we woke up, he was gone."

"Have you called the police?"

I heard the hesitation in her voice and knew what she would say before she said it.

"Randall didn't want to. He was so angry and embarrassed. Tough love, he said." A sob escaped her. "You know how stubborn he is."

"How is Caitlin taking this?"

"She's heartbroken. And confused." I heard a sharp intake of breath. "Can you find him, Jared?"

Receiver tucked between my jaw and shoulder, I rubbed my temples. Of all times for Josh to pull a stunt like this. Couldn't he have waited until I got my life back?

I sighed and said, "I'll do my best. Do you know of any friends he might have gone to stay with? Any teachers he was close to?"

"I don't know," she said, her voice small and ashamed. "He hardly talks to us any more. I know there used to be a girl named Sharon and a boy named Curt he used to hang out with."

"Last names?"

"Um. Let me think." There was a long pause on the other end of the line. "Sharon . . . Blankenship, I think. And Curt Holland. Or Hollis. Does that help?"

"They live in Old Hickory too?"

"Yes. But zoned for Mt. Juliet. They went to school with Josh. There was a teacher he kind of liked, too. She lives in Shiloh. Ms. Casale. English."

"All right," I said. "Don't worry, Wendy. I'll find him."

It wasn't difficult to find Sharon Blankenship. There were four Blankenships in the phone book, and I found her on the third try. I explained the situation to her.

"I'm sorry, Mr. McKean," she said. She sounded very young. "I haven't seen Josh all summer. He hangs with a different crowd now."

"Could you tell me how to reach any of them?"

"I could give you some names. But they probably won't talk to you. They're into the Goth scene."

"What?"

"Goths. You know. Death worshippers." A chill crept up my spine and lodged between my shoulder blades. "Black lips, real white skin, always wear black. Kinda like vampires. They all come from these great families and sit around and rant about how bad their lives have been."

"Death worshippers?"

"I mean, like, always talking about death, and vampires, and how the world is such a mess and it's never going to be any better. It's a real downer to hang with them."

"Is that why you and Josh split?"

"Yeah." She sighed. "He got weird. Like, his art. It got to be a total gorefest. All daggers and monsters and stuff. And he never wanted to do anything fun. He said there was no point, because the world was going to end soon anyway. I figure, if the world's about to end, let's have some fun before it does, right?"

"Sounds reasonable." I wondered if Josh was as disturbed as Sharon made it sound, or if it was mostly teenage posturing. "Listen, do you know where Josh and these Goth kids hang out?"

"Um. You could try Elliston Place. It gets kind of crazy down there after dark. And there's this place on Second Avenue. It's a Goth hangout called The Underground."

"Thank you, Sharon," I said. "You just earned yourself some real good karma."

"No prob. Josh used to be totally cool. I hope you find him."

"Do you know if he was into drugs?"

"I don't know. Maybe some pot. Are you the cop?"

"Not anymore."

"Um. Okay. I never saw him use anything but pot, and sometimes beer."

"Do you know a guy named Curt Holland? Or Hollis?"

"Curt Hollis. Sure. He used to hang with Josh and me. I mean, he used to hang with Josh. He still hangs with me."

"Do you think you could give me his number?"

"Sure." She rattled it off. "But you won't be able to reach him until next week. He's at football camp."

I thanked her again and hung up. No sense calling Curt, then. But Sharon had given me a place to start.

I reached Elisha Casale on the first try. She was the only Casale in Old Hickory. I introduced myself and explained my situation, asking if she could offer any insight into what Josh might be thinking.

"Josh is a talented young man," she said, carefully. Her voice was deep for a woman's, with a sexiness I didn't usually associate with schoolteachers. I found myself wondering what she looked like. "I'm sure you've seen his artwork?"

"Not lately. But I know he used to be real good."

Her laugh was throaty, almost sultry. I was suddenly aware that I was nearly naked. "That's an understatement, Mr. McKean. The boy is a gifted artist. And, I might add, an excellent writer, though his subject matter was a bit disturbing."

"Meaning?"

"He wrote a lot about death. And his father. I don't know all the details, Mr. McKean, but I got the impression that things weren't very good between Josh and his father. He used a pseudonym in his work, Joshua Nightbreed, as if he were disavowing his family name."

"There's been some tension lately."

There was a pause. "I think—and I may be overstepping my bounds here—but I think Josh is . . . Conflicted . . . about his sexuality."

"He didn't seem too conflicted yesterday when he told his father he was gay."

"Ah." Somehow she managed to infuse that single syllable with understanding, concern, and confirmation.

173

"You knew?"

"I suspected. He skirted the issue in his writing, but I thought it was fairly clear. He was angry and confused. And he was afraid of his father."

A wave of heat crept up my neck. "He was never afraid of Randall. If he said he was, he was lying."

"I didn't mean physically afraid," she said. "I meant, he was afraid of his father's disapproval."

All right. That I could understand. "Mrs. Casale—"

"Miss."

"Miss Casale." *Miss* Casale. "Do you have any idea where Josh might have gone? Who he might be with?"

"I know some of his friends." She reeled off some names I didn't recognize, and I scrawled them on a Post-it note. "They're all . . . I hesitate to say outcasts. Outsiders. Rebels. Mostly passive-aggressive. I get good work from them, because they're creative children, and they like to write, but generally, they have contempt for what they call standardized education."

Standardized education. Josh was getting to be quite the little elitist.

"Do you have any of Josh's writing? I'd like to see some of it."

"I have a few samples at the school. But I'm sure Josh has stacks of it at home."

"I'll check with his mom. If we can't find anything, would you mind giving me a copy of what you have?"

"Not if his parents don't object. But you should be prepared. You might find some of his work upsetting."

"Miss Casale." I tried not to sound judgmental. "Why didn't you tell Josh's parents he was so disturbed?"

"Disturbed?" I imagined her frown, the little furrow between the eyebrows. Auburn hair, I thought. Blue eyes. "I wouldn't say disturbed. In turmoil, perhaps."

"Is there a difference?"

"Disturbed implies permanence. Turmoil ends. To answer

your question, I didn't contact his parents because he would have seen it as a betrayal. Whatever trust he had in me would be lost, and he would have lost one source of adult support and guidance. My students write what they write, Mr. McKean, because they know it's safe to write it."

I sighed. It was water under the bridge now. I thanked her for her time and hung up, annoyed and disgusted with myself for being aroused. It was just a voice on the telephone, for Christ's sake.

I pulled on a pair of jeans and a Donelson Tae Kwan Do T-shirt. Thought about everything I needed to do. Hunt for Heather. Research the men in Amy's life—Hartwell, Carrington, and Avery. Run background checks on all of the above plus Valerie's boyfriend—ex-boyfriend, if the afternoon I'd spent in her bed was any indication. I ran out of fingers before I ran out of things to do. If I was racing the devil, it looked like the devil was winning.

But family came first. I called Jay and asked him to take care of the horses if I wasn't back by morning. Then I grabbed a cheeseburger and fries at the McDonald's drive-through on my way downtown to Elliston Place, where I hoped to talk to the vampires.

# 24

ELLISTON PLACE, ON THE WEST end of downtown, cut from the northwest corner of Baptist Hospital to the southeast corner of Centennial Park. To its north was Centennial Medical Center, to its south, Vanderbilt Hospital and University. Perhaps because of its proximity to the college, it boasted an eclectic mix of music, food, and business. Elder's Bookstore, which carried antique and used books squatted between Rock Block Guitars and a cutting-edge clothing shop called Dangerous Threads. Next to the guitar store was the Elliston Place Soda Shop (best milkshakes in town), and across the street were a Mosko's novelty store and the Sherlock Holmes Pub, which served Shepherd's Pie for supper, crumpets and scones at tea-time, and English beer on tap all day long. Some nights, they had live Celtic music. I'd taken Maria there a few times when we were married.

Down the street from the Soda Shop were the Gold Rush Saloon, Obie's Pizza, and Rotier's, immortalized by Jimmy Buffet in "Cheeseburger in Paradise."

In daylight, Elliston Place had a quirky, understated personality.

After dark, it swarmed with a blend of ordinary tourists, punk rockers, metalheads, and drag queens. Mardi Gras meets Mayberry. Nothing understated about it. I'd been down here on weekends before, working cases as a cop and, later, as a P.I. The only trouble was, it was a Thursday night, and it was dead. The Soda Shop and most of the businesses were closed. I went into Mosko's and asked the guy behind the counter what time the Goths came out.

"Not 'til after midnight, man," he said. "Things don't get hopping down here until about two in the morning."

Great. "How about that club on Second Avenue. What's it called? The Underground?"

"One Seventy Six Underground."

"Same thing there? Dead 'til after midnight?"

He laughed. "Dead. That's a good one. No, they open up at ten and close whenever."

I thanked him and went back to the van. Since there wasn't much I could do in the way of finding Josh until later, I started hitting other bars, looking for Heather. It was like trying to find a specific needle in a stack of needles. She could be anywhere.

Anywhere, apparently, except where I was.

At one A.M., I went back to Elliston and found the place transformed. Groups of mostly young people stood in clumps or milled about, dressed in leather, lace, and pseudo-medieval finery. Clumped beside Obie's Pizza were a plump girl stuffed into a long red velvet dress with a thigh-high black lace insert; a wild-eyed, cadaverous girl in a black leather miniskirt and bustier; and an older blonde in a black fishtailed dress with cleavage almost to the aureoles. The blonde had a silver cigarette holder and elbow-length black gloves a la Morticia Addams.

The guys prowled the street in blousy pirate shirts and tight black pants, some with metal studs, some with laces. One wore a tux, complete with top hat and a long black cape lined with red silk. They all had punked-out hair and painted faces. White skin, black lips, dramatic, kohl-ringed eyes. Death masks.

They wore enough silver and Celtic jewelry to outfit a renaissance fair for a year.

Along with the Goths, there was the usual assortment of young punkers and regular Joes looking to see what all the fuss was about.

I got out of the car, the Colt at the small of my back a reassuring weight.

I didn't expect to need it, but it was nice to have it there.

I approached the Obie's Pizza group. The smell of clove cigarettes was strong, but not unpleasant. They looked at me and blew smoke in my direction.

"Hi," I said.

"Hi," said the chubby girl in the red velvet dress.

I pulled Josh's picture out of my wallet. It was a school picture from the year before, and I didn't have a lot of hope, since he barely resembled it these days. "I'm looking for a Goth kid. Name's Josh. Anybody seen him?"

She took the picture, looked at it, and passed it to her friends. "You a cop?"

"I'm his uncle."

"Which doesn't answer my question." Her expression was defiant, but there was more than defiance in her tone. She wanted me to know how smart she was.

"I'm not a cop."

"Why are you looking for him?"

"Because his family is worried sick about him."

The girls exchanged glances. The one in red took a long drag from her scented cigarette. "I wouldn't worry about it. He's where he wants to be."

"He's fifteen years old."

"So? Goth kids are smarter than other kids. More sensitive. More open. His parents don't get it. So what? It's his life."

I felt my jaw tighten. "Let him run off when he's eighteen. Plenty of time to break their hearts when he's of age."

She snorted. "What do you know about broken hearts? You're so white bread, you're practically a Brady."

"You think I don't know life's tough because I don't dress like a freak? Yeah, that's real open. Real sensitive."

She stared at me. "You don't understand."

"I understand that Josh has parents who would drink acid if it would help him. That his sister cries herself to sleep at night worrying about him. That he thinks he's the only one with feelings, so it doesn't matter what he does or says to the people who love him. I understand that he's a coward."

"Having the courage to be yourself isn't cowardice," the girl said.

"Running away when things get tough is."

"Maybe he didn't run away. Maybe he's running *to*."

"Semantics," I said.

"You say that like it's a bad thing."

I sucked in a deep breath, then blew it out. Count to ten, mom used to say. "Look, do you know him, or not?"

"I don't know," Red Dress said. "What's his name?"

"Josh. Josh McKean."

"No. I mean, his real name. Like, I'm Absinthe. This is Medea." She gestured toward the wild-eyed young woman in the miniskirt. Two feral-looking young men strolled toward us, and Absinthe waved in their direction. "Over there is Barnabus, and that's Dark Knight. What's your nephew's name?"

I started to say I didn't know. Then I remembered what Miss Casale had said about Josh's writing. "Nightbreed," I said. "He calls himself Joshua Nightbreed."

"Joshua Nightbreed. Sorry. I wouldn't tell you if I did know him. We don't rat out our own."

The young man she'd called Barnabus stepped up to us, tucked his silver-tipped walking stick under one arm, and swept his top hat off his head and across his body in a formal bow. "Ladies. Is this mundane bothering you?"

Mundane.

I gritted my teeth. Arrogant little bastard.

"No, it's all right," said Absinthe. "He was just leaving."

It was like that everywhere I went, with everyone I talked to. One girl spoke of the Goth's love of beauty and darkness. Another spoke of a life of sadness. One young man with an engaging, impish grin laughed and said it was all a big joke, a chance to leave reality and visit in a comic book. Another, with a smoldering anger that seemed more incubus than imp, told me Josh—Nightbreed—was with "his people" and should be left alone.

One went so far as to assure me that Nightbreed was being taken care of by his "true family," and that I should go back to the suburbs and mind my own business.

About an hour before dawn, when the street was all but empty, I did.

AT 6:00 A.M., I PULLED into the driveway of ValeSong Stables. Since the red Chevy was parked by the barn and there was a light on in the kitchen window, I dialed Valerie's number and asked if I could come in.

"Just in the neighborhood and thought you'd stop by?" Her voice was rich with sleep and a heat that made me glad I'd come.

"Something like that."

"It's kind of early."

"I'll help you with the horses."

"Deal."

Breakfast was good.

Dessert was better.

Afterward, I kissed her again and rolled out of bed. "Where's your bathroom?"

She pointed. "Down the hall and to your left."

The first door I tried was a spare bedroom. The second was locked, and the third was the charm. I washed up and went to muck stalls while Valerie fed her horses.

When I turned Dakota out into his paddock, he nuzzled my hand before trotting out into the sunlight. I left him with a flake of hay and went to muck out his stall. He was something of a neatnick, choosing one corner of the stall to relieve himself in. Some horses are like that. Others seem to think life is a challenge to see how much of their stalls they can cover with manure.

I wasn't really looking for a horse, but it was another point in his favor.

When the soiled bedding had been scooped out and I'd spread on a layer of clean straw, I bent to even out the bedding beneath the feed bucket. Something small and dark caught my eye, and I reached in to retrieve it. It was wedged between two boards, but I pushed hard on one to widen the crack and it came free. I held it up to the light, a spiny seedpod with shriveled brown skin that still held a tinge of green.

I carried it into the feed room, where Valerie was measuring out sweet feed and vitamins.

"You got a problem," I said, holding out the pod.

She looked up. "What's that?"

"Milkweed. I found it in Dakota's stall."

"Milkweed?" She frowned. "Let me see."

I handed it to her. "Looks like maybe you got a bad batch of hay. Could be what caused his colic. You have a problem with any of the other horses?"

She shook her head, eyeing the pod as if it were some new and disgusting kind of insect. "A couple of the mares were a little off their feed for a few days. Nothing like what Dakota went through." She made a face. "I've never had a problem with toxic plants before."

"Happens sometimes. You want me to get rid of what you have and bring you a new load?"

"I finished up those bales about a week ago." She dropped the pod into the trashcan. "What I'm using now should be all right."

"Better safe than sorry."

"You're probably right."

We spent most of the morning hauling away her old bales and replacing them with new ones from my own supplier. A spot check of the new bales showed no sign of the contamination.

Then she thanked me in an inimitable way, and I drove home to catch a few hours of shut-eye before I had to hit the streets again.

THAT EVENING, AFTER DINNER, I practiced my Tae Kwan Do forms until it was late enough to venture back into Josh's world. I started with the white and yellow belt forms—Chon-Ji, Dan-Gun, Do-San, Won-Hyo—and worked my way through the patterns to the second degree black belt forms—Choong-Jang, Ko-Dang, and Sam Il.

Then I showered and put on a pair of black jeans, black boots, and a black T-shirt. When in Rome and all that jazz.

I hit the Underground Club first. Because the traffic on Second was murderous and the parking even worse, I parked at Mean Billy's place on Seventh and walked down.

Nashville's Lower Broadway, including Second Avenue, used to be a seedy place dominated by adult bookstores, peep shows, and tired saloons, but in recent years, it had undergone a radical renovation. I'd heard it compared to Bourbon Street in New Orleans, which might be an apt comparison if you took away the beads, the "Judgment is Nigh" crusaders, and most of the debauchery. Bourbon Street Lite. The Family Friendly edition.

A man in a cowboy hat played guitar in front of the Wild Horse Saloon, where, for the cost of a BMW, you could buy a burger and fries with a side order of line dancing. I tossed a dollar bill into the cowboy's guitar case. He stared at the dollar for a moment, then turned his head away and squirted a stream of tobacco juice onto the sidewalk.

I gave him a what-the-hell look, then shrugged it off and strolled on, up the street and past the Old Spaghetti Factory, where the line snaked out the door, through the wrought-iron gates, and halfway down the block.

On our first date, Maria and I had stood in line there for two hours, bursts of awkward small talk finally giving way to genuine conversation. After dinner, we sauntered through the Second Avenue Emporium, nursing ice cream cones while she tried on vintage hats and held up knickknacks and essential oils for my appraisal. A cut crystal teardrop with a silver chain made her eyes light up; I plunked down too much money for it and placed it around her neck with suddenly trembling hands. We finished the evening in Printer's Alley, listening to jazz and sipping draft beer, and she fell asleep on the way home, her head in my lap, warm against my thigh.

The memory left a hollow ache in my stomach. My family was fractured; I wouldn't let the same thing happen to Randall's. I lengthened my stride and surged ahead to the Underground—officially called One Seventy Six Underground in honor of its street number. A small group of Goths, both male and female, clustered by the door, smoking and talking in low tones. I eased past them and paid the five-dollar cover charge.

Nobody thought to check me for weapons.

I showed my photo I.D. at the bar, ordered a $7.50 rum and Coke, and looked around. Kids dressed in a blend of modern and medieval styles danced to a mix of music the DJ called Goth/Industrial. The bands had names like Switchblade Symphony, Christian Death, Red Temple Spirits, and The Shroud. When he announced a group called Creaming Jesus, I slumped down in my chair and waited for lightning to strike. Felt relieved when it didn't.

I saw a lot of the same people I'd spoken to the night before. Absinthe and her friends had snagged a table near the dance floor. I nodded to them, raised my glass. They stared back with undisguised hostility. A few minutes later, Absinthe made her way to the ladies' room. On her way back, she stopped by my table.

"Just because you're wearing black doesn't make you one of us."

"No sense sticking out like a sore thumb," I said.

She was squeezed into a black gown with a froth of lace at the hem. In spite of her weight, she might have been pretty if not for the death's head she'd made of her face. I wanted to tell her that when you've really suffered, when you've lost the people and the things you love most, you don't need to announce it to the world.

Instead, I asked, "What happened to you guys to make you all so miserable?"

"Life is miserable," she said, and shrugged. "Only death is constant. You can't really live until you've learned to live with death."

"We all live with death," I said. I thought of my mother and my father. I thought of Jay. "Most of us don't fall in love with it."

"That's because most of you are afraid of it."

I couldn't deny that. The thing was, she was young, with the immortality of the young. She could flirt with Death because he wasn't looking over her shoulder.

"Seen Josh?" I asked her.

"You mean Nightbreed?"

"Whatever. Sure. Nightbreed."

"No. Why don't you try The Masquerade?"

"What's that?"

"Little club off Elliston. Caters to the vampire crowd."

"The vampire crowd. That's different from the Goth crowd?"

She rolled her eyes. "You really are a mental deficient, aren't you? I'm talking about vampire games. Live action role-playing and stuff. Posers, mostly. A lot of them share blood."

My stomach heaved. "You saying Josh is into that? Blood-letting?"

She shrugged again. "It's not that big a deal. I did it once or twice, but it didn't turn me on."

I tried not to wince. "You ever hear of AIDS?"

"Hey," she said. "We all die. What does it matter when?"

"If you believe that," I said, "why are you still alive?"

She sighed, her dark eyes wide and mournful. "Sometimes I wonder that myself."

# 25

THE WALLS OF THE MASQUERADE were draped in crimson velvet and lit by candles flickering in sconces. Black tablecloths covered all the tables, with a crystal vase in the center of each. Each vase held a single rose, white, red, or black. The patrons were dressed in Goth styles with a certain funereal flamboyance, all dark colors, silks and velvets. Some had painted fake wounds on their throats or foreheads. A couple of kids danced in slow motion to some eerie music written in a minor key.

At one table, I saw a young man sucking on his girlfriend's neck. At another, a girl held a razor blade between her thumb and forefinger and sliced a thin line of red horizontally across her boyfriend's wrist. As I watched, she lowered her lips to the wound.

A movement from the back of the room caught my eye, and a shadowy figure darted toward the door farthest from me. The build and the way it moved told me it was Josh.

I started after him.

A tall, leather-clad man dressed like Edward Scissorhands stepped into my path and said, "You Uncle Jared?"

A second man, this one in biker pants and a lace-fronted white shirt, sidled up beside him, cracking his knuckles.

I said, "What if I am?"

"He doesn't want to see you," said Edward. "*Capische*?"

"I don't care if he wants to see me. I want to see him."

"Screw you," said Lace Front.

"He wants to be free of me?" I said. "Then he's going to have to see me. Otherwise, every time he turns around, I'm there."

"Eat shit," said Lace Front. He was nothing, if not eloquent.

"Tell him," I said, and left.

Of course, I ducked around the back to see if I could catch a glimpse of Josh, but by the time I got there, he was gone.

ON SATURDAY MORNING, I followed Samuel Avery to the Piggly Wiggly, the post office, and finally a florist's shop, from which he emerged with a cauldron-sized basket of red and pink carnations. Next stop, St. Thomas Hospital. He went in with the basket and came out without it.

How sweet.

I tried, without success, to repress my cynicism.

When he went straight home from the hospital, I called it a day. I didn't like the reverend, but I had no concrete reason to consider him a viable suspect. Nothing but an unsubstantiated hunch and his uncanny resemblance to a dead man. I couldn't spend all my time on him. Especially not with my nephew missing.

At two o'clock on Saturday, I knocked on my brother's front door.

Wendy answered, looking wan, her hazel eyes swollen and bloodshot. When she saw me, she opened the screen door and stepped aside to let me in.

"Did you find him?"

"I have a few leads. I'll have him back soon."

She pressed a trembling hand to her mouth and stifled a sob. "Thank God. Is he all right?"

"He's fine." I didn't know if this was true or not, because I didn't know who he was with or what he might be into, but he was alive and whole, and for the moment, that was enough.

She turned away, her shoulders shaking. If it were Maria, I'd take her into my arms and hold her while she cried. I'd known Wendy since I was nineteen, and I still felt like an intruder on her pain.

"Is Randall in?"

Her laugh was full of tears. "Is Randall in? What makes you think I'd know if he was in?"

"What's that supposed to mean?"

"Nothing." She swallowed hard and smoothed her skirt with both hands. "Why don't you ask him? Ask him where he goes when I wake up at night and he's not there."

"He goes for walks," I said. "Always has."

"Walks?" Her voice rose. "Where have you been? He can barely walk across the room."

I ignored that. His limp was worse, but he was walking. "Drives, then," I said. "You've been with him for seventeen years. You know sometimes he has to get away."

"Away from what," she said, but it wasn't a question. "Forget it. I shouldn't be laying this on you. He's in the study. Unless he's gone out the back."

I found him sitting cross-legged on the floor, surrounded by stacks of old photo albums and loose photographs. Old family pictures. Disney World. Opryland. Picnics at the lake. Josh's fourth birthday. Caitlin's third.

I saw Josh laughing out at me from a hundred different angles. Josh on his first birthday, slamming his whole fist into the cake. Josh at two, dressed as a pumpkin for Halloween. At five, learning to ride a bike. At six, with missing teeth. At seven—roller skates. Josh at ten, posing like Babe Ruth at home plate, smile a mile wide and lighting up his face.

"He was beautiful, wasn't he?" my brother asked, not looking up.

"Yes. He is."

He picked up Josh's sixth grade school picture with trembling fingers. "I can't believe I named this . . . thing . . . after our father." His chest hitched, and he rubbed at his eyes with the heel of his hand. "Dad would have been so ashamed."

I hardly remembered our dad, except from photographs and the stories Mom told. In his pictures, he's almost always smiling. There are two exceptions. In one, he's holding me in his arms, fresh from the hospital, and Randall is hanging over his shoulder like a sloth. Dad's face is soft with wonder, and he looks very young and very vulnerable. In the other, he's leaning on the front porch post, watching a summer storm roll in. He's wearing jeans and a white muscle shirt, and he seems pensive and saddened, bewitched by the roiling clouds. That is the picture I have sitting on my dresser, and it's how I imagine him in Vietnam, watching muzzle flashes in the dark and listening to the distant thunder of mortar fire. It's the personification of my earliest childhood and the hovering specter of the war.

"I don't think he'd be ashamed," I said. "Josh is a good kid. He's just . . . lost himself for awhile."

"He says he's a faggot."

"Randall . . ."

"I know. I know. You don't like that word. Your queer friend doesn't like that word. Although I've heard him use it often enough."

"It's different when they use it."

"Did you ever stop to think that if you hadn't kept bringing that little fairy around here, Josh might not have thought it was so cool to be gay?"

I'd been expecting this—and dreading it.

"Randall, it isn't about being cool or not cool. It's just who you are. Or aren't. Jay knew he was different from the time he was in grade school. It just took him a while to understand why."

"Of course, Jay has to say that. What else could he say?" He looked up, eyes glistening. "What did we do wrong? Was I too strict? Not strict enough? I loved him so much." His voice broke. "I loved him just so damn much."

"I know you did." I pushed aside a stack of albums and sat down beside him, Indian-style. "I know you *do*. He knows it too. He's just all messed up right now."

"I think he enjoyed telling me. I think he wanted it to hurt."

I laid a hand on my brother's shoulder. "What if he did? He's hurting, so he wants everybody else to hurt too. Have you found any of his writing? Journals? Poetry? His English teacher thinks we might learn something from them."

He gestured toward a dog-eared spiral notebook that looked like it had spent most of its life in the bottom of a teenager's backpack.

"There. It's all death and anger and...I don't want you to read it. My son hates me, and it's all there in that book, in every stinking page of it."

"He doesn't hate you," I said, picking up the book. "Randall?"

He made a gesture that I took for acquiescence, and I opened the notebook.

*At night, the old man*
*Covered in brick dust*
*Drinks his coffee black*
*Too tired to speak to*
*His invisible boy.*

A few pages later,

*Man-boy, with muscles rippling*
*Do you have a moment*
*For a skinny boy-man*
*To trace your ripples*
*With my tongue?*

And:

*Death bends across your pillow,*
*her cold palm pressed*
*against your fevered cheek.*
*Kiss her icy lips, my son.*
*Embrace the pale maiden.*
*Plunge the knife deep, as*
*She bends to lick the*
*Edges of your soul.*

The poetry was interspersed with long, rambling journal entries. Reading the passages with Randall's eyes, I could see why he read hate in every line. But with my own eyes, I read love there, and the pain and fear of a boy who knows he is not the son his father always wanted.

"This isn't a hate letter," I told Randall, when I had finished it all. "It's a fucking love poem."

Randall scrubbed at his face with his hands. "What do you mean?"

I read a passage, "'My dad is so perfect. He's so strong. Why can't he understand I can't be him?' He's crazy about you, Randall. And he's scared to death that when you know him, you won't be crazy about him."

"My son is not a homosexual."

I splayed my fingers on my thighs. "I don't know if he is, or if he isn't. Neither do you. But whatever he is . . ." Randall looked up to meet my gaze. "He is what he is. He didn't choose it, and he can't change it."

"I don't believe that."

"I can't argue this with you. I just know that I for one could not wake up tomorrow morning and decide to get a woody for Mel Gibson and not for Madeleine Stowe. Neither could you."

"It's not the same thing."

"Nobody chooses to be pissed on and beaten up and treated like a monster because of who he gets it up for. If Jay could have *decided* to be straight, I promise you he would have."

"You don't know how lucky you are," he said. "You'll never go through this with Paul."

I sucked in a sharp breath. "You don't mean that, Randall. You know you don't wish Josh was mentally retarded."

"I wish to God he was," my brother said. The earnestness in his voice made my stomach clench. "I'd rather he was. I'd rather he was dead."

I DROVE HOME WISHING for a magic pill that would make things all right. Star light, star bright, and all that jazz.

When I walked in, Jay said, "I have something for you on the insurance. Sorry it's taken so long, but my guy at the company was in the hospital. Broke his leg parasailing in the Bahamas and just got back to work today."

"Great." I tossed my briefcase onto the couch. "Shoot."

"You wanted to know if there was a life insurance policy on Amy Hartwell."

"Right."

"My friend says there was one. Half a million dollars."

"The beneficiary?"

"Calvin Hartwell. Also, there's a policy that ensures that if one of them died, the house would be paid for. The house is appraised at $250,000."

I whistled. "So Calvin is about $750,000 richer. And free to marry his soul mate."

Jay shrugged and took a sip of his water. "Sure beats having to pay alimony."

AS SUSPECTS WENT, Calvin Hartwell was a good one. He had motive, opportunity, and an alibi that was unreliable at best. With one wife missing, another dead, and a history of philandering, he was looking less and less like the Good Christian Man Glenda had called him. Had he decided to end his painful marriage and cash in on Amy's life insurance at the same time? If so, it seemed the wages of sin were three quarters of a million dollars.

That afternoon, I stopped by Bluefield, parked a few doors down, and watched Cal Hartwell play softball with his girls. With only three of them, it was really just a hit, pitch, and catch practice session, with the three players alternating positions. Katrina loped around the bases, long legs pumping, cornsilk hair flying behind her. The younger, Tara, scrambled after the ball, a bright smile on her broad, sunny face.

Calvin slid to third base as Tara scooped up the ball in her tanned fist and flung it to him. He tipped it with his fingers and let Katrina fly past him toward home.

I didn't want to see him this way, warm and unguarded with his girls. I wanted him to be a villain.

The game ended, and they disappeared into the house, the girls on either side of Calvin, each with an arm around his waist. There was no sign of the distance I'd noticed between Calvin and Katrina.

I stayed long enough to make sure they'd gone in for the night, then drove by Maria's place to pick up Paulie. I felt a little guilty about not keeping after Josh, but he'd be harder to find now that he'd been alerted. Let him think I'd given up. I'd go back tomorrow night.

D.W. met me at the door with Queenie close behind. She hobbled over and leaned against my legs, and I stroked her head, knowing that the day was coming when the pain of her arthritis would outweigh whatever pleasure she got from the rest of her life.

"Is she getting her arthritis medicine?" I asked.

"Of course."

"Do you think you could increase it? She seems to be hurting."

"The vet said we could double it if we needed to."

"I want you to."

"Sure. We were going to try that in a couple days, anyway." He closed the door behind me. "Before you call Paulie, there's something I want to show you."

I followed him downstairs to Maria's darkroom and photo gallery. Then he stepped aside to let me pass. The pictures from the picnic had been added to the collection. Paulie blowing out his candles, Paulie opening his presents, Josh sulking on the dock, Caitlin swinging on the swing set, her yellow sundress tucked around her hips. Wendy, shoving a deviled egg into Randall's laughing mouth.

D.W. grilling the hamburgers, a strained smile on his face. Me, playing my guitar on the picnic table. Me, holding Paulie on my lap. Me, talking to Randall. Me, licking birthday icing off my fingers. Me.

D.W.'s voice came from behind me. "Sometimes I am so damn jealous of you."

Even I could hear the bitterness in my voice. "You have my wife, my kid, my house. Even my dog. What do you have to be jealous of, man?"

"That's just it. It's your wife. Your kid. Your dog." He gestured to the pictures. "She still loves you, Cowboy. She loves you more than she loves me. I know that, and I have to live with it, because I'll be damned if I'm going to let her go. Just don't rub my nose in it, okay?"

I thought about it for a moment before I nodded. It wasn't supposed to be like this, I thought. Divorce should be a clean severance, like an amputation. But what was it they said about phantom pains?

"Hell of a world, isn't it D.W.?"

He nodded back, solemnly. "It is that."

# 26

ON SUNDAY, I DRESSED in jeans and a meerkat T-shirt Maria had given me, then went downstairs to find Jay and Paulie eating Cocoa Puffs and cinnamon toast in the living room. Queenie was stretched out at their feet like an Akita rug.

"Bugs Bunny, Daddy," Paulie said, pointing at the TV. "What's up, Doc?"

I bent down for a milky kiss, and squeezed onto the couch next to my son.

Jay asked, "Found Josh yet?"

"Working on it."

"He'll be all right. He's a sweet kid."

"I don't know." I thought of the sullen white face, the gray eyes burning with hostility. "Sweet isn't the word I'd use these days."

The phone shrilled, and Jay reached across Paulie and me to answer it, which meant he was still hoping for a call from Eric.

He held the receiver to his ear, and his crestfallen expression told me it wasn't Mr. Perfect on the other end of the line.

"It's for you," he said, and handed me the receiver.

It was Birdie Drafon.

"Mr. McKean, I hate to bother you," she said. "But I think something is wrong at Amy's house. I mean, the Hartwells'."

"What do you mean, something's wrong?"

"Well . . ." She sounded tentative. "It may be nothing. But Calvinand the girls didn't go to church today. The car is still out front. That isn't like him."

"Maybe he's sick," I suggested. "Or one of the girls is."

"Yes, I thought of that. So I went over to see if there was anything I could do. And there was no answer. It was . . . so

194

quiet, Mr. McKean. Too quiet, if you know what I mean."

"Ms. Birdie, have you called the police?"

"Oh, no. It isn't anything I can put my finger on. The police would think I was just some hysterical old loon. It just feels wrong somehow."

"All right. I'll come and check it out. Do the Hartwells have a dog?"

"No. Calvin doesn't like hair on the furniture."

"One more thing, then." I was already sliding off the couch. "Do you happen to have a key to the house?"

The Colt was tucked away in the top of my closet, like it always was when Paulie was around. I pulled it down and loaded it, then tucked it into the Galco small-of-back holster and strapped it on. Regretfully, I untucked the meerkat shirt and tugged it down to hide the gun.

So much for sartorial eloquence.

"Can you take Paulie home for me?" I asked Jay. "There's something I have to do, and I'm not sure how long it will take."

"Sure," he said. "Is it about the Amy Hartwell thing?"

"It's about the Hartwells. I don't know if it's about the thing."

Thirty minutes later, I strolled up the walkway to the Hartwell home, Ms. Birdie's key in my pocket. With a handkerchief around my hand to keep from leaving fingerprints, I rang the bell.

No answer. I wasn't surprised, but a hollow feeling settled in my gut all the same.

Ms. Birdie was right. It was too quiet.

With the handkerchief still in hand, I pushed the key into the lock and turned it. Cracked the door open, and the stench of human waste rocked me back a step.

"Cal?" I called. "Calvin Hartwell?"

I stepped inside and closed the door behind me, knowing there would be no answer.

Cal slumped on the couch, one hand still gripping the Browning Hi-Power. I knew, even before I saw the spray of blood on the wall and on the couch behind his head, that he was dead. He hadn't begun to decay, but his muscles had relaxed, releasing the contents of both bowel and bladder. Beneath the smell of feces and urine was the delicate scent of potpourri.

I circled the body, careful not to touch anything, and looked at the entrance wound. The bullet had entered beneath the chin, and there was a ragged, oozing asterisk where the explosion gases had expanded between the skin and the bone and blown out a starburst around the bullet hole. Beside him, spattered with droplets of blood, was a crumpled piece of paper that said, "God forgive me."

His eyes were glazed and unblinking. I didn't need to check for a pulse.

Instead, I peered into the kitchen and the den, then took the stairs two at a time to the second floor, where the bedrooms must be.

First room on the right, the master bedroom. I pushed the door open and glanced inside. Empty. I didn't waste my time there, but my mind registered the shoes lined up neatly on the floor of the open closet, the clothing arranged by color and type, everything ordered with military precision, except for the bed, which was still rumpled. Odd. A man like Cal, I'd have thought he'd make the bed before he offed himself. He would have wanted to leave everything in order.

The next room was a bathroom, empty.

The next door had a sign on the front. Rainbows. Butterflies. A smiling teddy bear carrying a basket of something. Berries, maybe. Or wildflowers. "Tara's Honey Tree," it said.

I pushed the door open a crack and peeked through. Brightly colored patchwork bedspread, yellow curtains, shelves filled with books, dolls, and antique teddy bears.

The little girl was sprawled across the bed, one leg dangling over the edge. Her arms were thrown up over her head, as if she'd been struggling when the gun went off. Her cheeks were streaked with blood and tears, and her nightgown was drenched with red.

Damn it. Damn it to hell.

I'd spent seven years solving homicides, seen death's thousand ugly faces, but the kids still got to me.

Somehow my legs carried me across the room. My fingers felt for a pulse, found her skin cool beneath my hand.

Too late for CPR, too late for anything.

Damn Cal.

I turned away sharply and crossed the hall, where a crayoned sign on the door was decorated with hearts, flowers, and a unicorn with a glittered horn. "Katrina's Magical Kingdom."

With a mixture of hope and dread, I opened it.

My mind let me see white lace curtains and a white lace canopy over a bed draped with a white lace-and-satin coverlet. A cut-crystal teardrop dangled from the window, splashing rainbows across the room, and over unicorn music boxes, unicorn posters, unicorn figurines, stuffed unicorns.

Only then would it let me see the splashes of red across the pillow, the spray of blood against the headboard, the thin, hunched figure half-covered by the bloody bedspread. At twelve, she was almost a woman.

It looked like she might never make it.

"Oh, Jesus," I heard myself moan.

I knew it was hopeless, but I pressed two fingers to her neck and felt a faint flutter, like the kiss of a butterfly.

She was alive.

# 27

I CALLED 911 AND FRANK CAMPANELLA, then jerked open a dresser drawer and snatched out a white Mickey Mouse T-shirt. Katrina had a single oozing entrance wound and an exit wound that had left a halo of blood on the pillow around her head.

With nothing to do but worry and wait, I held the shirt against the wounds and tried to picture the sequence of events. Cal, stricken with guilt, decides to kill himself. But he has his daughters to think of. He could send them away, but how will they survive without either parent? How can he leave them?

He steps into Katrina's room and fires the gun into her head at point blank range. Then he goes into Tara's room. Awakened by the earlier shot, she struggles against her father, but to no avail. He presses the barrel of the gun to her temple and pulls the trigger. She falls back, and, enraged by her defiance, he empties the gun into her chest. Finally, he goes into the living room, writes his plea for forgiveness, places the barrel of the gun beneath his chin, and blows his brains all over the wall behind him.

End of story.

End of guilt.

Only, it didn't quite make sense. The unmade bed still bothered me, as did the bloody stains on Tara's gown. One bullet to Katrina's head—that might have been an act of desperation, or even, in some twisted way, mercy. But someone had emptied a magazine into Tara's body. That kind of over-kill said something very different.

I remembered Cal's face at the memorial service as he hustled his children away, the way he had gotten out of the car at the school for one last hug, the way he had looked playing softball with his daughters in the front yard. And I knew that, whatever his flaws, Cal Hartwell had loved his girls.

Then there was Amy's murder, which had taken months of planning. A man who could arrange his wife's death coldly and efficiently and set up an innocent man to take the blame was not a man who would be driven to suicide by guilt.

Blessedly, the ambulance arrived, and I was hustled out of the way so the paramedics could do their jobs.

I was never so glad to turn over a task to anybody.

I met Frank and Harry in the living room, where they were examining Cal's body with their hands jammed in their pockets.

Obeying the first rule of a crime scene: Don't touch anything.

Harry nodded as I came over to them wiping the blood from my hands on the handkerchief. He said, "Things not exciting enough for you, you have to go looking for trouble?"

I grimaced at him, but something uncoiled from around my heart. If he was joking with me, he wasn't thinking of me as a murderer. I said, "The younger daughter's dead. Older one's still hanging on, but I don't know for how long."

Frank looked up at me and blinked. "What are you doing here, anyway?"

I showed him the key. "Lady down the street called me, said there was something weird going on, but she didn't want to call the police, since it was just a bad feeling. Birdie Drafon." I gave him the address.

Frank's bushy eyebrows merged into a V at the bridge of his nose. "You think Hartwell did this to himself?"

I shook my head, shrugged. "I don't know. I thought so at first, but . . ."

"But?"

"He didn't seem the type."

"You can't always tell."

"That Hartwell's handwriting?"

199

Frank leaned over the couch and peered down at the paper. "Too soon to tell. Plain block letters. Not too many distinguishing characteristics. Harry, you ready to start with the photos?"

"Uh huh."

Frank and I stepped out of the way while Harry photographed the crime scene. Standing in the doorway, he began to his immediate left, then panned around the room, taking overlapping shots. Between each shot, he stopped to painstakingly label each one. When he had completely circled the room, he went to the opposite wall and took a shot of the place he had been standing. Then he started on the body.

"You know I have to look at you on this," Frank said.

I didn't know what to say to this, so I kept quiet.

The paramedics hurried past us with a gurney, an oxygen mask over Katrina's face. Outside, the street was beginning to fill with police cars as the uniforms, the medical examiner, and the other significant personnel arrived on the scene. There was a van with the Channel 3 logo on the side.

Surprise, surprise.

I nodded toward the van. "Looks like you've sprung another leak."

"She's a stunner," he said. "Too bad she's a cockroach." He stared out at the chaos that was swiftly forming in the Hartwells' front yard.

Harry came out, blinking in the bright sunlight. "We won't know for sure until we do the gunpowder residue tests whether Hartwell did it or not. You ought to hang around until it's done."

"Harry. You don't think . . ."

"No." He gave me a half-smile. "Just, better safe than sorry."

They tested my hands and let me wash them when it was clear that I hadn't discharged a firearm recently. Then I cooled my heels at the kitchen table while Frank and Harry processed the scene. It felt strange. I knew that evidence was being placed in bags and tagged, that a technician was swabbing Cal's hands with a five percent solution of nitric acid and checking the swabs for traces of nitrates, barium, and antimony, the presence of which would prove that Cal had fired a gun shortly before his death. I wanted to be part of it all, not relegated to the kitchen hiding from the cameras.

While I waited, I tried to envision what had happened in the Hartwell house and how it related to Amy's murder. With Cal dead, the equation had suddenly and dramatically changed.

After awhile, Frank came in and said, "He did it."

"Gunpowder residue?"

"That's right."

"It doesn't fit."

"Well, maybe we'll get lucky, and Katrina will be able to tell us what happened."

"Maybe." I thought about the spray of blood on the headboard and knew the girl wouldn't be talking soon. If ever. "Any of the neighbors hear anything?"

"Nada. Not a thing."

It didn't mean much—maybe the neighbors were sound sleepers—but it made me wonder if whoever had done this had used a suppressor.

I was as certain now that Cal was innocent as I had been sure before that he wasn't.

Maybe the killer, or killers, had overpowered Cal.

Maybe.

But sitting there in the kitchen, knowing Cal had fired the Browning, I imagined a different scenario.

I LEFT THE HARTWELL HOUSE and trotted over to Ms. Birdie's. From the Channel 3 van, Ashleigh called my name, but I pretended not to hear her. She started after me, but a couple of uniformed policemen blocked her path.

Ms. Birdie's eyes welled with tears when I told her the news.

"How much more must that poor child endure?" she asked, when I got to the part about Katrina. "Will she be all right?"

"I wish I could say. Head shots are unpredictable. She could make a full recovery, or she could have varying degrees of brain damage."

"I don't know what that means. Are you saying she could be a vegetable?"

I sighed. "Ms. Birdie, it could mean anything."

She picked at a loose thread on her sleeve. "I can't believe Calvin would do such a thing. He wasn't a good husband, but he wasn't a bad man."

"I know," I said. "But there's no doubt he fired the gun that killed him. I just need to find out why."

Her moist, black currant eyes met mine. "Of course, dear. Just let me know if there's anything I can do."

"Do you know who inherits if Calvin and the girls die?" I steeled myself for the answer. "Is Valerie the next of kin?"

She cocked her head, birdlike, to one side. "Well, I suppose so, dear, but she doesn't inherit anything. She isn't even beneficiary of their insurance. Cal's will stipulates that if he and Amy both die, everything goes to the church."

"Everything to the church? What about the girls?"

"That minister of theirs gets custody. Amy wasn't really happy about that, but there was no one else."

"What about Valerie?" My stomach churned at the idea of Avery taking the girls. If he was really Walter . . .

She waved her hands. "Oh, heavens no. She didn't even like the girls that much."

"Grandparents? Aunts and uncles?"

"I don't think so. Calvin's parents were dead, and Amy's were estranged. Then her mother died just a few months ago. It's like a black cloud's been hanging over that family."

If Avery had killed the Hartwells in order to inherit, the string of deaths should end here. But if someone was systematically destroying Amy's family, then Valerie was next.

I PARKED THE VAN in her driveway just as a red Corvette with flames painted across the hood pulled out. I recognized the guy behind the wheel—limp blond hair, chiseled jaw. He looked like a British rock star. The last time I'd seen him, he was orchestrating the sound and lights for Amy's memorial program. The first time I'd seen him, he was climbing into Valerie's red Chevy.

Valerie came out of the house, holding a glass of ice water.

"I thought you weren't seeing that guy anymore," I said, trying to sound casual and not quite pulling it off.

She brushed my cheek with her lips. "Jealous?"

"Maybe a little."

"I never said I was only seeing you."

Fair enough. "Can we go in and talk for a minute?"

"I have a lot to do. Can't we talk while I work?"

"It would be better if we went inside."

She grinned. "My God, you're insatiable." Then she looked into my eyes and the smile faded. "What's wrong?"

"Let's go inside."

I led her into the living room, sat on the sofa, and patted the cushion beside me. She plopped down and tucked one leg beneath her, one arm resting across the back of the couch behind my shoulders. Her face was pale and perfectly still.

I took her hand and told her, as gently as I could, about Calvin and the girls. Then I told her my suspicions about Avery and the Church of the Reclamation and about my belief that all the deaths were somehow related and that she might be in danger.

She listened wordlessly until I'd finished. Then, "You're insane," she said. She scraped a fingernail across a stray thread from the southwestern throw that protected her sofa. "My mother's death was an accident. And Cal . . ." She stopped and gave a deep, animal moan. "Oh, God, Cal."

I pulled her into my arms. She resisted at first, then buried her face against my chest and wept.

"I don't think he did it," I said. "Not on his own. I wish you'd stay somewhere else for a few days. Until I get this sorted out."

She snuffled into my armpit. "He must have done it. Don't you see? He must have been crazy."

"He may have been crazy, but not the way you mean."

"Because the *bed* wasn't made?" She gave a little shriek of laughter and sat up. "Calvin never made a bed in his life. He thought that was woman's work."

My jaw set. "I'd still feel better if you'd find someplace else to stay. You could crash at my place for awhile."

"No, no, there's too much to do. Katrina, and the estate, and . . . Tell you what." She wiped her eyes with the heels of her hands. "If you haven't caught the bad guys in a week, I'll come to your place for a while."

"Anything could happen in a week."

"Nothing's going to happen."

"Let me stay here, then. Just in case."

"Look." Her cheeks were still wet, but she seemed to have cried herself out. "I don't blame you for being freaked out. I'm pretty freaked myself. But I got along just fine before you came along, and I'll get along just fine after you're gone. I don't need some guy to take care of me."

"This is a little different."

"Jared." She snuggled in and gave me a peck on the jaw. "I'll be spending my nights at the hospital with Katrina. Security guards all around. How much safer could it be?"

I DIDN'T LIKE IT, but there wasn't much I could do. There had been months between her mother's death and Amy's, weeks between Amy's and Cal's. Whoever was behind all this was taking his time. How long could I play Valerie's guard dog? Awhile, but not forever. All the killer had to do was wait. Which meant I had to find him first.

Thinking bleak thoughts, I swung by the office. Opened the door to the communal stairwell I shared with four other tenants. The air in the hallway was hot and dank, like a pile of old blankets in a steam room. A sharp exhalation of breath burst from the cubby hole beneath stairs, and I had a moment to register another smell, a layer of sweat and cheap after-shave, before a human pile driver surged out of the darkness wearing LeQuintus's face.

He hadn't been bluffing when he said I'd see him again.

I was too slow turning, and he hit me shoulder first, square in the chest. All the air punched out of my lungs, and the force drove me backward into the door so hard I heard the wood crack. A jolt of pain shot through my back, up through my neck and down through my tailbone. A millisecond later, the back of my head smacked the door frame. Another burst of pain, and something warm and wet trickled down the back of my neck.

Head reeling, I ducked under his arm and came up behind him. He turned to face me, pulling a ten-inch hunting knife from his belt. His eyes were cold, but he was grinning. The grin said he could think of nothing more fun than slicing me into pieces and eating my heart.

"Told you you'd be sorry, asshole," he said. "Fuck with me. Anybody fucks with me be sorry."

Shit.

I knew I should try to reason with him. Maybe it would even work. But I felt like coiled muscle and nerves scraped bare, and I couldn't seem to find the words. With the smell of Katrina's blood still in my nostrils, I reached behind my back and came up with the Colt.

"I've had a bad day, LeQuintus." I pointed the gun at his head. "Blowing your brains out might actually make me feel better."

He froze, the grin dissolving into a hard, thin line. His eyelids fluttered. In the quiet, I couldn't even hear him breathe. "You crazy, man," he said.

"No. *You* crazy, man. But I tell you what. If you get out of here right now, I won't kill you today. And if I never see you around here again, maybe I won't kill you at all."

His eyes narrowed. "You bust my ass in front of the whole fuckin' jail."

I didn't try to explain the concept of self-defense. "That's what this is about? Your reputation?"

"Ain't nothin' else worth nothin'."

Couldn't argue with that. "Then tell your buddies you came here and kicked my ass. I don't care enough to tell them otherwise. But if you try anything like this again, I swear I'll shoot you just for being stupid."

He looked at me, thinking it over. Looked down the barrel of the .45. I could almost see the tumblers in his mind turning as he tried to decide if I'd really pull the trigger.

He wasn't sure I'd shoot him.

I wasn't sure I wouldn't.

Then his big shoulders sagged and he turned away. "Crazy man like you," he said. "Shouldn't even be on the streets."

I watched his retreating back and thought back to our first encounter. I hadn't wanted to kill him then. I hadn't wanted to kill anyone.

It seemed like a long time ago.

# 28

IT TOOK SEVERAL MINUTES for my heart rate to return to normal. Then I went up to the office and bolted the door behind me. I'd planned to stay just long enough to check my messages and clear up some paperwork, but before I left, I made a quick call to the sanitation department and learned that Avery's garbage pickup was on Tuesday morning.

On the way home, I stopped by Randall's place to tell him what I'd been doing and how close I was to finding Josh.

"I think I'll find him in a day or so," I finished. "I just need to lay out your options, see how you want to handle it. One, you can leave him where he is. Two, you can call the police and have them pick him up. Three, you can charge in there like gangbusters and get him yourself. Four, I can get a friend of mine and we'll go in and get him."

He thought it over for a moment. I could tell he wanted to be the one to rush in and bring Josh home to momma. It was what he knew, that men take care of their own problems.

"What do you think I should do?" he asked. As far as I could remember, it was the first time he'd ever asked me for advice.

"Honestly? I think you should let someone else be the bad guy."

Slowly, he nodded. "Let someone else be the bad guy. Sure. That makes sense."

"I know you don't want to bring the police in on this. I don't mind doing it, Randall."

"You sure?" He searched my face, and I knew he was looking for some trace of reluctance. "I don't want him to resent you, either."

"He'll forgive me. I'm not his father."

He nodded again. His eyes brimmed with tears. "Go get my son, then, Jared," said my brother, who did not, after all, wish his oldest child dead. "Bring my boy back home."

I WAS DEAD ON MY FEET by the time I pulled on a pair of black jeans and a black Harley Davidson shirt, warmed up some vegetarian stroganoff Jay had put in the fridge for me, popped a couple of No-Doze, and went back downtown to stake out The Masquerade Club.

On the best of days, there's nothing glamorous about a stakeout. You sit in your car, and you wait for something to happen, trying not to eat or drink too much because the Murphy's Law of Surveillance said that, if anything exciting was going to happen, it would happen while you were taking a leak.

I knew there was a chance Josh wouldn't show up at the club—that I might have spooked him on Friday night. On the other hand, I hadn't been there last night, so he might have been lulled into a false sense of security. Granted, he should have known me better than that. But his judgment of character seemed to have been skewed lately, and I wasn't sure he'd give me credit for brains enough to feed myself, let alone to find him and bring him home.

At two in the morning., I finally saw him. He was wearing a purple, lace-front shirt, tight black pants with D-rings down one side, and a short black cape with a deep blue lining. He looked like a bruise. He was holding hands with a man in a scarlet pirate shirt and black leather pants. From where I was, I couldn't see the partner's face well, but he looked older than Josh. Late twenties, early thirties. Too old to be holding hands with a fifteen-year-old.

I was halfway out of the car before I reined myself in and took a deep breath. Slid back behind the wheel and clenched my fists around it. If Josh had run away to be with the Pirate Shirt, I needed to know where the Pirate Shirt lived.

At four-thirty, I followed them to a run-down Richardsonian Romanesque house just off West End. Two minutes after the door had slammed behind them, I was knocking on it.

The man in the scarlet shirt opened the door. I could see candles flickering inside. "Who are you?" he demanded.

"I want to talk to Josh."

"Oh." He curled his lip. "You're the cop. He doesn't want to talk to you."

"He doesn't have a choice."

His eyes narrowed. He'd darkened the area around them so it looked liked he'd been punched. "This is my home. You don't have any jurisdiction here."

"My nephew is a minor," I said pleasantly. "You can let me talk to him, or explain to the police what he's doing here. How old exactly *are* you, Mr . . ."

"You can call me Razor," he said. "And you can go fuck yourself."

"I'm getting that a lot lately," I said, and called past him, "Hey, Josh! You going to make me call the cops on your boyfriend?"

"Get out of here." Razor tried to shove the door closed, but I jammed my foot into the opening. Winced as the door slammed hard against my instep.

Josh stepped out of the darkness and said, "It's all right Razor. I'll talk to him."

"You don't have to."

Josh scowled at me. "You don't know him. If he says he'll call the cops on you, he will. He's pigheaded, like my father."

"Seems to run in the family," I said.

He glared and said, "Well, don't just stand there. Come inside."

Razor's house was decorated in late *Dark Shadows*, early *Addams Family*. It had a certain morbid elegance, from the livid purple velvet draperies to the red satin throw pillows on the black leather couch. An authentic-looking fiberglass skull, flanked by candelabras, leered at us from the mantel. Josh gestured toward the sofa, then sat down in the chair opposite.

Razor disappeared into the kitchen.

"Do you want something to drink?" Josh asked. "Or are you afraid I'll poison you?"

"I'm fine, thanks," I said. I didn't think Josh would poison me, but I wasn't certain about Razor.

"I'm not going back," he said. "You can't make me."

I arched an eyebrow. "You think I can't?"

He sighed and crossed his legs at the knee. "All right. I guess you can. But you can't make me stay." He gestured to his crossed legs. "Does this bother you?"

"No. Should it?"

"I just wondered. You and my father. So irredeemably masculine. It bothers him."

"Josh, I live with a gay man."

"Yeah." He blinked. "But it's different when it's your own blood, isn't it?"

"This isn't about you being gay."

"Isn't it?"

I rubbed my temples. "If you're gay, Randall will learn to accept it. But this other . . ."

"It's who I am."

"Girl at the Underground says you drink blood."

His cheeks flushed. "What if I do? It's between two consenting . . ." He stopped.

"Adults?" I finished for him.

"People. Two consenting people."

"Ever heard of AIDS?"

He uncrossed his legs and leaned forward. "I'm not going to get AIDS. But what if I do? Look around, man. The world sucks. Life sucks. Things are getting worse and worse, and there's nothing we can do about it. Death's not something to moan and cry about. It's—"

"But life is?" My tone was sharper than I'd intended.

"You don't understand. Life is . . . what it is. You have to suffer through it. But death . . . that's something to be embraced."

210

"Yeah?" I asked bitterly. "Jay might disagree with you."

He looked down at his lap.

"You make me sick," I said. He looked up sharply. "I mean it. You have a father who'd eat nails for you, a mother who thinks you hung the moon, a little sister who adores you, no matter how weird you get. You have a strong, healthy body, which Jay would give anything for, and a sharp, intelligent mind, which I'd give anything if Paulie had. You have everything, and all you can do is sit around and whine about how bad your life is."

He looked away, eyes glistening. "I didn't expect you to understand."

"I understand," I said. "I understand that you're sitting here like a spoiled child while your parents grieve their guts out for you."

Razor stepped into the doorway. "I think you'd better leave now."

"Not without Josh."

Josh opened his mouth, but Razor cut him short. "He isn't coming with you. He's not going back to that hellhouse, where nobody understands or gives a damn about him."

I looked at Josh, then to the door behind Razor, where three men in black regalia poured into the room.

"You see?" said Razor. "Five of us. One of you. Bye-bye."

"Go home, Uncle Jared," Josh said. "I don't want you to get hurt."

"Josh—" I started, then stopped. I knew I could do some serious damage to this mob and still end up getting my ass kicked. I looked at Razor and his buddies. I looked at Josh. He couldn't meet my gaze.

A dull ache pulsed behind my left eye.

I laid a hand on Josh's shoulder and said, "I'll be back."

I WANTED TO GET AN ARSENAL and go back after him. Instead, I did the next best thing. I called Billy Mean. "You up for a little adventure?"

"Any time, man. What's up?"

I filled him in. "I don't think there'll be trouble, but there could be."

"*Could* be," he said. "Aw, you're just tryin' to get my hopes up."

I picked him up in the van and we drove down West End and back to the house where I'd just seen Josh.

This time a wild-eyed, emaciated young woman answered the door. She was the same girl I'd seen on Elliston Place, the one Absinthe had called Medea.

"Where's Josh?" I asked.

"Not here."

"And Razor?"

"Not here, either."

"Oh." I moved forward, leaving her no choice but to step aside or use bodily force to stop me. She gave my chest a feeble thump, and then I was past her. Mean Billy followed me in.

"We'll wait," I said.

"They won't be back 'til late."

I sat down on the sofa and put my feet up on the black glass coffee table. "We'll wait," I said again. Billy sat down in the chair Josh had used just a few hours before.

"You can't stay here," she said, with a smug smile. "I'll call the police."

I smiled back. "Please do."

Her smile faltered. "You have no right to be here. Nightbreed doesn't want you."

I stretched my arms across the back of the sofa. "Nightbreed, as you call him, is a minor. What he wants doesn't matter. Not this time. His parents sent me here to bring him back, and I plan to do that, with or without your cooperation. Or his, for that matter. Now, either you go fetch Josh, or my friend and I are camping here until Hell freezes over."

The hostility that leaked from her eyes would have fueled several small wars. I looked at Billy and grinned. Billy heaved a sigh and clomped his size eleven biker boots onto the coffee table.

Medea whirled and stalked from the room, her long lace skirt swirling around her legs.

It was Razor who came in, which was just what I expected. "Barbarians," he said. "Take your filthy feet off of my furniture."

"Sure, Buddy. Happy to." Slowly, I removed my feet from the table. Mean Billy scraped his heels across the glass and set them on the floor.

Razor ground his teeth and said, "I told you you weren't welcome here."

"Oh, that's right." I slapped my forehead with the heel of my hand. "You did."

"I want you out of my house."

"People in Hell want ice water, but they ain't gettin' it. I want my nephew. Is he listening, by the way? Because it would be better if he were."

"Just say your piece and get the hell out of my house."

"I'd like to save you some trouble," I said. "More trouble than you can imagine."

"You can't do anything to me."

"Oh, but you're wrong, Razor. I can do plenty to you. How old did you say you were?"

"I didn't."

"That's right. But you said this was your house. You own it?"

Warily. "Yes."

"Which makes you over eighteen. Which makes you guilty of, at the very least, contributing to the delinquency of a minor. Now, if you and Josh have had sex, *that* makes you guilty of statutory rape. If Josh leaves now, maybe his parents won't press charges." Yeah. Right. "If he stays here . . ." I shrugged. "Prison is a nasty place, Razor. I don't think a young man of your obviously sensitive nature would survive it. What do you think, Mean Billy?"

Billy clicked his tongue. "Dead in a month, would be my guess."

Razor's lip twitched. "You're just trying to scare me."

I grinned as menacingly as I knew how. "That's right, Razor. We are. Because you're going to be scared now, or you are going to be worse than scared later."

He drew himself up to his full height, five-nine or so, and I uncoiled myself from the couch and stepped into his personal space. He flinched away from me, but didn't give ground.

"How dare you?" he demanded, in a voice that might have seemed imperious if it hadn't been trembling. "How dare you threaten me in my own home?"

"Razor," I said. "That boy is my flesh and blood, and I'll do a lot worse than threaten you if he's not in my car within the next fifteen minutes."

"Lancelot!" he called. "Nightshade! Hellwind! To me!"

The three ghouls from earlier in the night charged into the room and stopped short as they saw me spin their leader toward me and wrap my arm around his neck. The palm of my other hand cupped his forehead. "Don't make me snap his neck," I said. Razor made a high-pitched, keening sound.

Mean Billy rolled to his feet, fast and fluid in spite of his bulk. He settled into a martial arts stance, left leg forward, right leg back, hands up and ready for action.

"I wouldn't," Mean Billy said, as one of the ghouls started toward him. "Special Forces, Vietnam. Back off, boys, and my buddy and I will let you live."

"Stop!" Josh's cry cut through the room like a katana. "Don't hurt him, Uncle Jared. Please."

I nodded. "Go get your things, Josh. Put them in the car, and wait there. Billy and I will be out in a minute."

"You won't hurt him?" he asked, eyes wide.

"I won't hurt him."

"I'm sorry, Razor," Josh said in a small voice.

Razor had stopped struggling. "It's all right, Nightbreed. It's not your fault you're related to assholes."

I released my hold on Razor enough to make him a little more comfortable, but not enough to give him any ideas. When Josh had taken his duffel bag—ironically, it was Randall's—to the car, I let Razor go. He lurched away from me, rubbing his throat.

As we backed out the door, one of the ghouls rushed us. Mean Billy dropped him with a meaty punch to the gut, and the others fell back, mumbling curses.

"Two of us. Four of you. Bye-bye," I said, misquoting Razor.

Billy hurled his bulk into the front seat, whooping like a wild man. "Man, what a rush. Only next time, pick some bad guys who can really fight."

Josh stared out the window, arms folded across his body like the sleeves of a straitjacket. "You should have left me alone," he said. "You didn't have to hurt him."

I sighed. "Josh, I didn't hurt him. I scared him a little. How old is he, anyway?"

He hesitated. "Twenty-eight."

"I know you think you have it all figured out, but…"

"I'll just run away again," he said. "I'll go somewhere else."

"Josh," I said. "You run away a hundred times, that's how many times I'll find you."

"Why?" His red-rimmed eyes met mine in the rearview mirror. "Why can't you just let me be?"

"Because, Kid," Mean Billy said. "He loves you."

I DROPPED BILLY OFF at his place, then took Josh home. I saw his tear-streaked face in the rearview mirror, and a knot formed in my throat.

"Josh," I said, pulling into the driveway and turning off the ignition.

"What?"

"I know you think your dad is mad at you right now. I know you think he's a heartless hardass who doesn't understand or care about you. But when I told him I knew where you were, he cried. He told me to do whatever it took to bring you back home."

He wiped at his eyes with one sleeve. "Yeah, sure. Like he cares."

"He cares so much it hurts. Look, he isn't like you. We grew up in a different time. Men didn't cry. We didn't talk about our feelings. We just sucked it up. This is hard for him."

His voice wavered. "It's hard for me, too."

"I know it is. But aren't you supposed to be the open-minded one? Aren't you supposed to be the tolerant and sensitive one?"

He nodded, hiccupped.

"Okay. Well, how about saving some of that stuff for your dad?"

"Why?" he cried. "Why do I have to be the one to understand everything?"

"Because," I said, gently. "He doesn't know how."

We sat in silence for a moment. Then the porch light flicked on and Wendy and Caitlin hurtled out the door in their bathrobes.

"Do you think he'll let me see Razor sometimes?" he asked.

I sighed. "I don't know. I know you think you're all grown up, but you're not old enough to be having a sexual relationship with a twenty-eight-year-old man."

He bit his lip. "I'm old enough to love."

Outside, Wendy stopped and hugged herself, gnawing at a thumbnail. Caitlin stood behind her, hair tousled, eyes uncertain.

"Give them a chance, Josh," I suggested. "No one could love you more."

He nodded slowly and pushed the car door open.

"Josh?" Wendy's voice cracked. Then she opened her arms and he stepped into them, tucking his head into the arc of her neck.

"Thank you," she mouthed over his shoulder.

Caitlin hauled the duffel bag out of the car, paused to lean across the seat, and kissed me lightly on the cheek.

As I pulled out of the driveway, Randall stepped out of the house and strode across the lawn. He looked at me for a moment, his expression unreadable. Then he turned his face away and gathered his family into his arms.

# 29

WITH JOSH SAFE AT HOME, exhaustion hit, and hit hard. My temples throbbed, and I couldn't seem to get my eyes to focus. I couldn't remember when I'd last gotten a good night's sleep. Maybe since Josh had run away. Maybe since Heather had stepped into my life. Too long, anyway. I headed blearily back to my place and crawled into bed.

Sleep didn't come easy. Every time I closed my eyes, I saw Tara's broken body behind my eyelids, the splashes of red on Katrina's white lace.

I'd been away from the Job for awhile, long enough for the protective veneer to crack. But I was a good homicide cop. I knew how to detach, and finally, fitfully, I slept.

On Monday morning, I settled in for another surveillance of Samuel Avery. When the black sedan pulled out of the driveway, I sighed and steeled myself for another exciting Piggly Wiggly run. This time, though, the sedan rolled onto I-40, edged into the downtown traffic, and made its way to West End, where a series of convoluted twists and turns led him to a dirty white clapboard building with a sign in the window that said, "Massage."

Ministering to the whores of Babylon?

I snapped a couple of photos as he went in and a few more when he came out an hour later, dabbing at his bald pate with a handkerchief. There was a spring in his step that hadn't been there when he went in, and while a good massage could do that, I suspected he'd had something a bit more intimate.

I stuck with him until he pulled into the driveway of the parsonage. Then I drove on past, stopped at an ATM to make a withdrawal, and headed back to the massage parlor.

A bell tinkled as I pushed the door open, and a pale

woman with tortured white-blond hair looked up from the scarred desk where she was polishing her nails.

"Help you?" she asked.

"What are your prices?"

"Thirty dollars for an hour. Swedish or Oriental."

I cocked my head and grinned. "What if I had something else in mind?"

She pursed her lips. They were fire-engine red. "We're not that kind of business."

"Friend of mine says you are." I gave her a conspiratorial wink. "Heavyset guy. Mostly bald. Mid-to-late fifties. He was in here just a little while ago."

"You a cop?" she asked. The standard ritual.

"Nope."

"'Cause you look like a cop."

I laughed. "What does a cop look like?"

She made a wry face and fanned her wet nails. "It's the way you walk. You walk like Marshall Fucking Dillon."

"I'll give you fifty for a blow job," I said, and she visibly relaxed. A police officer wouldn't have made an offer. "Or whatever my friend had."

Now she was all smiles. "Sammy? He likes Leona. Hundred-and-fifty for a full massage and a blow job or hand job. Fifty more if you want to get laid."

I whistled. "I didn't know Sam was such a big spender."

"Yeah, well, you can never tell." She held up her hands to admire her nails. "So, you want to book Leona or not?"

I pretended to think it over. "Why not? You only live once."

The massage room was cramped and dingy, with the dank smell of sex and mildew.

A dark-haired woman with café-au-lait skin met me at the door. She was wearing three-inch heels and a black satin robe with a crimson dragon embroidered on one lapel.

"You must be Leona," I said.

The woman from the desk waved me in. "Give him the

219

works," she said, and returned to her manicure.

Leona stepped around me and closed the door. "The works, huh?" She traced one cherry red claw down my arm. "Mmm. I like a man with muscles. Why don't you get undressed and lie down on the table?"

She reached for my shirt buttons.

I caught her wrist and stepped back. "I'd rather talk about Sammy." Her eyes narrowed, and I could tell she knew who I meant. I described him anyway. "What can you tell me about him?"

"Nothing." Her tone was hostile, but there was something else in her eyes—fear, helplessness, a sense of resignation. "It's none of your business."

"Look," I said. "I'm not here to hassle you. It would be a shame to have to call my friends in Vice to come in here and shut you down. Especially considering the valuable service you provide."

"Damn straight, valuable service. You gonna bust me?"

"I'm not a cop," I said. "I just want to know what you can tell me about Samuel Avery. The guy who was in here about forty minutes ago." I pulled a fifty from my wallet and held it out between two fingers.

She snatched it away and stuffed into the crease between her breasts. "What do you want to know?"

"Whatever you know. How often does he come here? Rough trade or pussycat?"

"Pussycat," she said, baring her teeth in an artificial smile. "Couple of times a week. Nothing kinky. An occasional slap on the ass, but no real rough stuff."

"He come in at the same time every week?"

She nodded. "Like clockwork."

"How about Fridays? He come in on Friday nights?"

"No, he comes in the daytime. During the week."

So. All that sinning, and it didn't even win him an alibi. It didn't mean he didn't have one—Margaret might be telling the truth—but it made me mighty happy all the same.

# 30

AT 2:00 A.M., A CRUISE THROUGH Avery's neighborhood told me he had two hunter green, thirty-nine gallon garbage cans and glossy plastic lawn and leaf bags with twist ties.

At 3:00, after a detour to Wal-Mart, I drove by again. This time, I stopped long enough to exchange two brand-new lawn and leaf bags stuffed with crumpled paper and cheap dishtowels for Avery's, which were, if fate was smiling on me, full of information.

In the pale circle made by Jay's side porch light, I dumped out the bags and pulled on a pair of rubber medical gloves. Then I sat cross-legged on the ground and sifted through the soggy detritus of Avery's week. Sodden paper towels, old coffee grounds, broken eggshells with a sticky sheen. The glamorous life of the private detective.

The smell wasn't as bad as a decomposing body, and it wasn't as bad as the mess I'd found at the Hartwell house. Still, I wondered if I'd ever get the stink of stale coffee, rancid yogurt and rotting vegetables off of my skin. Even through the gloves, I could feel the slimy slickness of decomposing broccoli.

The screen door creaked open, and Jay stepped out onto the side porch wearing a pair of tartan pajamas. "My God," he said. "What's that stench?"

"Just fishing," I said. "I didn't mean to wake you."

"You didn't." He sat down on the steps and hugged himself. "I couldn't sleep."

I didn't ask why. Bad dreams. Night sweats. If he wanted me to know, he'd tell me. I held up a blackening banana peel and said, "Wanna play?"

"I'll pass."

"Chicken."

While I sorted through the trash, I filled Jay in on everything, from Avery's fondness for hookers to the grisly scene at the Hartwells'.

"Does Frank have any theories?" he asked, when I'd finished.

"He thinks Amy's murder may have been incidental to framing me. Beyond that, he's not saying. Look at this." A pile of stained strips of paper told me Avery was a shredder. And since people don't usually shred things like letters from Aunt Mabel, I set the strips aside.

"What do you do with those?" Jay asked.

"I'll show you when we get inside."

When I'd been through it all, I had a couple of ice cream cartons and four Dixie cups that might have Avery's fingerprints and three piles of shredded strips, each about the size of a pith helmet. I stuffed what was left back into the bags, scooped up my treasure trove of shredded paper, and went inside to dump it on the kitchen table.

"I don't see how you're going to get much out of those," he said, whisking the salt and pepper shakers to the safety of the counter. "They all look the same."

I showed him how to match the perforations and the fragments of type on the strips and then glue them onto poster board to recreate the original. It was tedious. Like watching paint dry. No, worse. Like painting your bedroom wall and blowing on it until it dried.

"Now, this I can do," he said. He pulled on a pair of gloves and picked up a strip, fluttered it at me. "Why don't you go out and investigate something while I put these together?"

I reached for the glue. "You don't want to spend your day doing this. It sucks. It's monotonous."

"I program computers," he said. "Monotony is my life."

"I'll let you help," I said. "But no way am I letting you do it all. I don't need that kind of karma."

By suppertime, we'd reconstructed Avery's credit card bill, his telephone bill, his most recent bank statement, the church's bank statement, and the reverend's social security number.

"Nice work," I told Jay, picking up one of his posters.

He looked tired but pleased. "It's not that hard once you get the hang of it. Just time-consuming. Is there anything here you can use?"

I gave him my passwords and showed him how to search the databases. It was like teaching Mozart how to play the xylophone. By bedtime, we'd learned that Avery had gotten his first driver's license at the ripe old age of fifty-four, that he'd married the well-to-do Margaret just this past April, that there were no personal or church records before February of this year, and that the church had paid out over $240,000 in maintenance fees to a company called "Fogerty and Sons".

Call me crazy, but that seemed like a lot of maintenance.

The next morning, I turned to the phone books and the courthouse records. There were four Samuel Averys of the right age in Nashville and the surrounding areas, but only one with the middle name Zebedee. Samuel Zebedee Avery, born sixty-three years ago to parents Lacey and Ozell Avery. I found an obituary for Ozell, but Lacey's last recorded address was Pine Ridge Nursing Home in Antioch.

It wasn't far, and twenty minutes later, I was at the Pine Ridge Home for the Aged and Infirm.

"Lacey Avery," I said to the woman at the front desk.

"Room 211."

I thanked her and walked down the long institutional-green corridor to Lacey's room. The hallway smelled of urine and cheap industrial cleaner.

Lacey's room was small, with pale yellow walls that made it look larger than it was. It smelled like the hallway, but with a dusting of baby powder. The bed, standard hospital-issue, was draped in a navy crocheted coverlet. The gaps in the design showed the pale blue bedspread underneath. Photographs festooned the walls. Her family, I assumed.

None of them resembled Avery.

On the far side of the room, a small, hunched figure sat in a rocking chair facing the window. A black leather Bible with gilt-edged pages lay across her lap.

"Mrs. Avery?" I asked.

She cocked her head to one side and smiled. Her ivory skin was clear and sweetly wrinkled, her refined features nothing like Avery's blunt bulges. I thought she must have been a beauty in her day.

"Yes?" she asked. "What is it? Time for my medicine already?"

"No, Ma'am." I stepped across the room and knelt beside her chair. Her cloudy blue eyes followed me. Not blind then, but nearly. "I'd like to talk to you about your son." I didn't tell her who I was, and she didn't ask.

"Jeremiah?" A look of alarm crossed her face, and her chin quivered. "Is he all right?"

"He's fine," I said, as gently as I knew how. "It's Samuel I need to ask you about."

"Samuel." She clutched her Bible to her chest and rocked, forward and back, forward and back. "Poor little thing." She reached out and touched my face with a gnarled hand. "Do I know you?"

"No. I'm just looking for some answers. What happened to Samuel?"

"They say I smell bad," she said. "Do I smell bad to you?"

I leaned in and touched my cheek to hers. "You smell fine. Nice. Like roses."

She gave me a sad smile.

I smiled back and said, "Samuel. Can you tell me what happened to him?"

Her eyes welled, and she rocked again, stroking the Bible as if it were a child. Then the words tumbled out of her as if my prompt had pulled out an invisible stopper. "I only left him for a minute. The beans were boiling over, and I went to lower the

224

heat. Young people know better now, but in those days...I only left him for a minute."

Her hand trembled, and I laid my hand across hers. It felt fleshless, fragile, like a newly hatched robin. "It was an accident," I said. "How did it happen?"

"The little creek," she said. Her eyes were glazed, and I knew she was seeing it again. "Who would have thought? Hardly ever any water in it, but we'd just had the spring rains . . . Poor little thing. He was only three years old the day he drowned."


SO, SAMUEL ZEBEDEE AVERY was dead.

The reverend had constructed a whole new persona from the dead child's identity. He'd searched the obituaries for an infant or toddler who would be the right age if he'd lived, obtained a copy of the birth certificate, and used that to apply for a driver's license and social security card.

It was the most common and least risky way to create a new identity. It didn't prove that Avery was Walter Christy, but it meant he had something to hide.

I took the ice cream cartons and the Dixie cups by Frank's office and asked him to run the prints.

"You're bringing me garbage now?" he groused. "After all I've done for you?"

"I'm solving your case. You should be grateful."

"My case is solved," he grumbled. "Calvin Hartwell. His girlfriend hasn't cracked yet, but she will."

"I don't think so."

"You're not clear yet, either, you know. Just because Hartwell offed himself doesn't mean he's the one who did his wife. Maybe he was overcome by grief."

I ignored the speculation. "You still got those pictures our guy planted in my car?"

"Yeah. Why?"

"Can I look at them again?"

He frowned. "What for?"

225

"Just let me see them."

He spun his chair around and reached into the bottom drawer of his filing cabinet. "Here." He tossed me the file. "I've seen sicker, but it's bad enough. They're doctored."

"Doctored, how?"

"Katrina's head, some other kid's body. Maybe got the body off the Internet."

I opened the file, and Katrina Hartwell's pensive features stared back at me. I was relieved to know she hadn't posed for the photos, but it was a small consolation. Someone had posed for them.

"You remember Walter's photos?" I asked.

"Christ, what's this jones you got for Walter? Walter's dead, for God's sake."

"Humor me."

"Okay. Yeah, I remember them."

"Little girls and white cotton panties. Wearing them, holding them. Always the white panties."

"So?"

I showed him the photographs. "The white cloth in her hand. Panties. I'm telling you, this is about Walter."

"You think Avery's Walter. But I met him, and I didn't think the resemblance was that strong."

"A lot can change in thirteen years. He would have aged, gained weight, gotten balder . . ."

"That doesn't change the fact that he's dead."

"*Maybe* he's dead. Explosion like that, I bet there wasn't much of an autopsy."

"I guess not." He stuffed the file back into the cabinet and picked up the bag with Avery's fingerprints in it. "I'll run these, if it will ease your mind. But don't get your hopes up."

"I never do."

His smile was smug. "Bullshit," he said. "You already have."

ON THURSDAY MORNING, I was wrenched out of a sound sleep by the shrilling of the telephone. I managed to force my eyes open and felt for the receiver of the cordless phone I kept on the bedside table.

"Yeah."

"Yeah?" I recognized Frank's gruff voice. "What kind of way is that to answer the phone? Your mama raise you in a barn?"

"Frank."

"It's ten o'clock. You still asleep?"

"Not anymore. What's up?"

His voice lost all its jocularity. "That woman you say you were with the night of Amy Hartwell's murder..."

"The woman I *was* with."

"Barbed wire and blue rose tattoo around the right ankle? Butterfly tattoo on the left shoulder?"

"Yeah. That's what I said."

"I think we've found her. But we need you to come down and I.D. her for us."

"Sure." My brain still wasn't functioning, but a vague uneasiness was seeping through the fog in my mind. "I can be there in an hour. Is that soon enough?"

His sigh was heavy. "Take your time, son. She ain't going anywhere."

"Aw, no. Don't tell me, Frank."

I could almost hear him nod. "She's in the morgue."

# 31

"I T AIN'T PRETTY." Frank stood beside the metal morgue table and unzipped the plastic body bag. "She's been dead awhile."

The smell knocked me back a step. In Nashville's humid heat, a body could be skeletonized within a matter of weeks, but the woman on the slab was still recognizable. Barely. I covered my nose and mouth with my hand and prayed for olfactory fatigue.

"What's awhile?"

"Probably since the night you picked her up. That's when she apparently went missing."

"Buried?" Burial would slow decomposition.

"He wrapped her in plastic first." He gave a little bark of humorless laughter. "Garbage bags."

Freudian, pragmatic, or a deliberate message? *This woman is garbage.*

What was left of her face and neck were dark red, indicating manual strangulation. A ring of deep, livid, broken bruises marked the place where the ligature had been.

Something besides insects had been at her.

"It's her," I said. "Any idea who she was?"

"Hooker. Worked the Dickerson Pike area."

My bowels clenched. Ninety percent or more of the hookers who work that area are HIV positive. "Any connection to Amy Hartwell?"

"Not that we could find."

I tried to keep the fear from my voice, tried not to think of the pills, the pneumonia, the purple lesions that advertised the presence of Kaposi's sarcoma. I tried not to think of AIDS.

I said, "There must be something."

"We figure she was hired to set you up. Fingerprints, DNA. Then whoever hired her decided she was more of a liability than she was worth."

"'Two people can keep a secret if one of them is dead.'"

"Exactly."

I remembered the fresh bruises on her face. "She must have let him hit her."

He zipped the bag. There was something sad about watching the opaque plastic close over her face. I thought of the note she'd left. *I'm sorry.* In spite of what she'd done to me, I felt a rush of sorrow for the person she might have been, for all the broken dreams, and for the pitiful, pathetic thing she had become.

"They didn't use your gun on this one," he said. "For whatever that's worth."

*They.* I cleared my throat before I spoke, but my voice still sounded strained. "You don't think I did it."

He rolled the body back into the freezer. "If I thought you did, we wouldn't be here. Anyway, a couple of hikers found the body out near the lake. Buried shallow, looked like something got at her, maybe dogs, maybe a coyote. That's why they found her. Saw a foot sticking out of the ground."

"Jesus."

"She's been dead about three weeks, give or take. Another hooker, works the same stretch of road, says she saw the victim get into a red Corvette at about seven-thirty the same night Amy was killed. We found gray fibers matching the ones on Amy Hartwell's body. We figure those came from the carpet in the Corvette. No license number, naturally."

"Naturally."

"Our witness was so hopped up on crank it was a wonder she remembered anything, let alone the license plate."

"Does Avery have an alibi for that time frame?"

"Home in bed with his wife."

Too bad. "She credible?"

"Credible enough, since there's no evidence against him."

"Heather's friend. Where could I find her?"

"Try driving up and down Dickerson Pike until you spot a white woman with her hair a kind of purple red. Street name's Shannon. This morning, she was wearing a leopard-print bustier and a black leather mini-skirt. Black panties. Ask me how I know."

I didn't need to. Lot of these girls got a rush out of flashing their arresting officers.

"Mind if I go see if I can get anything else out of her?"

"Be my guest."

I didn't ask the other question I had, the one I wasn't sure I wanted the answer to. He answered it anyway.

"There's something else you want to know," he said.

"What's that?"

He looked at ceiling, at the shiny metal instruments, at the slanted metal tables with their faucets and gizmos. Anywhere but at me. "She tested positive."


I'D USED A CONDOM, I told myself. I couldn't have been infected; I'd used a condom. But I'd performed cunnilingus on her, which was not without its risks.

If I'd known she was a whore . . .

But I hadn't known. And what difference did it make? The risks were what they were. Only suddenly, the risk factor had multiplied.

Whoever she was, I should have been more careful.

The worst part was, it would be months before I knew. I'd have to be tested in three months, then again in three more. That was a heck of a long wait to know if you were dying.

My mouth filled with the metallic taste of genuine fear. Beatings by thugs, broken bones, a quick bullet—I'd never been too afraid of those. The quick rush of adrenaline when a gun was pointed at my head, that sudden awareness of mortality, that wasn't fear. That was preparation. Even at Caleb Wilford's hunting lodge, with my blood pooling beneath Frank's hands, I'd felt more shocked than frightened. But the thought of the long slow death that was AIDS, the wasting, the cancers, the eventual dementia . . . I wondered how Jay lived with this crushing fear.

"You okay?" Frank pushed me down into a metal folding chair and handed me a cup of water.

"I'm okay." I took a sip, noticed that my hand was trembling. Thought of Valerie. We'd used condoms. We hadn't done anything that might put her at risk.

"You been thinking about what I said?" Frank asked. "About this being about you?"

"I've been thinking about it. But this pretty much proves Amy was the target."

"How you figure that?"

"If all that mattered was framing me for murder—just any murder—they could have just planted all that evidence on Heather and left photos of *her* in my car."

"Hope," he said.

"What?"

"Her name was Hope. Heather was her street name."

"Hope." The irony of the name wasn't lost on me. "They could have just framed me for her murder. Why kill *two* women, if all that mattered was I go to jail? And if they were going to kill both women anyway, why not just frame me for both?"

He grunted. "Who says they haven't? Just because I don't think you killed her doesn't mean nobody else will."

"They didn't use my gun on Hope, and they hid her body. Somehow it was important for Amy to be the one I was supposed to have killed, and somehow it was important for you to think I'd taken those pictures of Katrina."

"Just think about it, okay?" He jangled the keys in his pockets. "Somebody about your height and build. Who knew you'd be a sucker for a lady with a hard-luck story. Who knew Maria called you 'Cowboy.' Someone who knew the combination to your glove compartment, and that you'd have your piece in there."

231

"What are you getting at?"

"I think you know."

"No."

"He knows the combination to the lock."

"Hell, everybody in the family knows. Ashleigh announced it over Sunday dinner, thought it was a big joke. 'He knows his horse's *birthday*. It's the combination to his glove box.'"

"But Randall knows the exact date."

"It wouldn't be that hard to find. Besides, if Randall hated me that much, he'd just shoot me and be done with it."

"All I'm saying is, somebody knows an awful lot about you. How sure are you that Randall wasn't banging Amy Hartwell?"

I thought of Wendy's tear-streaked face. *Ask him where he goes when I wake up at night and he's not there.*

"I'd bet my life on it," I said.

"Good." His voice was somber. "Because that's exactly what you're doing."

HE WAS WRONG about Randall. My brother might have reason to resent me, but he would never kill a woman or take pornographic pictures of a child.

I drove up and down Dickerson Pike for an hour and a half, looking for Heather's—Hope's—friend, seething at Frank's suspicions and reminding myself that he had my best interests at heart.

Then I saw her, a tall girl with purple-red hair, maybe five-nine without the three-inch spiked heels she was wearing. She had on black fishnet hose under her miniskirt, and nothing under the bustier, which had been laced so that a three-inch gap showed most of her cleavage and a fair amount of torso. Her nipples were covered, barely, but as she turned to face me, I caught a glimpse of aureole.

I pulled over, reached across the seat, and shoved open the passenger side door. "You Shannon?" I asked.

She stared at me, chomping on a wad of gum the size of an apricot. "Who wants to know?"

I grinned and arched my eyebrows. "I have a hundred bucks says, what do you care?"

"Show."

I slipped a hundred out of my wallet. On a normal case, this would be considered an expense, and the client would reimburse me for it. This time, I was the client, so once it left my pocket, it would stay gone.

I waggled the bill at her.

"You a cop?"

"Nope."

She got in.

"Okay." She slammed the door, hard. "For a hundred bucks, what the hell?"

I shook my head and pulled away from the curb. They'd go anywhere, these girls. With her friend newly dead, it still hadn't occurred to Shannon that she might be in danger. Or maybe it did, and she just didn't care. "Buckle up," I said.

She gave me a funny look, but pulled the seat belt across her lap. "What gives?"

"You were friends with a girl named Hope? Called herself Heather?"

Her eyes narrowed. "I thought you said you weren't a cop."

"I'm not."

"What you want to know about Hope for?"

There were track marks on the inside of her arms, but she seemed to have come down from the high she'd been on when Frank questioned her.

I glanced at her from the corner of my eye. "Cause I'm the guy she helped set up for murder."

She shrank back against the door. "Oh, my God."

"She tell you about that, did she?"

"She called me from the dressing room when the john was buying her new clothes. Said he gave her five hundred bucks to let him beat her up, and she'd get five hundred more if she could get you into bed and bring him something with your fingerprints, a couple strands of hair and the used rubber."

"And it never occurred to her to wonder why?"

She popped her gum and shrugged. "Hey, man, a thousand bucks. Nobody gonna turn that down."

"Some people would."

She shrugged again. "Girl's gotta live."

A flush of anger started at the top of my head and washed downward. "You gonna live, Shannon? You got the virus? Gonna pass it to some poor schmoe who never did you any harm?"

"Hey, man." It was her turn to redden. "You pays your money and you takes your chances. Anyway, some pig wants to pay me to rut around like some kind of animal, what do you expect? Guy's an exploiter. He deserves what he gets."

"For buying what you're selling?"

"For being a pig."

It hadn't been like that. Had it? I'll admit that Heather—Hope—had meant next to nothing to me. A night of pleasant company, an enjoyable diversion from the thought of Maria with D.W. But the desire had been mutual—or so I'd thought. If anyone had been exploited, it had been me.

"So." I decided not to argue the point. "Who's the guy who hired her?"

She snorted derisively. "You think he gave her his name?"

"Could be."

"Well, he didn't."

"He have a face?"

"I expect he did."

I gave her a look of annoyance, held up the hundred between two fingers. "Did you see it?"

"Naah. Never met him. It was s'posed to be some big secret, never tell a soul, yadda, yadda, yadda."

"But she called you from the dressing room."

"A thousand bucks. She got to tell somebody. Besides, I'm

234

her best friend." She rolled down the window and tossed the plug of chewing gum at a pedestrian. "Shit," she said. "Missed."

"She tell you what he looked like?"

"Don't remember."

"Hundred bucks," I reminded her.

"Ain't worth squat if you ain't alive to spend it."

"He know about you?"

"How should I know? I don't know what she might of told the guy before she died."

"You figure the guy who hired her is the one that killed her?"

"Sure."

"What makes you think so?"

"Had to keep her quiet, didn't he?"

"Then, if she'd told him about you, I reckon you'd be dead by now." I gave her a minute to think about it. When fear flickered across her face, I said, "You see him when he picked her up?"

Her eyes were wide. "Uh-uh."

"She tell you what he looked like?"

She leaned her head back and squeezed her eyes shut. "I don't know." A tear trickled from the corner of her eye and down into her ear.

"You do know."

"Blond," she said. I could be called blond, but there was no reason for me to try to frame myself.

"Did you tell the police all this?" I asked.

"Hell, I don't talk to cops."

"Today you do."

"The hell I am."

"The hell you aren't." I gave her an icy smile. "See, it works like this. You tell Frank Campanella everything you just told me, and probably they'll just leave you alone. Frank works Homicide. He doesn't care if you turn tricks. But if you don't tell, things will start to get very interesting. Cops hauling your ass in to the station at the drop of a hat. Could get very hard to make a living."

I didn't know if I still had that kind of pull, but whether I did or not, it didn't really matter. All that mattered was that she believed I did.

If looks could kill, I would have spontaneously combusted. "You threatening me?"

"You bet your sweet ass I am."

I dropped her off at the police station with Frank's card and the hundred bucks. She wasn't happy about it.

AN HOUR LATER, I SAT BEHIND the desk in my office, considering Shannon's description of the man who had paid a thousand dollars for my DNA and fingerprints. A blond man, about my height and build. I thought of the possibilities. Ben Carrington, not blond. He could have worn a disguise, but my instincts told me he was wasn't involved. I typed his name into my favorite search engine and did a brief background check that raised no alarms.

D.W. Shorter and stockier than I and not blond. He had access to my schedule and personal information. He might even have known Tex's birthday, but I couldn't see him in the role of predator. Safe, reliable D.W., murdering people? I wasn't sure I liked him, but the idea was ludicrous.

Eric the Viking. Funny, how he'd shown up just as I was being framed for murder. I deleted Carrington's name and did a search for Eric's. There were about a dozen hits. Art shows, gallery openings. He'd been at an open house the night Amy was killed; photos of the event were posted on his studio's web site. Too bad. I would have liked to nail the little shit to the wall.

Samuel Avery, or whoever he was. He was hiding something, but a near-sighted witness on a foggy, moonless night would have had a hard time confusing him for me. He could have been pulling strings, though. Had he hired or persuaded someone to murder Amy and impersonate me?

Walter was a manipulator, and if Avery was Walter, he'd had thirteen years to perfect his craft. He had plenty of motive—three quarters of a million dollars worth. And then there were the photos. Who but Walter would want to incriminate me with those particular pictures?

Then there was Valerie's ex. Or not-so-ex. I pulled out the pamphlets I'd gotten from Avery and skimmed until I found a photo and blurb for Sonny Vanderhaus, a mastering engineer at AudioStyle recording studio. An Internet search showed that he was a busy boy, working full-time at the studio and hosting a nighttime radio show on weekends. The show was live, which meant that, unless he could be in two places at once, he had an alibi for Amy's murder. Still, his relationship with Avery kept me from crossing him off the list.

A quick search through one of the databases I subscribed to showed a six-year gap in his activities, and I made a mental note to find out if he had a record.

I moved the cursor to exit the database. Paused. The program's final question taunted me. *Do you want to make another search?*

I typed in my brother's name and stared at the screen some more. What did I think I could learn? Financial problems? Hell, who didn't have those? An old arrest record? What difference would it make?

The words looked stark against the screen. *Randall James McKean.*

Even to consider it was a breach of trust. I cleared the screen and exited the program.

# 32

I'VE GOT SOMETHING FOR YOU," Jay said. "But this one's going to cost you."

"That good, huh?"

His smug expression said it was.

"Okay, what's it going to cost me?"

"Dinner at Amerigo's. And I want to go dancing."

I groaned. "Jesus, Jay. Dancing?"

"We can go someplace with line dancing. I don't care. We don't have to slow dance or anything."

"You want me to take you to a gay bar?" I tried to wrap my mind around this. "Me?"

He laughed. "It will be an educational experience."

I gagged and gasped, rolled around on the couch and pretended I was dying, but he didn't relent. Dinner and dancing it was.

To be honest, I knew he would give up the info for nothing if I asked him to. But I also knew how bummed he was about Eric the Viking. He could use a little cheering up.

All the same, I hoped Randall wouldn't find out.

Or Frank.

Or pretty much anybody else I knew.

"I'll take you," I finally agreed. "But I won't dance." It was as good a compromise as he was going to get, and he knew it.

I wasn't sure what a straight guy was supposed to wear to a gay club, but Amerigo's Italian restaurant was upscale so I dressed up for the occasion in a dark gray suit and a silk tie with tigers on it. I knotted the tie with a pang of regret. Maria had bought it for me, and the last time I'd worn it, she was the one who had tied the knot and smoothed the tie flat against my shirt.

Jay's suit was the color of ash. One corner of a silk handkerchief protruded from his suit pocket. He looked ironed and creased, like he had just stepped out of GQ. He gave me an approving nod as we went down the driveway to the car. "What a waste," he said. "A tragedy for gay men everywhere."

"Let's not get carried away," I said, and he laughed.

At dinner, he ordered a vegetarian pasta dish, while I settled on grilled salmon with new potatoes and grilled vegetables. I don't eat red meat when Jay's around. Once I ordered lamb and thought he was going to vomit.

"All right," I said. "You've got your dinner, and I promise to take you dancing. Now, give."

"Her name is Shirleen Roystan. She and Calvin married thirteen years ago. Divorce papers filed two years later."

"No unmarked grave, then?"

"No unmarked grave." He handed me a slip of paper with an address and phone number on it. "This is where she lives. I guess someone will need to call her."

"I'll pass it on to Frank and Harry." This was one thing I didn't miss about the job. *I regret to inform you . . .*

A familiar voice interrupted my thoughts. "Hey, Jared! Jared McKean!"

I turned to face the owner of the voice and found myself face to face with Louis Wilder. Lou was about my height, but stockier, with short red hair cut in a buzz and a broad, square face with a thick neck. His shoulders strained at the jacket of his double-breasted suit. He would have looked more natural in cleats and a football jersey.

"Hey, Lou."

Jay stepped aside, as if announcing we were not together. Which in a way, made it look even more like we were.

Lou's eyes darted from me to Jay, then back again. I saw the question in his face, but he didn't ask it. Instead, he said, "I been trying to call you."

"I got your message. Sorry I haven't been able to catch you."

He shuffled his feet, cleared his throat. "I heard about that little mess you got yourself in."

Only Lou would call being arrested for murder a little mess.

"Yeah. I'm working on it."

"Well, I thought you should know. I did a job on you awhile back."

"What?"

"I had a client, wanted me to follow you, find out where you went, what your routines were, all that stuff. Wanted to know everything. He was real interested in what went down with you and Ashleigh Arneau last year."

"Was he?"

"Yeah, well, this guy wants to know all about what happened, how serious you were with Ashleigh. He wants to know where you go on Friday nights. He wants to know how often you see your kid. Everything."

"And you did this?"

"Hey, man. A job's a job. Somebody hires you to shadow me for a couple weeks, you gonna turn it down?"

"I'd want to know why. But yeah, I'd probably turn it down."

He flushed a deep red, laughed a short, harsh burst. "Yeah. Well. Maybe. You're a better man than me, Cowboy. Anyway, I thought you'd want to know, under the circumstances. I heard Ashleigh Arneau say you were claiming that some mystery chick had set you up. And I thought, hey, maybe he's right."

"Who, Lou?" My fists clenched. I took a deep, calming breath and forced them open. "Who hired you?"

"Aw, now, you know I can't tell you that." He backed away, hands raised chest-high. "Client confidentiality and all."

"Lou, I want to know who hired you." I moved toward him, and he backpedaled as fast as he could go.

Jay caught me by the elbow.

"No, Jared. Don't."

"This bastard knows who set me up," I said through gritted teeth. "And he is by God going to tell me who it was."

"Sorry, Charlie." Lou slipped into the crowd with unusual grace for a muscle-bound hulk. "Gotta run. Lotsa luck."

I went after him like a shark after chum, grabbed him by the back of the collar and spun him around. "You call Frank Campanella. Homicide. You call him, you hear? Tell him what you just told me."

"Take your hands off me, McKean, or people are going to start calling you Captain Hook." His Neanderthal jaw jutted out, and I knew he meant it. I was past caring.

"Try it, Wilder."

"Jared . . . ," Jay started, and clamped his mouth shut.

I shoved my face in close to Lou's. "Listen to me, you lard-brain, no-neck piece of crap. My ass is on the line here. I'm looking at life in prison, and you know who put me there. You don't want to tell me, fine. But you get your ass on the phone, and you tell Frank Campanella someone hired you to get information on my personal habits. You *do* it, Lou!"

A vein in his forehead bulged, and for a moment, I thought we just might have to kill each other. Then his jaw unclenched. His muscles relaxed. I felt the stubbornness leak out of him like water from a cracked glass. I sighed and let him go.

"Do what you can, okay, Lou?" I said, suddenly exhausted. "I'd appreciate it."

He stepped back and gave me a broad smile, smoothing the front of his jacket with his hands. "Well, sure. All you had to do was ask nice."

He turned and stepped into the crowd we'd gathered, and they parted for him like the Red Sea parting for Moses.

I sank into my chair as the meaning of what had just happened hit me.

It wasn't Randall.

Randall wouldn't need to hire a detective. He could have gotten anything he needed from me. Or Jay. Or even Maria.

Even though I'd known it, relief washed over me.

"Well," Jay said. "That was unique."

"Sorry."

He shrugged. "Oh, that's all right. You're entitled to the occasional outburst, under the circumstances."

A young man wearing jeans, a Rolling Stones T-shirt, and a Dodgers baseball cap stepped out of the crowd and spat on Jay's two-hundred-dollar Italian shoes.

"Jesus hates faggots," he said, glowering at the two of us.

Jay looked stricken. My right hand curled into a fist, but I knew punching the little bastard would just make Jay feel worse. Not to mention possible assault charges.

Instead, I scowled and said, "As much as He hates bigots?" Then I took Jay's elbow and guided him across the street to the car.

"I'M SORRY," JAY SAID. He was hunched so far over on the passenger side I was afraid he might meld with the door.

"*You're* sorry?" I glanced over at him, then back to the road. "What do you have to be sorry about? I'm the one who nearly got into a street brawl."

"I wasn't trying to look like a couple."

"I know."

"It just oozes out of me, doesn't it? I shine like a beacon, even to people with lousy gay-dar." Gay-dar is the ability to sense when someone else is homosexual. It's short for gay radar, and Jay's is finely honed. He can spot another gay man from a thousand yards.

"Don't worry about it."

"I don't want to embarrass you. Maybe we should go home."

"I promised you dancing. And I always keep my promises."

"It's all right. I don't mind." He eased himself away from the door. A good sign, I thought.

"Jay," I said, "we are going to a dance club if I have to

carry you there in a sack."

He laughed, though without much humor.

"Now, please tell me where to go," I said. "And make it a gay club, because I don't want to meet anybody else I know."

"Oh, I don't know about that," he said. "You might be surprised."

It wasn't as bad as I expected, which is to say, it wasn't as bad as getting your foot shot off, or even as bad as a root canal. I got hit on more times than I cared to count, which was both flattering and upsetting; I never got hit on that much by women.

"Men are more aggressive," Jay said when I groused about it. "Even gay men. Don't worry. I have very good gay-dar, and I promise you, you're one hundred percent straight."

"Tell me something I don't know."

He shook his head and pushed away from the bar, went off to mingle with the crowd.

He didn't ask me to dance, and I didn't volunteer. Instead, I sat at the bar, fending off advances and watching Jay work the room. Then I saw his back stiffen. I turned my head toward whatever had caught his attention, and there he was.

Mr. Perfect.

Mr. Eric-Fucking-Cad.

My jaw tightened, and I started toward him.

He saw me coming too late to avoid a confrontation.

"Hey, man." He laughed nervously. "I didn't expect to see you here."

"No shit, Sherlock." I took his arm firmly, but probably not too painfully, and turned him toward the dance floor, where Jay was pretending not to notice us. "You see that guy in the gray suit? Blond hair. A little thin. You see him?"

Eric swallowed hard, eyes flitting like caged butterflies. "I see him."

"You said you'd call him."

"I . . ." He looked at me and seemed to get his courage back. "Hey, man. I got busy."

"Yeah? You too busy to act like a decent human being?"

His face flushed. "Hey, you got no call to—"

"I got call," I snapped. "I *got* call. I'm the one who has to watch him beat himself up when dickheads like you lead him on and use him and then dump him like yesterday's trash. I got call, all right."

"All right." He backed away, looking for an escape, but I had him firmly by the arm. "All right, man."

"It's not all right. You understand? You hurt him. He thought you were something special, and you treated him like junk. You want to know a secret, Dickhead? You're not good enough for him. A dozen of you wouldn't be good enough."

"I meant to call," he said.

"Oh. You meant to call. You know what? Then call."

"I will. Let go. I'll go talk to him now."

"If you're just going to dump on him again, then you can just leave him the hell alone."

"I'm not. I mean it, man. I really meant to call him. It's just..."

"Just what?'

He sighed. "It's just that he's so damn needy."

"So what? He gets a lot, he gives a lot."

"He's got the virus."

"I see." I let go of his arm. "You think he's going to get sick and you'll be stuck with nursing him."

He had the grace to look ashamed. "It happens, man. I've been there before, and believe me, it sucks."

A muscle in my cheek pulsed. "Let me put your mind at ease. Jay doesn't need you to nurse him, and he doesn't need you to take care of him. I'm there for that, Eric, and I will always be there for that. What he needs is someone who will love him."

"And you don't?" He rubbed his arm where I had grabbed it. "Coulda fooled me."

"I'm not gay," I said.

"Uh huh."

244

"You going to ask him to dance, or you going to give up what might be the best thing that ever happened to you?"

He looked at Jay, slow dancing with a young man wearing tight black jeans and a black mesh muscle shirt. The look that crossed his face was almost enough to make me sorry I'd called him a dickhead.

He started toward the dance floor. "I'm going to ask him to dance."

# 33

FIRST THING MONDAY MORNING, I put in a call to Frank.

"You talk to Shannon?" I asked.

"Yeah. I did."

"The guy in the red car. I think it might be Sonny Vanderhaus."

"We checked him out. For Amy and Hope both. He was on the radio both nights. Live show. So, unlikely as it seems, we're looking for another blond guy in a red Corvette."

"Is he about the same size as me?"

"Pretty close."

"The guy served time. Could you look up his record for me?"

"No need. We already pulled it. Sonny Vanderhaus. There was a series of B&E's in his old neighborhood, and word on the street was he was behind them. Sharp guy for a junkie, always had some sugar mama to look after him."

"They catch him for the breaking and entering?"

"Porn. Mostly doctored photos, mix and match stuff, Marilyn Monroe's head on some stripper's body, stuff like that. Some kiddie stuff too, that's what got him. Indications are, he wasn't into it himself, but he'd make photographs and video for other people. For a price, of course."

"And he only did six years?"

"He didn't take the pictures himself. Just doctored 'em. Plus, he made a deal. Ratted out some of his clients."

A child pornographer and a rat. I bet that made him a popular boy in prison.

"So he could've made the pictures you found in my truck. Do you know if he and Walter were in at the same time?"

246

I heard him shuffling papers on the other end. "Looks like it," he said. "How'd you ever guess?"

SHORTLY BEFORE ELEVEN, I took Interstate-40 downtown to Demonbreun, then took a sharp left off Music Square to the office complex where Sonny Vanderhaus worked at Audio-Style Recording.

At noon, I saw him come out and get into the custom-painted Corvette. When he'd turned the corner and was out of sight, I got out of the van and went inside.

The woman at the desk looked to be in her mid-forties. Rich, coffee-brown skin, thick-lashed, sloe-shaped eyes so dark they looked black, elegant understated makeup. She wore a light green, short-sleeved sundress with matching earrings and a necklace of large, brightly colored beads.

Nice.

I flipped my wallet open to my detective's license and held it across the counter to her.

"Afternoon, Ma'am," I said. "Would it be possible to ask your mastering engineer a couple of questions?"

She looked at me doubtfully. "Which one?"

This was unexpected. I'd expected her to tell me he was gone, and I would say that I could talk to someone else, then. This was better.

"It doesn't really matter. I need to know about the job, not about a specific person."

"Oh." She looked relieved. "Just a minute."

She spoke into the intercom on her desk. "Mr. Schroeder, there's a detective here who would like to talk to you about mastering. Do you have a moment for him?" She was silent for a moment. Then she gestured toward the hall behind her. "He says you can go back. End of the hall, first door on the right."

The mastering room had ninety-degree angles on three sides, with the fourth wall resembling half a hexagon. Three video screens and two speakers adorned that wall, and parked directly in front of them was a desk with a computer, a mixing board with a mind-boggling array of slide controls, and a swivel chair which held, barely, a burly man with bushy brown hair and glasses. He looked like a bear wearing spectacles. There was some kind of maroon cloth covering the walls. I poked it with my finger, and the cloth gave beneath the pressure.

"It's girl-cloth," said the man behind the desk. At least, I thought that's what he said.

"*Girl*-cloth?" I asked.

He gave a boisterous laugh. "*Grille*-cloth. It absorbs sound, keeps the echo down. That's why the room has these crazy corners, too. No square rooms in the recording business."

"I wondered. You're Mr. Schroeder?"

"Kerry. Kerry Schroeder. You wanted to know about mastering?"

"That's right."

"What do you want to know?"

I wasn't sure, but I took a stab at it. "You guys do the audio work for that Sunday morning preaching show, right? The one they do for Road to Glory Church of the Reclamation?"

"Sonny does that. It's kind of a personal project for him. We don't make much on it."

"Well, let's just use that as an example. He records it at the church, right?"

"Right. It would cost too much to rent the studio time every week."

"So, he records it at the church. And then?"

"Well." He picked up something that looked like a miniature videocassette and handed it to me. It was about two inches long, an inch and a half wide, and maybe a half inch thick. "That's a DAT tape. D-A-T. That's Digital Audio Tape. We just call them dats. They're not real reliable, because they're so tiny, which makes them really delicate. Lots of stuff can go wrong, so you always have a backup DAT."

"Why use them, then?"

"Because they're so easy to use. He records the service onto DAT first. He does that at the church, sets up the mikes, balances the tape machine, and so on."

"When you say 'balance' . . ."

"Sets the mike level so they're not too low and not too loud."

"Okay. Then what?"

"Then he brings it back to the studio and edits it."

I waited.

He gestured toward the computer. "Okay. What that means is, he puts the tape into the tape deck, which loads it into the hard drive of the computer. Then he can do pretty much whatever he wants to with it. The software we use is called SADIE. That's Studio Audio Digital . . . something. We just call it SADIE."

I looked over his shoulder at the computer. "What can you do with that?"

He shrugged. "Well, once it's digitized, you can do pretty much whatever you want. Say there's a baby crying in the church. You can separate that sound and take it out. Or if the altos are too loud, or the sopranos are too soft, you can fix that. You EQ the sound. That means you equalize it. You make everything all beautiful and even. We have compressors, which kind of . . . squash . . . the sound a little bit; it fine-tunes everything, squashes the loud sections and brings up what's too quiet. You can clear up any static. Or extraneous noises." He leaned back and laced his fingers behind his head. "We have this one machine, it's called CEDAR, that's Computer Enhanced Digital Audio Restoration. It clears up poor sounds, filters out stuff. We used it to help out the FBI a couple years ago. They had this tape, like on an answering machine, and there was some kind of stuff going on in the background. Like an airport terminal, or something. We cleaned it up and pulled up the station sounds, took out the other stuff."

"Like in *The Fugitive*."

"Yeah. Just like."

"Where was he? The guy on the answering machine."

"Oh. Somewhere out of the country. Sweden. Norway."

"If you have a DAT with someone's voice on it, can you change the words around? Make it say something it didn't?"

"Sure. It's like that software program, 'Photoshop'. You put in a picture, and then you can do anything you want to it. Well, it's the same with sound. There's software designed just for editing, and you can do pretty much anything you want to with it."

"And the pitch?"

He frowned. "I don't know what you mean."

I grimaced, trying to put my question into words. "Well, if I say 'my bitch is about to have puppies', and 'that horse is getting too fat', and 'Aries was the Greek god of war', and somebody turns that into, 'My God, that bitch is fat!', wouldn't the inflections be all off?"

He nodded. "I get what you're saying." He gestured toward a small black machine that sat to the right of the mixing board. "See this bar? You can see the shape of the music—or whatever—on it. A wide splash represents something loud. Getting smaller means diminishing sound. Once it's in SADIE, you can take sounds out, put them in, change the pitch speed, which raises or lowers the pitch. So you could do what you were talking about. Mix and match to make a different message."

"Any way to figure that out? If that's been done?"

"The FBI could probably do it."

"If I called you on the phone and recorded your voice, would that give me a good enough recording?"

"Mmmm. It might be. But the quality might not be so hot. It would be better if you had some kind of recorder on the phone. If you got my voice on an answering machine, it might do."

Or if I had a recording device in your receiver.

"Sonny Vanderhaus," I said. "He's pretty good at this stuff?"

A smile flashed beneath his beard. "Man, Sonny is an absolute genius. Tapes, video, CD's, Photoshop. He's multimedia."

"He DJ's too?"

"Yeah. He does a live show three nights a week on WCNE. Same guy runs it who does AudioStyle. They broadcast out of here; the station's just down the hall. 'Raising Caine' is their slogan. Cutting edge stuff."

"But the Sunday show . . ."

"WPRZ. PRZ for Praise. Sonny isn't really into all that stuff. He's more into alternative rock, shock rock, industrial. But the church gig pays okay, and his girlfriend sings there sometimes."

"Anybody else here when he does the show?"

"Not usually. Why?"

"Just wondered." I was beginning to see how Sonny might be in two places at one time. "The live show. Is it music? Call-in? What?"

"Music, jokes, discussion. Whatever Sonny feels like doing."

So he could have pre-taped his "live" show and left the studio without anybody knowing. The perfect alibi.

I thanked Kerry for his help and left. I had no doubt Sonny would hear that I had been here, but that didn't matter. Let him worry. It might make him careless.

FOR SOME REASON, ASHLEIGH SEEMED less than delighted to hear from me. "This is not exactly a good time..."

I cut her off. "What did you do with the tapes? The ones you got off my phone?"

"I . . . What? I don't know what you're talking about."

"I saw you take the device out of the receiver."

She was silent.

"Come on," I said. "What did you do with them?"

"Are you recording this?" she asked. "Is that what this is about?"

"Am I . . . Oh, for Christ's sake, Ashleigh. If I was going to nail you for this, I would have done it a year ago."

"Then I don't see what this has to do with anything."

"And you won't, unless you tell me what you did with the tapes. Did you destroy them? Please, tell me you destroyed them."

"No." Her voice was thin and breathless, as though the air were being squeezed from her lungs.

"Did you give them to someone?"

"No, of course not."

"So you still have them?"

"Jared . . ."

"Ashleigh." I could hear annoyance and exhaustion in my voice. "Go and see if the tapes are where you left them."

She heaved a deep sigh. "If it will make you happy, all right. Hold on."

She was gone a very long time. Too long. I heard her breathing on the line for some time before she actually spoke. "They're gone."

I almost felt sorry for her, wondering where the tapes had gone, wondering who might hear them. It could mean the end of her career. It could mean federal prosecution. Nothing good could come of this for her, and she knew it.

"Did you take them?" she asked.

"No. Tell me, were they labeled?"

"Just with your first name."

"Ever met a guy named Sonny Vanderhaus?"

Silence.

"Ashleigh."

"He's in radio. He interviewed me once, for that show he has."

"And did you tell him about the tapes?"

"Not on air."

"Of course, not on air." I wanted to add a few choice epithets, but somehow I managed to stay calm. "Did you tell him about them, *ever*?"

252

Her voice sounded like someone was pinching off her air supply. "We went out after the show. He's a really charming guy. And very cute."

"You went out after the show. And then?"

"Well, we went back to my place. And we drank a little wine. And we got to talking about the worst things we'd ever done. He'd been arrested once, for joyriding." *Yeah*, I thought. *Among other things.* "But that wasn't the worst thing. He said the worst thing was, he once dated a woman just because she had some money, and she was going to back his show. And I said the worst thing I'd ever done was tap your phone."

"And did you tell him where to find the tapes?"

"No. I just said I'd kept them. You don't think he would have stolen them? How could he have gotten in?"

"That break-in you had a few months ago. Your buddy, Sonny, has some experience with breaking and entering."

"But why—"

"Any chance you told him about the combination to my glove compartment?" When she finally answered, her voice was small. "I thought it was funny, that's all. That you know your horse's birthday."

"Yeah. Real funny. Here's a word of advice, sweetheart. Next time you tap someone's phone, remember to destroy the evidence."

# 34

RUVEN TOMEY REACHED ACROSS the table at the International House of Pancakes and plucked a crisp slice of bacon from my plate.

"Sonny Vanderhaus," he said, thoughtfully. He stuffed the whole slice into his mouth and talked around it. "Yeah, I 'member him."

Ruven was a guard at DeBerry Correctional Facility, where Walter Christy and Sonny Vanderhaus had served time. An amiable giant, Ruven not only knew every convict in the place by name, but also each one's favorite foods and what he'd wanted to be when he grew up.

"You remember anything about him?"

"Uh huh." He picked up a pitcher of warm maple syrup and drenched his pancakes with it. "He was real, real smart. Had a rough time, though."

"How so?"

"Too good lookin'. From the first day, he was everybody's punk. Up until ol' Christy made up to him."

"Walter Christy?" I tried to keep my voice steady.

"Uh huh. That's the one." Ruven shoveled a dripping hunk of pancake into his mouth and chomped. "They wasn't supposed to be in the general pop, but you know how that goes."

Sure I did. 'Accidents' happen. 'Mistakes' are made. Just like the one Hal Meacham had made when he shoved me into a cell with the likes of Breem and LeQuintus. "Christy and Vanderhaus were friends?"

He wiped at his mouth with one huge paw. "Sure was."

"How'd that happen?"

"I'm tellin' you how it happened. Sonny got a craw full, finally. Some asshole or another goin' at him all the time. One

254

day in the laundry room, one of the cons tried to get Sonny off by hisself. Sonny blew a gasket. Big ol' fight broke out."

"Walter was there?"

"That's right. And Walter'd had hisself a hard time with some of these shitheads too." He scooped a forkful of scrambled eggs into his mouth and washed it down with a long swallow of orange juice. "He was standin' by the steam iron, and when one of these guys came by, Walter tripped him up and shut his head in the press. Lordy, you shoulda seen it. Christy holding the lid to the iron down, and that guy—name of Bulldog Landry—kickin' and squealin'. They had to pull Christy off the iron, and when they finally got him off, Bulldog didn't hardly have no face left."

"Jesus."

He flashed a smile that rounded his cheeks and made the skin around his eyes bunch. "That's ezzackly right. Nobody messed with Walter after that, and Sonny was right up under Walter's wing. So nobody messed with him any more either."

"Were they lovers?"

"Well, Sonny was into women and Christy was into little girls, but you know how it is in prison."

"So they might have been."

"Be surprised if they wasn't." His plate empty, he gestured toward mine.

I pushed it toward him. "You think they were tight enough to keep it going after prison."

"Oh, definitely, man." He bobbed his massive head and stuffed another piece of bacon into his mouth. "Ol' Christy used to say Sonny was the son he never had. Then, when Sonny got out, he'd come back to visit Christy. Guess that father-son thing went both ways. I bet Sonny flipped a lid when Christy blew hisself to kingdom come."

"THERE'S DEFINITELY A LINK between them." I held the cell phone to my ear and eased onto Old Hickory Boulevard.

"Forget Walter," Frank said. "He's not your guy."

255

"You're sure about that."

"Just got your prints back. One set of prints we figure belong to the wife. No record on her. Another set belongs to one Eddie Krutcher. Two-bit scam artist. This whole Church of the Reclamation thing is just a big racket."

"Pay your money and sin to your heart's content." I was no paragon of Christian virtue myself, but the idea rankled.

"That's about the size of it. There are warrants out for him in three states. We've got a car out after him now. So get this Walter-obsession out of your head."

"What about Sonny's connection to Walter? What about the photographs? That's Walter's trademark."

"He's not the only child molester with a fetish for white panties."

All right. I was willing to concede that Avery wasn't Walter. That Walter really had died in that car crash, and that maybe Sonny had taken up with Avery because of his resemblance to Walter. But what if Sonny really had cracked up when his father figure died? What if he was going after everybody he thought had betrayed Walter? What if he'd been sleeping with Valerie to get close to her family?

I punched the gas, and the van bucked forward. At this time of day, I'd be lucky to make it in an hour.

When I finally arrived, the custom Corvette was in the drive. A quick glance into the Corvette told me the interior was gray, and a search of the barn told me Sonny and Valerie were probably in the house. But what if I'd read the situation wrong? What if I went barging in only to find them in *flagrante delicto?* I shook my head to clear away the fog. Was I acting out of concern or jealousy?

I took a deep breath and ticked off the evidence. Sonny had been close to Walter. He had a history of breaking and entering. He knew about Ashleigh's tapes and had the skills to obtain and use them. He'd been involved in child porn and knew how to doctor photos. He was blonde and drove a red Corvette, the interior of which was gray.

It may have been circumstantial, but it was an impressive list. And that meant that, sooner or later, Valerie would be in danger.

I didn't want to startle him, so I crept to the mudroom door.

Listened.

Nothing.

Almost every cop knows how to pick a lock. It isn't a skill we use often, but it's something we all learn. Gotta know how the bad guys do the things they do. As locks went, Valerie's was no pushover, but it wasn't all that tough. It took me maybe three minutes—three minutes of sweating and praying nobody drove up to the barn—before the tumblers clicked. I eased the door open and listened again.

When I was sure they weren't in the next room, I stepped inside and closed the door behind me.

The living room was as I remembered it, nothing out of place, no sign of a struggle. The tan carpet and cream-colored living room set gave the room a sandy feel, broken by the Navajo blanket thrown over the back of the couch. One wall was devoted to Valerie's trophies, some for riding, some for singing, a few for local beauty pageants.

They were from a long time ago.

Three wooden tack trunks lined the floor in front of the display, prizes for High Point Champion in Shelbyville's Festival of Horses. A silver-studded show saddle straddled one of the trunks.

A set of car keys with a Grateful Dead key chain lay on the coffee table. They weren't Valerie's.

Cautiously, I made my way down the hall, opening each door a crack to make sure no one was inside. The silence bothered me, reminded me too much of the stillness at the Hartwell house.

*She's all right.* My heartbeat pounded in my ears. *He isn't going to hurt her. Not yet.*

No one was in the bathroom, no one in the linen closet. I

tried the door that had been locked before, and this time it swung open. Photographs and clippings lined the walls.

I moved in for a better look. Candid photographs of me—Lou's surveillance shots?—were splashed between newspaper clippings from Walter's trial and 3x5 photos of Walter and his family. A wife with hair the color of buttered toast. Two little girls with haunted eyes. A graduation photograph of Amy with the eyes gouged out. One headline had been copied multiple times and pinned up throughout the rest of the display: "Child Molester Dies in Fiery Crash."

Valerie's voice broke into my thoughts. "He was my father," she said. "And you killed him."

I turned to look at her and found myself staring down the barrel of a pistol.

Everything clicked into place. The book on incest. The history of promiscuity. Ms. Birdie saying, *those girls didn't have much of a father figure.* Ben Carrington's suspicions that Amy had been abused by her father. Two women stumbling across a parking lot.

Or one woman stumbling under the weight of another, drugged out of her head? It suddenly made sense that Amy hadn't mentioned her affair with the phantom Jared McKean to Birdie or to Ben. There had never been one.

And Dakota's colic? Had Valerie dosed him with milkweed and gotten Sonny to doctor the tapes?

The gun in her hand trembled, but I didn't think that meant she wouldn't shoot me. If anything, it meant the opposite.

"He killed himself," I said.

"Because of you."

"Because he was a monster."

Her mouth worked. "He never hurt anyone. He was gentle and kind and had a beautiful spirit."

"He told little girls that if they didn't jerk him off, he'd get cancer and die."

"You just don't understand."

"I get that a lot," I said.

"You ruined my life."

"Okay, I get it. You're pissed at me. But why kill Amy?"

"Figure it out, smart guy."

"Because she testified?"

"Among other things." She stepped back and gestured toward the living room with the gun. It looked like a Glock, a little smaller than the one police had confiscated from my truck, but plenty big enough to punch a hole in me. "Let's go someplace more comfortable, shall we, lover?"

I led the way, and Sonny came out of the bedroom and stood behind her. She handed him the Glock. "You hold this one. I'll get his." She reached around me and unsnapped the holster, slid the Colt free.

"You kill your mother, too?" I asked.

"Mother was an accident. I didn't even have to do anything. Just watch her die."

"You mean, let her die." I glanced around the room for something I could use as a weapon. A lamp. A trophy. Maybe a sofa cushion. "Quite a body count you've got going. Amy, your mother, Heather. I mean, Hope."

"Whores die every day," she said. "Nobody cares."

"I get that. And I get Amy. But why Calvin and the girls? You still pissed because he dumped you?"

Her eyes narrowed into slits. "I would have had him crawling to me on his belly. But that little bitch, Tara, answered the phone that night. Couldn't keep her mouth shut." She rolled her eyes and added in a child's voice, "'Oooh, Aunt Valerie, why did mommy go to see you?' Cal started asking questions. So . . ." She shrugged. "I wish it hadn't happened."

"Made things messy, did it?"

"Well, it definitely muddied the waters. It was too hard to pin that one on you. But I'm flexible. I wanted you to suffer through everything my father went through, but I guess I'll just have to kill you instead."

Behind her, Sonny nodded.

Valerie went on. "Of course, it will be self-defense. You killed my sister, and now you've come to murder me. You'll shoot at me, but in your chaotic mental state, you'll miss. My boyfriend will have no choice but to shoot you. It's all terribly traumatic."

I cocked an eyebrow and tried to stay cool. "What am I supposed to have shot at you with? You know a nitric acid swab will prove I haven't fired a weapon."

"I'm sure Sonny will figure out something."

"Like he did with Cal?"

"Cal shot himself."

"I know. But you were holding his children hostage. You don't have mine. Did you tell Cal you'd let the girls go if he pulled the trigger? Did you tell him you'd take care of them?"

"Shut up," Sonny said. "You don't know anything."

I swung my attention his way. "It's not just about Walter for you, is it? It's about Valerie. I had her, you know that? She jumped me in the laundry room, and we fucked like rabbits."

His face blanched. "Shut up," he said again.

Valerie rolled her eyes. "Oh, just kill him," she said to Sonny, and turned away.

I didn't wait for him to pull the trigger. A man can't outrun a bullet, but sometimes he can outmaneuver another man. I ducked and threw out my left leg in a hook kick that knocked the Glock from his hand just as it discharged. It flew across the room and bounced off the curtains and onto the floor.

Valerie jerked the Colt around, and I dived for the Glock.

Time seemed both to slow down and to speed up at the same time. I heard three sharp cracks, a strangled cry, a stream of curses that might have been mine.

My hand closed on the Glock and I rolled to my feet and pointed the gun at Valerie's head.

She froze, Randall's Colt trained on my chest.

Stalemate.

Beside her, Sonny sank to one knee, a flower of crimson blooming in the center of his chest. "Shit," he said softly.

Valerie's gaze flicked to her lover and back to me.

"He get in your way?" I asked. I noticed with an odd sense of detachment that the calf of my jeans was soaked with blood and that it had left a streak of crimson on the tan carpet.

"He'll be all right," she said.

"He needs a doctor."

"So do you."

I couldn't argue with that. The wound hadn't begun to hurt yet, but I could tell it was a bad one because of the little pool of blood that was forming on the carpet around my boot. It felt surreal, the two of us chatting, our semi-automatics trained on each other.

"Tell me about Avery," I said. "How did Calvin get involved with him?"

"Calvin didn't have anything to do with it," she said. "Amy introduced them. She said Reverend Avery reminded her of Daddy. Can you believe that?"

"I had the same thought myself."

"He was nothing like Daddy," she said sharply. "But she was all, 'oh, he even has the same voice.' It was guilt, if you ask me."

I thought of Amy crossing a Wal-Mart parking lot, plucking a pamphlet from beneath her windshield wipers, glancing down at the photo on the front and seeing Avery's face, so much like her father's. Seeing a chance to relive the good parts and make up for the bad, to recreate the father she'd both loved and hated.

A dull ache settled inside my ribcage.

"She didn't have anything to feel guilty about," I said.

"I'd expect that from you, since you helped her kill him."

"What did Calvin think about all this?"

She gave an angry laugh. "Calvin just liked his message. He *would*."

"But you went to his church too."

She shrugged. "One big happy family. Besides, he let me sing."

261

My head felt light. The room slowly listed to one side. Hang in there, I told myself, and shook my head to clear it. My left hand fumbled for my cell phone, which was still clipped to my belt.

"You're bleeding to death," Valerie said, calmly.

"Your concern is touching."

"Don't flatter yourself. It's just an observation."

My fingers found the keys. Punched one of them.

Another wave of dizziness swept over me, and I stumbled back, gun wavering. I steadied it.

"You're a smart man, lover," she said. "For a dead man. You have a good story, but you have no evidence. Cal shot himself. The girls were shot with the same gun. There's nothing to connect either Sonny or myself to their deaths."

I could barely hear her through the ringing in my ears. "Unless Katrina talks."

"Katrina is a vegetable."

"You've made mistakes." My voice sounded hollow, and very far away. "The police already know I didn't kill anyone. Where do you think they're going to look next?"

She bit her lip and thought about it.

Sonny slumped against the wall, pressing his wound closed with one hand. Good idea. Maybe I should do that too. I would, if Valerie would put the stupid gun down.

Sonny coughed, cried out again.

"You going to let him die?" I asked.

Something in her expression warned me. A flicker of indecision. The tension in a muscle. I leaped to one side as she fired Randall's Colt, and my finger, on the trigger, jerked.

The ringing in my ears intensified, and above the ringing, sirens, and then the sound of my brother's voice.

# 35

THEY'RE RIGHT ABOUT BULLET WOUNDS. I hadn't even known I'd been hit until I saw the blood, and two hours later, I felt like someone was digging through my calf muscles with a serrated knife.

The doctor gave me two units of blood and plenty of morphine and said I'd probably be up to speed in six or seven weeks.

Randall was waiting outside, and when the doctor left, a grandmotherly nurse with *Calvin & Hobbes* scrubs let him in.

"You okay?" he asked.

I nodded. "I dreamed you were there at Valerie's."

He gave me a quizzical look. "I *was* at Valerie's. You called me, remember?"

My fingers, fumbling at the keys. I'd punched three instead of Frank's less familiar four. Or maybe some part of me had meant to call for Randall all along. "I'm sorry," I said.

"For what?"

*For ruining your military career. For not salvaging my marriage. For thinking, even for a heartbeat, that Frank might have been right.* "I think I lost your Colt," I said.

"It's just a gun. I'll get another one. Besides . . ." He smiled. "Now you owe me."

I leaned back against my pillow and said, "Randall, I always have."

"HOW'S EVERYTHING?" I asked Jay.

"You tell me." He crossed his arms and rested them on my bedrail.

"I meant, how are you feeling, and how are things with Mr. Perfect?"

263

"Fabulous," he said. "Couldn't be better. I don't have any bullet wounds, unlike some people I know. My T-cell count is holding steady. And Eric is being a regular Prince Charming. Truth to tell, I think he's too scared not to be."

"Good," I said.

"It's a sad day when men have to be threatened to go out with me."

"I didn't threaten him. I merely reminded him of what he was missing."

"For which I'm eternally grateful. But I do have one more favor to ask."

"Never satisfied." I forced a grin. "What's the favor?"

"Do you think you might get through the next week without getting beaten up or shot at?"

It was a promise I was happy to make.

By the time Frank and Harry came in, I remembered to ask about Valerie.

They exchanged glances, and I read something in their faces that I didn't want to see.

"Ah, no," I said.

After an uncomfortable silence, Frank cleared his throat. "Good news is, the D.A. dropped the charges."

"You could come back to work," Harry said.

Frank nodded. "Now that everybody knows what happened with the Arneau bitch."

"Maybe someday."

I missed the force, but you know the old saying: You can't go home again. The force was home, and I had left it—or been made to leave—and it would never be the same. There would always be the stares and the suspicions, the whispers and the smug, knowing smiles.

Maybe one day I wouldn't care.

"Just as well, maybe," Frank said, but he sounded like he didn't mean it. "Word is, the new chief's planning to shake things up a lot. You take care, Cowboy." He tapped two fingers to his forehead and turned to leave.

"Frank?" I stopped him at the door. "How'd you know I didn't do it?"

"I didn't know. You had me worried for a while there."

"Yeah, but then . . . you started to believe me. You had a shitload of evidence, and you still believed me. Why?"

"I know you, Mac. The voice print made me lose sight of it for a while, but you're not that kind of guy." He gave me a small smile. "Besides, there was your gun."

"My gun?"

"You might have forgotten to wipe the prints off the glasses, and you might have got carried away and left a message on her machine. But you would have thought to ditch the gun."

I remembered how close I'd come to doing exactly that. *Two points for doing the right thing*, I thought. How often does that happen?


I SLEPT, AND WHEN I AWOKE, the room was dark and my leg was throbbing. Moonlight streamed through the slats of the window blinds and made the bed rails and the metal edges of the bedside table shine.

I fumbled for the remote, clicked on the TV, volume on low, and checked the time. Nine-thirty. It felt later. A news report came on, and I clicked the TV off again. Thought about how one thing leads to another, about unexpected consequences. Walter Christy fumbles beneath a little girl's dress, and years later, Valerie aims a pistol at another child's head.

Confluence.

Events converge. Strands meet, leading to inevitable endings. But at what point do they *become* inevitable? If you could unravel them at the beginning, could you change the course of fate? I squeezed my eyes closed and remembered.


*"My God," Frank says, pressing Caleb's rambling letter into my hand. "He's going to kill her."*

*There is no time to wait for SWAT; a paranoid schizophrenic with an arsenal in his basement is holding them at*

265

bay in a normally quiet Donelson neighborhood. A sniper will eventually take him down with a single shot to the temple, but not in time for them to save Melody Wilford.

"The hell he is," I say.

The hunting lodge squats at the end of a rutted gravel road fifteen miles from the city. Caleb's pickup truck is parked a few feet from the front steps.

Frank climbs from the driver's seat of his Crown Vic.

"Caleb!" he calls. "Caleb Wilford!"

He prods the front door with two fingers, and it creaks open. Caleb is inside, his daughter clutched to his chest, his hunting knife pressed to her throat.

I slip around the corner and head for the back of the lodge.

Frank says to Caleb, "You don't have to do this."

He keeps Caleb talking as I pick the lock on the back door and creep inside, keeps him talking as I tiptoe through the mud room, cross the kitchen, and ease into the great room, where Frank and Caleb face each other across the scuffed hardwood floor.

There is an unstrung bow propped against the hearth, and beside it, a quiver of arrows.

A floorboard creaks beneath my feet, and Caleb turns toward the sound. His blade bites into Melody's throat, and the child lets out a squeal of fear and pain. A thin red line appears across her neck.

My fault.

Moving fast now. My fingers close around Caleb's wrist, and I draw the knife away and up, twisting until he cries out. The knife clatters to the floor. With my other hand, I push the girl toward Frank.

My gaze follows the child—is she safe? Did we save her?—and in that split second, Caleb lunges for the quiver, snatches out an arrow, and drives it into my chest.

The pain is blinding. It drops me to my knees, drives all thought from my mind. The titanium tip enters my chest two inches to the left of my heart, tearing flesh and severing the *small blood vessels in its path. A gun goes off, and Caleb Wilford and I crumple to the floor in a pool of mingled blood.*

Confluence.

I opened my eyes and stared at the ceiling. Thought about Melody Wilford and Katrina Hartwell, about the scars, both visible and invisible, they'd wear for the rest of their lives. I thought about Tara.

The kids I'd saved and the one I hadn't.

I lowered the bed railing and slid my legs over the edge of the bed. A blade of pain sliced through my calf. My teeth snapped together, and a gasp whistled between them. I perched there for a moment, waiting for the pain to ebb. When it had become a dull ache, I eased onto my feet and, IV apparatus in tow, made my way down the hall. The nurse at the desk looked up when I passed. She was wearing pink Snoopy scrubs and a pink barette in her hair.

"Can I get you something, Mr. McKean?" she asked. "Something for pain?"

"Just needed to move around a little."

"It's late."

"I won't be long."

IT SEEMED A LONG WAY TO PEDIATRICS, and by the time I got there, my calf was throbbing. I stepped inside Katrina Hartwell's room and let the door swing shut behind me, waited a moment for my eyes to adjust to the dimness.

Katrina made a slender lump beneath the thin blanket. Her pale skin glowed in the light from the window slats, and a tangle of wires and tubes stretched between the girl and the machines that monitored her vital signs. They made her look like an abandoned marionette.

A shadow by the window shifted, and a woman emerged from the darkness as if she had been formed from it. A sheet of cornsilk hair fell across her shoulders like a waterfall.

267

I had never met her, but I would have known her anywhere. Her daughter wore her face.

"Mrs. Hartwell," I said.

She gave me a wan smile. "Not anymore. Not for a long time. I'm Shirleen Roystan now."

"Jared McKean."

"You're the one who saved her." She stepped forward, touched my sleeve. "Thank you."

I didn't know what to say. *Aw, shucks, Ma'am. It was nothing.* Nothing seemed quite like enough. Instead, I said, "How is she?"

"Stable. Or so they say. There's brain damage, but no one can tell me how much."

"Hard to tell with head injuries sometimes. Sometimes there's less damage than it seems at first."

"And sometimes there's more." She stepped to the bed and laid a hand on Katrina's forehead. "I've been standing here for hours. Just watching. Thinking about what it would be like to take her home, take care of her."

"My son has Down Syndrome," I said. "It gets easier with time."

"I was a terrible mother," she said. "I'm not proud of that, but it's true. I was never any good with kids, how am I supposed to handle a handicapped child?"

"You grieve, you go on, that's all. You love her."

She went on as if I hadn't spoken. "And the expense. The medical bills alone would break us."

"Us?"

"I remarried. He doesn't want children at all. How am I supposed to plop a brain damaged child in his lap?"

A sharp pain started in the back of my neck. I thought of Caleb Wilford, knife to his little girl's throat, and knew there was more than one way to break a child's heart. "She's your daughter, for God's sake."

"I'm sorry," she whispered. "I just can't."

She brushed past me, a sheen of tears on her cheeks. I

should have felt sorry for her. Instead, I just felt a leaden sorrow for the daughter she was leaving behind.

I glanced toward Katrina. Her eyes were open, one skewed to the side, the other fixed on the door that was just swinging shut behind her mother.

I sank into the chair beside the bed. "It's okay, kiddo," I said. "You're gonna be all right."

She lifted one thin hand. In the light from the window, I saw a smear of blood beneath the tape holding the IV needle in place.

Such a small hand. I reached through the bars of the bedrail and slipped my hand beneath her palm. Her fingers closed over mine.

I sat beside her in the dark until her breathing became even and her grip loosened. Then I carefully slipped my hand from hers and limped back to my own room.

THE DAY I WAS RELEASED, Jay helped me hook up the horse trailer, loaded my crutches into the passenger seat, and drove to ValeSong Stables.

An auction had been scheduled for the following week, the proceeds of which would go to Valerie's estate. Dakota, unbroke and blind in one eye, was probably destined for the killer market. Instead, I left a thousand dollars in an envelope on Valerie's desk, loaded him into the trailer and hauled him back to Jay's place.

Some might have called it stealing, despite the thousand bucks, but I figured she owed both of us.

Sonny Vanderhaus survived and was sentenced to life in prison. In his house, the police found the tapes he'd made of his "live" show, as well as the ones he'd used to splice together the message on Amy's voice mail.

Ashleigh was persona non grata for a while, but nothing came of it. Apparently, she has friends in high places.

I still don't know if Heather gave me HIV.

I try not to think about the woman I killed, the sudden

brilliance of her smile, the warmth of her body, how she fiddled with her braid, how she rolled her lower lip under her teeth.

And I try not to think about the early morning hours when Cal Hartwell was awakened by his sister-in-law and her lover. I wasn't there, but I can see it in my mind as clearly as if I had been.

This is how it happened.

Sonny, with his all his expertise in picking locks, hadn't needed any of it. Valerie had a key. In his jacket pocket, Sonny had the Beretta and the Browning, and Valerie had a little snub-nosed .22.

Valerie hauled Katrina out of bed at gunpoint, while Sonny went for Tara. Both girls were told in whispers that if they made a sound, their father would be killed. Tears streaming down their cheeks, the girls were led into their father's room, where Sonny shook Calvin awake, showed him the guns they had pointed at the girls, and ordered him to get up and get dressed.

Hands trembling, Cal complied.

When Cal was dressed and ready, the little group trooped downstairs to the living room, Sonny behind Cal with the Beretta to Tara's head, Valerie behind Sonny with the .22 at Katrina's.

"Get on the couch," Sonny ordered Cal. "Sit there where I can see your hands."

Unarmed, with guns to both his children's temples, Cal arranged himself on the couch according to Sonny's instructions.

"There's a piece of paper and a pen on the end table. Take it and write what I tell you. Write 'God forgive me.' Slowly now. No sudden moves."

Obediently, Cal wrote, then turned the paper for Sonny to approve.

"Good. You're doing real well." Still pressing the barrel of the Beretta to Tara's temple, Sonny pulled the Browning, fitted with a suppressor and wrapped in a handkerchief, from his jacket pocket and tossed it onto the sofa beside Cal.

"If you think you can kill us both before we blow your babies' brains out, go ahead and try." He grinned. "I don't think you can."

Cal's chest hitched with what might have been a sob, but there were no tears in his eyes. He made no move to touch the gun. The girls were silent, except for little gasps and sniffles that told their captors they were choking back tears.

"Good boy," Sonny said. "Now, I want you to pick it up, very slowly, and place the barrel under your chin."

Cal hesitated, and Sonny lifted Tara off the ground by her throat. She gasped and sputtered, kicking and clawing.

"Daddy," she whimpered.

Behind her, with Valerie's arm around her chest and the .22 pressing into the soft place beneath her jaw, Katrina whispered, "Daddy, no."

"Ten," Sonny said, tapping the barrel of the Beretta against Tara's temple. "Nine. Eight. Seven..."

Calvin placed the Browning under his chin.

Sonny smiled and set Tara's feet back on the ground. "Now," he said. "Pull the trigger."

"No," Katrina said. "Daddy, don't."

Tara cried harder.

"Do it, Cal," Valerie said. "Or don't you believe we'll really kill them?"

"If I do," said Cal, "will you let them go?"

"Cal," she said. "I promise you, we'll let them go."

He had to know they wouldn't, that they couldn't. Not after the girls had seen their faces.

But his choices were to do it and hope the woman he had loved and betrayed would have mercy on his children, or refuse and watch his daughters die. His third choice, to fire the Beretta at one of his attackers and pray he didn't hit a hostage, was a death sentence for at least one of his girls.

How could he choose which one?

"Swear," he said. His eyes filled and overflowed, but his voice was steady. "Swear by all you hold sacred that you'll keep my daughters safe."

"I swear," Valerie said. "I'll look after them as if they were my own."

I have replayed this scene over and over in my mind, only I am there instead of Cal, and it is Paulie and Maria with the guns to their heads. In my fantasy, I disarm one opponent with a roundhouse kick and place a bullet squarely in the middle of the other's forehead. My wife and son are spared, the bad guys brought to justice. I think maybe, on a perfect day, I could possibly have pulled it off.

Calvin didn't have a prayer.

"Girls, I love you," said Cal. His eyes squeezed shut. "The Lord is my Light and my Salvation. I will not be afraid."

He pulled the trigger.

Both girls screamed, but the hands that clamped over their mouths muffled the sound.

"All right," Valerie said, as Sonny retrieved the Browning from Cal's lifeless hand. "I promised your daddy you'd be all right, so you just get on up to bed now and tuck yourselves in. Katrina, you first."

I don't know what was going through Katrina's mind as she climbed the long stairs to her bedroom, climbed into her bed, and pulled the white lace and satin bedspread up to cover herself. Maybe she believed she and her sister would live.

Her aunt straightened the covers—no need to worry about fingerprints in a house that surely had her prints all over it—and bent to kiss the top of her niece's head. Sonny passed her the Browning, and she pressed it to Katrina's temple.

And fired.

Tara, Sonny's hand clamped over her mouth, squealed and struggled, kicked and squirmed and bit and clawed. He dragged her into her bedroom and flung her onto the bed, where Valerie fired a quick shot into the side of her head.

She fell back, limp as a rag doll, this child who had stolen

Calvin away, this bastard get of Judases.

"Good night, sweetheart," Valerie said, and emptied the magazine into the child's chest.

Then they unscrewed the suppressor, wiped their prints from the gun, and pressed it back into Calvin's hand.

I HADN'T LIKED CAL HARTWELL.

He was a cheater and a hypocrite. His religion made a mockery of Christianity, and his arrogance had made Amy's life a misery.

A bad husband, Ben had said, and I couldn't disagree. But a bad man? The jury was still out on that one.

After all, King David had Bathsheba, and Jacob cheated Esau of his birthright. The Bible was full of flawed, yet faithful, men. Who was I to say Calvin Hartwell wasn't one of them?

People were complicated.

Sitting in my brother's back yard, sipping Heinekens and watching our kids play a bastardization of touch football, I thought of family, and of Amy Hartwell. If it was true that people were murdered because they got too close to evil, how could Amy have avoided her fate?

She had been born too close to evil.

"So," Randall said. "That little girl going to be all right?"

I took a swallow of my beer. "Too soon to tell. They think she may be blind in one eye, maybe have some motor damage. They don't know how much of her intellect might be affected. But at least she'll live."

On the playing field, Caitlin swept her arms around her brother. "Get Josh, Paulie!" she squealed, and my son plunged into the fray. They called their version of the game Tickle football, because instead of tackling, the ball carrier was tickled to the ground. Paulie loves it.

*It's hard with only three,* I thought, remembering Cal and his daughters playing softball.

Caitlin wore blue jeans and a Marvin the Martian T-shirt, while Josh wore black jeans and a black shirt with a tie-dyed circle on the front. I took the splash of color for a good sign. His hair was still dyed black, but he was sans makeup, which I thought was an improvement. He was seeing a counselor every Tuesday. On Fridays, the whole family went together.

There were no quick fixes.

Randall and Wendy had fought bitterly over whether to press charges against Razor. Randall thought it was a reasonable alternative to killing him. Wendy thought it would further alienate Josh. In the end, Josh settled it by refusing to testify.

In less than a month, Josh found himself replaced by another underage boy with a shitty home life.

Surprise.

A quick call to Barry Sheldon, and Razor was scrambling to find a lawyer who could get him off with a fine, a slap on the wrist, and a promise to confine his relationships to boys over the age of consent. Not the most satisfying ending, but I supposed it could have been worse. I wondered how many times he'd gotten out of similar situations.

Jay stood at the picnic table, helping Wendy and Maria with the lemonade, while D.W. picked at the deviled eggs. It was a sort of welcome home party, a freedom party, so to speak, celebrating my exoneration.

"What happens to the little girl now?" Randall asked, drawing my attention back to the matter at hand. "Where does she go?"

"I don't know. Frank reached the mother. I saw her at the hospital. So sorry, she says. She's not good with handicapped kids, her new husband doesn't want the responsibility, they can't afford the medical expenses. Katrina will probably end up in foster care. There's no one left to take her."

He ran a callused hand through his hair. "Sad story."

"Yeah."

"Josh thinks we should take her."

I considered it. "Big responsibility."

"Yeah. But he's good with kids like that. Look at Paulie."

"He is good with Paul. But it would be you and Wendy with all the headaches."

"I know. We've talked about it, and neither of us likes the thought of that poor kid being stuck in some institution, or bounced from foster home to foster home."

"Things are okay, then? With you and Wendy?"

His shoulders hunched. "We went through a patch. We'll get past it."

A lump formed in my throat, and I took a swig of beer to wash it down. "I think it would be great," I said. "If that's what you want."

We sipped in silence. Then I asked, "How's the knee?"

"I'll live." I knew the subject was closed.

A maroon Monte Carlo pulled into the drive, and Josh broke free of the game and sauntered over to greet it.

"Hey, Uncle Jared," he called. "Somebody wants to meet you."

She had caramel skin, wide sloe-shaped green eyes, and long molasses-colored hair that tumbled over her shoulders like a waterfall. She wore white shorts and a white peasant-style shirt edged with lace. The top of her head came to the bridge of my nose.

Randall handed me my crutches, and I hopped over to meet her.

"Hello, Mr. McKean." She held out a slender hand with short, perfectly manicured nails.

I knew who she was as soon as she spoke.

"Miss Casale."

No tangle of auburn hair. No blue eyes. I wasn't disappointed. Her smile was dazzling. "I'm not usually so forward, but Josh said you were shy."

"Gun-shy might be a better word. Would you like to join us for a beer? Tea? Watermelon?"

Josh laughed. It was a beautiful sound. "Jared and Elisha, sittin' in a tree." He darted away, dodging as I swatted at him with a crutch, and went to talk with Jay.

275

"That's your friend?" she asked, nodding toward Jay.

"That's him."

"I think he's good for Josh."

"I think so too."

We walked back to the picnic table, where the football players, hot and drenched with sweat, clamored for lemonade.

"Hey, Daddy." Paulie flung his arms around me. I winced as he pressed against my calf. "I win."

"Everybody wins." I propped my crutches against the table and scooped him into my arms.

"Is that your son?" Elisha asked. "He's beautiful."

Behind her, Randall winked, and I suddenly had the feeling that my streak of bad luck with women might be coming to an end. At least, I'd be more careful this time. Take it slow. Maybe ask for references.

"This is Paul," I told her. "Paulie, this is Miss Casale."

"Oh, no." She laughed. "Not Miss Casale. At least let's make it Miss Elisha." She held out her hand and Paulie, still in my arms, solemnly shook it.

I looked around at the jostling mob around the picnic table. My family. Paulie and Randall. Wendy, Josh, and Caitlin. Maria, with the new life inside her. Jay. And even, in an odd way, D.W. The family I had been given and the one I had chosen.

Across the table, Maria's eyes met mine, and I saw the loss and insecurity in them.

Then she smiled. *Goodbye. I love you. Goodbye.*

I tilted my head back and let the sun warm my face, as the laughter and cries from the ball game filled my ears and threatened to burst my heart.

# Author's Note

No book is created without the help and support of many special (and sometimes longsuffering) people. Thanks to everyone who helped make this book a reality.

Above all and always, thanks to Mike Hicks for his constant encouragement and support. Thanks to my mother, Ruthanne Terrell, and my brother, David Terrell, for their love and loyalty; Craig Combs for his friendship and for coming up with the perfect description of Jared ("Magnum PI meets Tim McGraw"); former co-worker and fellow author Jim Winfree for giving me my first "break," and agent Robbie Robison, for believing in me, even when nothing seemed to be happening.

Thanks to Officer Dan DeFranzo, Homicide detectives John Knowles and Pat Postiglione and the Metro Citizen's Police Academy for information about homicide detectives and the Metro police force; Charles Harlan, Medical Examiner, and the UT Knoxville forensics department for explaining about decomposition and answering all my forensics questions; Ken Mastri, Mastering Engineer, for the information about the recording industry; Assistant D.A. Bobby Hibbett, for his long-term friendship and being one of the first readers of this book; David and Lana Adkins, for the inside scoop on living with a family of police officers; George Chicazola, for helping with the Spanish phrases; Tamelyn Feinstein Mastri, for providing inspiration and encouragement since the sixth grade; Travis Baldwin, for cultivating a love of reading and storytelling in me; Michael Mill, for his advice and constant friendship.; Christina Wilburn for her grace, goodness, and editorial advice; Joe Clark, for bringing a fresh eye to Jared's story; and Ben Small, for leading the charge against typos.

I'd also like to thank the following people for their friendship and support: Brad Jones; Jeff Bibb; Barclay and Cathy Randall; Allan Barlow; C.J Breland: Sherry Langford; Mark Jones; Brett Bias; Henry Faust; Jeff and Lila Smith; Bob

Blanton; Gary Lane; and Chris Clark; all my wonderful friends and co-workers from MI, including Chris McCown, Kathy Palmer, Mary Beth Ross, Steve Jones, Scott Coulthard, Phil Perry, Lane Wright, Alan Lee, Michael Panasuk, Jerald Starr, Pat Thomas, Brian Thomas, and Louis Allen.

The Quill and Dagger Writer's Group deserves a special thanks: Nancy Sartor, Richard Emerson, Hardy Saliba, Nikki Nelson-Hicks, Nina Fortmeyer, Jeannie Arnold, Robert Helbig, and especially Chester Campbell, who went above and beyond the call of duty.

That the book exists at all is thanks to the support and encouragement of these fine people. Any errors are my own alone.

# Location, Location, Location

I have tried to capture the essence of Nashville and to keep the description of the city as accurate as possible. However, certain liberties were taken in the interest of creating a better story (and also in the interest of not strewing literary bodies across the doorsteps of local businesses).

Dark Horse Saddlery no longer exists in Franklin, but its memory lives on in these pages. The First Edition Bar& Grill is my own creation, inspired by the Front Page Bar & Grill, which used to sit at the "T" where Donelson Pike meets Lebanon Road. I have invented or adapted various other locations, especially those where murders or other unsavory acts take place.

LaVergne, TN USA
07 February 2010
172308LV00002B/79/P